# DEADCORE

# DEADCORE

## 4 HARDCORE ZOMBIE NOVELLAS

RANDY CHANDLER
DAVID JAMES KEATON
EDWARD M. ERDELAC
BEN CHEETHAM

EDITOR:
CHERYL MULLENAX

RED ROOM PRESS
WWW.REDROOMPRESS.COM

DEADCORE

A RED ROOM PRESS BOOK

*Deadcore*
copyright © Red Room Press, 2010

"Dead Juju"
copyright © Randy Chandler, 2010

"Zee Bee & Bee (a.k.a. Propeller Hats For The Dead)"
copyright © David James Keaton, 2010

"Night of the Jikininki"
copyright © Edward M. Erdelac, 2010

"Zombie Safari"
copyright © Ben Cheetham, 2010

ISBN: 978-0-9820979-8-4

Red Room Press website: www.redroompress.com
facebook.com/redroompress
twitter.com/redroombooks

FIRST RED ROOM PRESS TRADE PAPERBACK EDITION,
SEPTEMBER 2010

# DEAD JUJU
## By Randy Chandler

Randy Chandler is the author of the two solo nov-
els *Bad Juju* and *Hellz Bellz*, and authored *Duet for the
Devil* with t. Winter-Damon (God rest his soul). Randy
has been a magazine editor/publisher, a freelance
book reviewer, a mental health worker, a gas-pump
jockey, an ambulance attendant, a soldier in Vietnam
and a funeral home flunky. He often haunts fields
of carnage where angels and devils do battle.

# PART I
# FUCK ME DEAD

*For without are dogs, and sorcerers, and whoremongers, and murderers, and idolaters, and whosoever loveth and maketh a lie.*
—Revelation 22:15

# 1
## The Big Blink

Starving herself to death wasn't cutting it so Peg Pope decided to jump off this Tucson bridge and onto the railroad track in front of an oncoming train. It wasn't much of a bridge but it would do the trick. Less drama the better. Nobody would see her gory remains on the tracks but the poor slurps who would have to investigate and clean up the mess. *Slurps* was Peg's word for the slobs whose purpose in life was slurping up all the shit the world dished out to them with a wink and a nudge and a Fuck You Very Much.

She leaned so far over the concrete rail that she got dizzy and almost took an accidental header. That would not do. It had to be an act of will to take her out of Shit World. A thumb-in-God's-eye act of great deliberation. And here came her ticket now. Chugga-chugga choo-choo grinding up the tracks. Right on time. Dead on time.

A chorus of sweet-faced devils from her childhood chanted: *Jump, Piggy Poop! Jump!*

She couldn't see them now but she knew well their devilishly cherubic faces with the thick green mucus dripping from their noses and their crooked teeth and dirty skin. The little fuckwads had followed her all the way from her grade-school years and were always close by to cheer on little Piggy Poop whenever Peg Pope was feeling the full force of Shit World's latest dump on her unbowed head. *Well guess what, dirty little devils! Piggy Poop's head is no longer shitty but unbowed. Slurp it up, suckers! Check the bowed head. She's ready to grab her Golden Ticket out of here right out of the fucking air on the way down to the tracks. And if the impact on the tracks doesn't finish her, that hulking locomotive sure as shit will.*

The train whistle blew and the sunny day suddenly darkened as Peg glanced left, then right (Look before you leap!) and cursed when she saw the white-haired old man hobbling along the bridge's sidewalk with a cane, coming toward her on her side of the street, talking to himself. Or was he talking to her?

"Hope you got a strong heart, old dude," she muttered to herself. "Tough shit you gotta see this but here comes my train."

She looked at the looming train and knew she had less than a minute till jump-off. But then the scrawny geezer did something so unexpectedly odd that Peg had to react. He stopped short, looked up, pointed his cane up at the sky and screeched: *"In a moment, in the twinkling of an eye, at the last trump: for the trumpet shall sound, and the dead shall be raised incorruptible, and we shall be changed!"*

Lapsed Catholic Peg recognized it as a Bible quotation. Corinthians?

"Look up, damn you!" the old man yowled.

She looked up. "Holy shit," she half whispered.

Awestruck. Mindfucked. She forgot for the moment her date with death, the tracks and the train. The thing filled her mind as it filled the sky. Im-fucking-possible, but there it was, nearly blotting out the sun like an immense spacecraft.

A colossal eye. Perfectly rendered on the canvas of the sky as if painted there by a supernatural hand with a gigantic paintbrush in sparkling clouds and rainbow colors.

Peg knew in her heart that this was no random formation of clouds. No, this was a sign. An omen . . . but of what? The train passed under the bridge, its whistle shrieking like a thousand banshees.

"You see?" shouted the old man with the raised cane. "It by God sees you!"

The crazy old coot's rant was beginning to harsh her sudden high and she was about to look away from the huge eye in the sky long enough to tell the old fart to shut up and fuck off but then the awesome eye blinked and Peg pissed herself.

# 2
# Lord of Flies

Bobby Cruz took an immediate dislike to the mescal-drinking coyote and liked the looks of the man's partner even less. At least Cruz assumed the creepy dude was the coyote's partner. It was hard to know for sure because the guy—the probable partner—wore a blood-red hoodie that covered his head and most of his face and he never said a word, just grunted when El Coyote said something to him in Spanish as the dozen crossers milled about like voodoo zombies awaiting word to get their asses back in the truck.

Cruz had the feeling that the hooded dude could see right through him, see into his heart and know that Bobby Cruz wasn't really a Mexican looking to cross illegally into Arizona from this stark stretch of Sonoran Desert, that Bobby Cruz was a U.S. citizen and a laid-off American newspaper reporter looking to score a book contract off this Wetback-Like-Me undercover escapade. And if that wasn't enough to give Cruz a case of the crawling creeps, Señor Hoodie had a squadron of big black flies buzzing round his head and shoulders, almost as if guarding him. Dude never swatted them away. The buzzing fuckers didn't seem to bother him at all. *Lord of the flies*, Cruz thought and shuddered.

But there was something else about the spooky guy. Some other thing that disturbed him, though he wasn't sure what it was. He only knew something was off, ass-over-tea-kettle wrong.

The wind carried the rumbling of a motor vehicle and Cruz turned to see a pickup coming up the road from the south. Then he realized what the other wrong thing was. Those noisy flies orbiting Señor Hoodie's head were not affected by the desert winds. It was as if they were protected by an invisible shield. Something else too. They were bigger than horseflies. The biggest goddamn flies Cruz had ever seen. What the hell were they, mutants? Wouldn't want one of those behemoths to bite you, he thought.

El Coyote said, "Listen up, my little chickens." Bobby Cruz knew just enough Spanish to catch most of what the man said. The coyote told them that at their next stop they would get out and walk across the border. A man would meet them there and he would lead them into the land of plenty. Once across the border, a van would take them to a stash house in Tucson and the very next day they would be put to work at the chicken ranch.

"But first, we have something to give you," the coyote said as the dirty pickup pulled up and stopped behind the painted-over U-haul truck Bobby and the other crossers had ridden this far in. "You will be given a backpack full of very valuable merchandise. We know to the exact ounce how much is in each one. You will be responsible for your pack. Don't even think about opening them. OK. Someone will collect them from you at the house in Tucson. Consider it part of your fee. It's still a good deal, no?"

El Coyote's *pollos* shot each other nervous glances. A couple of them looked as if they might go ahead and shit their pants then and there. One, an attractive woman in her thirties, said, "I will not do it. I never agreed to smuggle drugs."

El Coyote walked up to her, got right in her face and said, "Crossing the border is a criminal act. What's one more broken law?" Then he pulled the knife from the sheath on his right hip, put the blade to her cheek and flicked his wrist. The woman yelped and backed away, her hand flying to her face to stanch the blood. "You will do what I tell you," he said with a teeth-baring grin, "or I will gut you like a fucking rabbit. And then I will murder your family. That goes for all of you." He brandished the knife.

Cruz pulled a folded bandana from his jeans pocket and offered it to the wounded woman. She accepted it with downcast eyes and held it to her cheek. "Keep it," Bobby said in passable Spanish.

A dark-skinned man in filthy dungarees and a plaid shirt got out of the pickup and gave each of the crossers a fully loaded backpack. With El Coyote standing by with his knife, the dirty drug distributor made sure everyone accepted a pack and slipped it on. Bobby did not doubt that the coyote would gut him if he didn't. A part of him was pleased with this unexpected turn of events. It would make for very dramatic reading—if he lived to write the damned story. That was the other part of him, the pessimist whispering that he would be lucky to live through the oncoming night.

"Back on the truck, my little chickens," El Coyote said with a dry laugh.

The Lord of Flies wordlessly watched from his shadowy cowl. The sun westered. A massive raft of ominous clouds darkened the sky. Cruz and the other *pollos* climbed back into the truck. The coyote rolled the door down and latched it and Cruz found a corner and sat down in darkness, thinking he and his fellow crossers were no longer chickens. The contraband on their backs made them mules.

The truck jolted into motion and resumed its journey over the desert road. Cruz wondered what the shit was. Smack, meth, weed, crack? He would have to find out later for the sake of the story. He relaxed a little and closed his eyes, thinking that a catnap wasn't a bad idea. He had a long night of hiking across the border ahead of him and he wasn't in the best of shape.

A few minutes later the truck lurched to a stop. Cruz's head bounced against the corner walls. He cursed. There were thuds and muffled cries as others were thrown to the floor. Doors slammed. Excited voices rose over the rumble of the truck's engine but Cruz couldn't make out the words. What the hell was going on out there? A run-in with the Border Patrol? A throw-down with a rival outfit of outlaws?

Then El Coyote's voice cried out clearly: "*¡Es el ojo del dios!*"

Cruz understood that simple Spanish well enough and it gave him a chill: It is the eye of God!

Then another voice, louder, closer, said: "*No, amigo, es el ojo del diablo.*"

Eye of the devil? Cruz impulsively pounded a fist against the truck's wall and yelled, "Hey! What's going on out there?"

Realizing he'd called out in English, he said, "*Mierda,*" as if saying *shit* in Spanish might cover his slipup.

The truck's engine died. The suddenly silent world seemed to catch its breath. Cruz held his breath as well and waited for . . . *what?*

The door all at once rolled up with a clatter and a bang and evening light flooded the interior and made him squint in irritation.

The mystery man in the hoodie stepped up into the rear of the truck, the Lord of Flies himself, making disturbing gestures with long fingers. Then he said something in a language Cruz didn't recognize and the squadron of black flies summarily swarmed forth and attacked Cruz and the other crossers.

The flies seemed to have doubled in number and their bites were fiercely painful. Cruz swatted and slapped, as did his companions, but the insects did not relent. Their wings seemed to cut like razors. Cruz thought the insects might be products of genetic engineering gone wild because these things could not be of the natural world.

Then everyone in the back of the truck belatedly got the same idea at once and bolted for the open door but before they got there, Señor Hoodie Lord of Flies rolled the door down with slamming finality.

The winged demons' shrill drone in the enclosed space became a buzzsaw roar.

Chaos reigned in the dark confines of the truck as people bumped into each other, slapped each other as they tried to swat the vicious flies, and screamed as the ravenous swarm fed on their flesh. The women's screams were the worst.

Cruz quickly found that he could scream with the best of them.

# 3
## Going Anal

"C'mon, bitch," she said, "fuck me harder. You won't kill me."

"I am," he said.

"Am *what?*" she prompted.

"Doing it harder," he said, pounding his pelvis into hers.

"Say it. Say you're *fucking* me harder."

"I *am* . . . fucking you harder."

She laughed. "Say it like you've got a pair, bitch."

"Ridiculous," he said, panting. "I obviously do. Have a pair. And don't call me *bitch.*"

"Sure thing, your holiness. Or should I say your ass-holiness?"

"Oh, you are a wicked woman," he said, explosive passion building deep in his balls.

"Fucking right, Reverend. I got the devil in me and you're trying to fuck him out."

She pumped her hips harder, her belly slapping his to accentuate each word: "Even . . . if . . . it . . . costs . . . you . . . your . . . fucking . . . soul."

"Oh Lord," he said through gritted teeth.

"You fuck your wife like this?"

"Shut up, whore."

She slapped his ass. "That's it," she taunted, "get me right with God. Save this wicked sinner, Preacher Thomas. Fuck the hell out of me."

"Yes. Yes. Yes!"

They came together, hard and fast and very messy. Then they were quiet for a while. He remained inside her, semi-erect.

"I'm *so* bad," she said, dipping her tongue in his ear. "I think Satan's still in me."

"No," he said, stifling a yawn.

"Oh but he is. And you're going to have to slip in the back way to root him out. That's the only way that will work now."

"Jamie, no. We can't."

"It's the only way, I promise."

She clamped her vaginal muscles on him and his penis responded with an involuntary twitch. She said, "See? The little bishop knows I'm right. You have to fuck me in the ass."

"Stop saying that."

"Okay. I won't say it. We'll just do it."

"No. It's wrong."

"Everything we're doing is wrong. Don't kid yourself that it isn't. What's the point of sinning if you don't go all the fucking way with it? Only then can you be purified by the fires of hell."

"That's nuts."

"No it isn't. And you know it. Follow St. Augustine's sterling example. Know sin from the inside out. And right now that means *inside my ass*."

She pushed him off her and rolled onto her tummy. She raised her ass, reached back with both hands and parted her cheeks. "Do it, Tommy. Don't tease me."

She slid her fingers into her sopping vagina and then lubricated her anus with them. "You know what they say? No, I guess you wouldn't. They say once you go anal you can never go back. It's true too. Which is why I'm begging you for it. It's a different kind of orgasm. You work the clit and put your fingers in my pussy while you fuck me up the ass. Do that and I'll be crazy for you forever. You'll own me body and soul."

"Don't talk like that," he said, looking away from her tempting rear. "It turns me off. It's beneath you."

"What? The dirty sex talk or the 'body and soul' part?"

"Both. I don't want to own anybody."

"Sure you do. What man wouldn't want a sex slave? That's why you're with me and not your wife. Because she's a dried-up prude who can't satisfy her man. Saving it for Jesus, right? You don't measure up, not in her book. How can you compete with Christ? With me you do. Measure up. And right now I want every fucking inch of you up my horny ass."

He turned away from her, grabbed the remote and turned on the plasma TV. Carnal images filled the wide screen. Soft-core porn in HD. He quickly changed the channel.

"Tommy . . ."

He pulled the sheet up to his waist so he wouldn't have to see his sex-slick penis.

"Let me tell you something," Jamie said. "Don't fuck with me. Or I'll fuck with you and you'll lose. Only one of us is going to be the real sex slave here and believe me, buddy, it ain't me. You're the one with a holier-than-thou wife and a whole lot to lose. Not me. I can ruin your life. I'll stand up in your church in front of your whole congregation and *testify*, brother. Give me what I want or by God I'll do it."

He stared at the TV screen. He punched up the volume.

"Are you listening to me?" Sitting up now, Jamie slapped his shoulder. "You're going anal. You just don't know it yet. You're well on your fucking way."

"Shut up. I want to hear this." He cranked the volume still louder.

Onscreen was what appeared to be a brilliant bit of CGI, an eye so big it filled the sky. It looked as if it had been painted on the clouds. Or somehow sculpted out of clouds. And yet it looked so real, so lifelike that it might be the actual eye of an immense angel.

"What the fuck?" Jamie said.

As if in answer, the cable news anchorwoman said: "It appeared overhead this afternoon and it hasn't moved since. Not only is it visible across all of America, it's reportedly visible over half the planet. No one at this point knows exactly what it is or how it came to be there. No one has claimed responsibility. Already there is talk of miracles and of the Apocalypse. If this isn't a natural phenomenon, then it must be supernatural in origin, so the speculation goes. All we know for certain at this point in time is that the big eye in the sky does not show up on Doppler radar, which means it isn't moving at all and might even mean it's there only in the sense of an optical illusion. It's apparently higher than aircraft can fly. Higher than clouds are supposed to be. And as we just reported to you, our contacts at the Defense Department tell us that the military has detected absolutely nothing to indicate that the thing in the sky poses any sort of threat or is anything other than benign. The only real problems so far have been the traffic jams and accidents its sudden appearance has caused.

I think it's accurate to say that thus far there is no physical evidence that the eye is there at all. For now, the phenomenon is entirely visual. Perhaps it will turn out to be nothing more than a fantastic optical illusion. There are nevertheless intriguing, perhaps even *disturbing* reports that the big eye actually appeared to blink at one point."

The anchorwoman paused, touched her earpiece, and then said, "My producer is telling me that we are in the process of getting cell-phone video from multiple sources that show the eye actually blinking. We will be showing you these momentarily. What this may mean is anybody's guess."

"My God," Jamie said, anal sex for the moment forgotten. "I've got goose bumps."

"Get dressed," Thomas said. "We have to go outside and see it before it gets too dark."

He climbed out of the big bed and into his pants.

"Screw the dark. You can bet your ass that freaking peeper can see in the dark. Probably sees right through ceilings and walls too. Been watching us the whole time, the whole fucking show."

# 4
## Rape Tree

Magda Menendez was going to die here by the rape tree. It was more bush than tree. And she was already more dead than alive. This was the only taste of life in America she would ever get. The bitter taste of forced sex. A beating so severe that she didn't think she could even drag herself away from this shameful tree hung with the underpants of the girls the coyotes had raped in recent weeks, or months. The men did it to mark their territory, to prove their manhood, to mock the gringos on land they said had been stolen long ago from Mexico. They worked for one of the drug cartels, so who would stop them? Nobody. The cartels were too powerful and the Mexican police and government were too corrupt.

Her faded blue panties were there on the end of a spindly twig of a limb, a sad tribute to her dream of a better life. It was a painful point of shame that Magda's panties were the shabbiest ones on the tree. The elastic waistband was frayed and there were two little holes in the crotch where the seam had split.

She reached a hand to the lips of her sex and verified that the bleeding had stopped. She closed her eyes against the glaring Arizona sky and asked God to forgive her sins, minor though they were. She crossed herself. Father. Son. Holy Ghost.

There had been three of them. After the two younger men were done with her, the older one with the evil eyes and the big scar on his face hurt her the most, showing the younger men how to handle a woman. For the scarred man, beating a woman was part of the sex act. Magda didn't think he meant to kill her or leave her for dead but he had been too rough with her when he picked her up and slammed her to the ground while he was still inside her. The small of her back had struck a sharp rock and everything below her waist went numb. And now she couldn't even wiggle her toes. She was already half dead, lifeless from the waist down. Naked down there.

Left for dead at the edge of the desert.

Feeling as helpless as an abandoned infant, Magda cried herself to sleep.

When she woke up the sky had opened its secret eye and looked down on her with no pity. A priest had once told her that heavenly angels could "translate" themselves into any shape or size, so it was no surprise to her that an angel's eye could fill the sky. But then she began to shiver violently and she came to fear that this eye might be the eye of great evil, perhaps of the Evil One himself.

"Diablo," she whispered.

Magda asked the Holy Mother to help her. As soon as she had spoken the words: "La madre santa del dios, me ayuda," a shrill voice said: "Si esto está infierno, después somos ya muertos." *If this is hell, then we're already dead.*

Then they were upon her, a band of bloody men and women wearing backpacks and looking for all the world as if they indeed *were* on a desperate trek through hell. The dozen of them halted when they saw her. She felt as if she should say something, perhaps apologize for her pathetic appearance and for being left to die under the rape tree, herself the ultimate trophy, but no words would come. She only looked at them with her sad eyes. Several of them swatted at big black flies that seemed to be tenaciously dogging them.

A man knelt beside her and asked if she could walk. She said she could not. She told him tearfully that she thought her back was broken. He frowned, then shrugged and stood. He glanced nervously at the sky's eye, then walked away.

Flies found her. They landed on her face and arms but most of them alighted on the sticky gumbo of blood, dirt and semen between her legs. Their bites stung her face and neck but she couldn't feel them at all below her waist, which she supposed was a small blessing.

One of the women said, "For God's sake, cover her." But no one did. The night would be cold out here and nobody was willing to give up an article of clothing. "Where are your pants?" the woman asked. Magda said she didn't know. The woman pointed to the tree and asked which panties were hers. Magda pointed them out and the woman retrieved them from the rape tree and was kind enough to slip them on, raising Magda's hips for her since she couldn't do it herself. She buttoned her blouse over her exposed breasts.

An older woman with bad skin and wearing a scarf on her head as if she were on her way to church said she was sick and didn't think she could go on. Then she threw up on the shoes of the man standing closest to her. He cursed her and shoved her away. She lost her balance and fell. She moaned. She did not get up. "Puta," the man with vomit on his shoes said to the fallen woman.

A man with a pistol on his hip appeared. A mule runner for the cartel. He took the sick woman's backpack and put it on his own back. Then he looked at Magda and at the retching woman on the ground a few feet from her and said they could keep each other company while waiting for the angel. "El ángel de la muerte." The angel of death.

Then Magda and the fallen woman were alone. Left behind to die.

The sick woman's breathing became labored. She rasped, "Es las moscas. Son matanza yo." Magda thought the woman was delirious. Why else would she say the flies were killing her? Poor woman. Poor *me*. Then she gave thanks that the flies had departed with the human mule train.

The sun set. The moon rose big and red. The eye above was luminous with sinister light.

Magda wanted water. She wondered if she would die of thirst or exposure. Not that it really mattered.

Suddenly the sick woman's rasping breath ceased. Magda stared hard at the woman's chest and saw that she had indeed stopped breathing. "Vaya con el dios," Magda said to the deceased woman.

She watched the giant eye watching the moon rise. Or was it watching Magda? No, of course not. She was too insignificant to warrant attention of the great evil eye of the Devil. She had to trust that God's angels would watch over her and come to her when it was time to transport her soul to Jesus.

She was feeling sick now. As if she might throw up. She shivered against the cold. I don't have long, she thought.

Something all at once blocked out the moon.

Magda's breath caught in her throat. The dead woman was standing over her, her eyes shining red in the moonlight.

"Oh mi dios," Magda said just above a whisper.

Then the dead woman fell upon her and began to snap at her with yellowed teeth. Magda fended her off as best she could, but being paralyzed below the waist was too great a disadvantage and the dead woman quickly overcame her and tore into her throat, ripped chunks of flesh from her face and then started on Magda's small breasts as if they were the finest delicacies. She stopped resisting and gave in to the savage assault. The pain became something else, a sensation she did not recognize, something well beyond mere physical sensation.

Something shifted inside her, knocking her off-center. She couldn't tell whether she was leaving her body or sinking deeper into its transient flesh.

Just before death took her, Magda looked deep into the Devil's eye in the night sky and knew God's angels were not coming for her.

At the last, she knew that Death was not taking her. Death was *joining* her, slipping inside her as evilly as her rapists had.

But unlike the rapists, Death had come to stay.

# 5
# Splat!

"Shut the fuck up," Peg said to the ghostly chorus in her head, the evil little cherubs going, *Piggy Poop, you've been duped. Duped by Death, don't hold your breath. Comes the hour round at last? No, says Death, you can kiss my ass.* "You're no Greek chorus. You're a fucking *Geek* chorus."

She would've offed herself eons ago (back when she was evil eighteen) if she hadn't become convinced that she was the honest-to-God antichrist in the fucking flesh.

Eons if she *was* the antichrist because the antichrist could exist outside of time like Jesus and the angels (by Peggy Pope's logic anyway), and why *not* a chick as antichrist? The dark female principle (as in *dark hole, Hell, the pit*) would make a perfect counter to the shining masculine light of Christ, right? *Sure as shit, Peggy Pissy Pants.* The possibility that she was the antichrist gave her a reason to keep living, to stuff the pin back in the grenade, so to speak. But then it was back to *Pull the pin, Piggy Poop* when she could no longer make herself believe the whole End Times schmear because she just couldn't swallow the preposterous notion that God actually existed. It was fantasy, a ginormous fairy tale, supernatural Pablum for thumbsucking shitheads and assorted slurps of Shit World.

The long and the short of it being that Peg Pope didn't exist eons ago because she wasn't the antichrist because there was no antichrist because there was no Christ because because because blah blah blah.

But now this big eyeball was up there looking at her and the frigging thing blinked and changed everything. Now she could believe *any*thing because *any*thing was possible. She could go back to being the antichrist if she'd half a mind to. She laughed, the idea of having half a mind tickling like a feather in her funnybone cerebellum. Say what? *Say amen, motherfuck. I'm still here.*

Still on the bridge after sundown. The geezer trying to raise Cain with his raised cane had moved on and was no doubt preaching the Word to elsewhere *slurps* dumb enough to hear it. When he'd got close enough to spray Peg with his spittle and to gaze into her Goth Girl whiteface, she put the fear of the Lord or Lucifer into him by saying: "Get the fuck off my bridge or I'll throw your narrow old ass off it." As he hobbled away tapping his cane on the sidewalk, she shouted: "I am the End Timer come to end Shit World!" A glance up at the eye in the sky put an end to that lie.

There was of course an easy way to find out who she was and what was what. She could go ahead and jump. "It is what it is," she said to the eye aglow in the night sky. "Or it ain't what it is. It's either splat! and die, or splat! and *Dig that bitching eye. Wow, dude.*"

She looked off at the Santa Rita Mountains to the south. A wind blew up so strong that she thought it might smack her off the bridge. Then it came to her that it was a devil wind from no place on this earth, a wind carrying something momentous. Just as quickly as it had come, it died. Or departed. Leaving in its wake a pair of buzzing flies. *Fucking flies?*

Big-ass horseflies. When the first one bit her she yelped and swatted at it in anger. Missed. Then the other one dive-bombed her and took a bite out of her throat.

This one she smacked good. Splat! Splattered its guts. She wiped the goo off her throat and examined the foul mess on her fingertips. Blood mixed with a sickening green gunk and a pallid pus-like substance.

It reeked.

It smelled like backed-up drainage from rotting corpses clogging a sewer line.

It reeked.

She retched. She held onto the concrete rail.

Dizzy.

Shit.

Horseflies from hell.

She looked one last time into the eye in the sky, wished she could spit in it but instead said, "That's it. I take no more shit. I'm ending Shit World right fucking now."

And she somersaulted over the side and went splat! when she hit the tracks.

A short while later, she got up and started walking on broken bones. Leaving behind a lot of blood and a bit of brain.

# 6
## A Dark Ride

The patio outside their Nogales motel room. Jamie chain-smoked and slapped at no-see-ums and a particularly persistent black fly. Thomas stared meditatively at the great eye overhead, occasionally shaking his head in wonder or disbelief.

"Can we please go in now?" she asked. "These bugs are eating me up."

Thomas grunted.

Jamie said, "How long can you sit and look at the goddamn thing? Let's go in. It's obviously not going anywhere."

"Um-hm."

She said, "I have to be home by midnight or John boy will get suspicious and once the son of a bitch catches scent he's like a fucking bloodhound. There ain't no quit in the man. Believe me, we don't want him sniffing us out. He'll kill us both. And his cop buddies will cover for him. So chop-chop. Get a move on. Hot night in Fuck City."

"I can't *believe* you," he said, finally taking his eyes off *the eye*. "Don't you know a miracle when you see one?"

"Jesus! We didn't come here for miracles. It's a no-tell motel, for Christ's sake. We came for screwing our asses off and so far you've let me down big time. I could've saved my money and stayed home with my vibrator. Mr. Mojo ain't afraid to go up my ass either. Unlike one ass clown I could name. Reverend."

"Could you be any cruder? My God . . ."

"Oh, I can be a lot cruder, Jesus boy." She flipped her cigarette into the deepening dusk surrounding the patio. "And I can make you love it."

A small plane with navigation lights blinking passed in front of the eye gleaming in the moonlight. Thomas looked up and said, "The thing must be outside the earth's atmosphere. As high as the heavens. I wonder what the space station sees."

She slid out of her chair and knelt between his legs and unzipped him. He tried to push her away and stand up but she kept him pinned to his seat. Her fingers found his limp cock, brought it out into the night air and took its bulbous knob in her mouth. It began to swell and quickly became a mouthful.

"Somebody could see us," he protested weakly.

"So what?" she said around his dick, sounding tongue-tied. "Nobody knows us here."

She sucked hard and bobbed her head until he groaned, then she pulled it out and said, "C'mon, we're going inside so you can fuck me proper." She yanked him out of his chair by his dick but this time he didn't object. She led him to the sliding-glass door, opened it and pulled him into the stale, frigid air.

She undressed in a hurry. "I'm itching like a bitch. Those little fuckers feasted on me. Didn't you get any bites?"

"A few, I guess. Mostly from you."

"Ha. So you did notice. I was beginning to think you were a fucking zombie. I'd hate for my best efforts to go unnoticed."

"I noticed. Why else would I let you lead me around by my . . . thing."

"Don't play the prude. It makes you sound like a phony. And don't kid yourself. When you whack off with your left hand your right *does* know what you're doing. Now get your clothes off."

She poked the head of his erect penis with her fingernail and said, "You're going to put that in my ass or I'll start screaming bloody murder. Don't think I won't."

"Jamie, please . . ."

She slathered massage oil between her legs, front and rear, and then climbed onto the bed, remained on her hands and knees and waggled her ass. "Come and get it, big boy. Climb on and pop it in the poop chute. It's a dark ride."

He obeyed. He positioned himself to mount her and she reached back to guide him into forbidden territory. He went in slow, an inch at a time.

"Oh . . . yeah," she said. "How's it feel?"

"Um, tight. Good."

"Bet your ass, baby. Now all the way. Reach around and finger me while you fuck me. Yeah. Yeah. Jesus Christ, that's wicked good!"

When the screams started in the next room, they paid no attention. They went on with their fucking and didn't finish until the police sirens screamed up outside.

# 7
## Killing Pedro

Pima County Sheriff Pedro Delgado wasn't going down easy. The Baddest Sheriff in America sure as hell was not going down without a wangdangdoodle of a gunfight. Funny thing was, Pedro didn't much give a rip if the three *chollos* killed him or if he killed them or they all killed each other.

Pedro was old. Sixty-six. Way he saw it, it was better to die by gunfire with his Old Gringo boots on than to die pissing himself in some reeking retirement home. The handcrafted boots were Tattoo Eagles, the style he'd made famous—so much so that the good folks at Old Gringo sent him a new pair free of charge whenever he wanted them. He didn't reckon he'd be needing another. Seeing as how he was likely to die here on this lonely stretch of desert road unless these *chollos* were as stupid as they looked—which hardly seemed possible. Nah, he figured they knew their business and business was pretty damn good, what with things going red hot along the border these days and politicians shooting off at the mouth, playing one group of folks against another, and with what some folks called The Machete War off some dumb-ass propaganda movie seemed about to break out for real between Mexico and the States, Machete being this Christ-like warrior avenger bent on taking it to white folks for being the white wicked spawn of Satan or something.

Lord knew Pedro had no shortage of enemies. When a lawman actually does his job, he makes plenty of enemies. The reason he was hated with so much venom was because his political enemies couldn't get away with calling him racist. Pedro Delgado was a third-generation Mexican-American. They couldn't very well accuse him of being racist for locking up illegals from Mexico. And that pissed them off so bad they couldn't shit straight. He was a stickler for enforcing the law and they couldn't tolerate that because it queered their deal, wrecked their grand agendas. They were desperate to knock his dick in the dirt but couldn't figure how to do it so it would stick. So they'd sent these three shooters with gang tattoos and blue bandana do-rags to gun down the Baddest Sheriff in America. *Tres amigos.*

"Bring it on, amigos," he said, hunkered down in an arroyo with his gun out and ready. "Let's get this hooraw over with. I ain't getting' any younger. And you boys ain't likely to get any older."

He should've seen this coming but when their pickup had barreled up behind his cruiser with lights flashing and horn honking, Sheriff Delgado had cut speed and pulled over to see what the trouble was.

Quick enough he saw trouble aplenty. That was when the three *chollos* jumped out of their truck with guns drawn, one of them waving a machete with his left hand. Pedro thanked the good Lord his reaction time was still pretty swift for a man of his age as he slid across the seat and ducked out through the passenger door and the assassins threw a hail of hot lead into the Pima County cruiser. One round knocked his hat off and a fragment of another clipped his earlobe and stung something fierce. Pedro drew and returned fire just to keep the boys honest, not to actually hit them because he had no clear shot.

The punk wearing a straw cowboy hat over his do-rag yelled "La raza!" and winged another shot at Pedro's hatless head. The shot punched a hole in the passenger-door window, missing his head by a good three inches. And that was when he decided to low-tail it for the arroyo just off the side of the road without trying to grab the cruiser's scattergun. He reckoned the 12-gauge would be of little use to a dead man. Then the *chollo* in the hat demonstrated that he wasn't as dumb as he looked when he reached into the cruiser for the scattergun. Pedro aimed his pistol and snapped off a shot at the man's head.

Missed.

He blamed the miss on the darkness, though the moon was plenty bright and there was good light from the pickup's headlights and the cruiser's too.

Pedro pulled his rosary from his shirt pocket and began to worry the wooden beads as he kept the pistol pointed toward the road and in the general direction of the three asshole hombres determined to kill him. His late wife had given him the beads years ago and made him promise to always keep them near his heart when he was on the job. He wasn't a devout Christian but hunkered in this arroyo he was no atheist in a foxhole either.

"Lord," he said, "I hope you can forgive me for having to kill these men. Or if it goes the other way, I hope you don't find my sins too offensive. Lord knows I most always tried to do the right thing. Forgive my failures if you can. Amen."

The pickup's headlights went out. Then the cruiser's lights went dark. The punks would be coming in for the kill now.

Pedro looked up at the sky. Whatever that thing was up there that looked like a giant eye seemed brighter than the full moon. Damndest thing. Like it was there just to witness this shootout. A worn-out Bible quote popped into his head and he said it aloud: *"If thine eye offend thee, pluck it out."* He chuckled at the sudden silliness of life. At the absurdity.

The scattergun boomed and took off the left side of his face. He hardly felt the pistol shot that hit him in the neck or the one that thumped into his breast. On his back now, he raised his pistol and fired at one of his killers and the *chollo* went down, gut-shot.

The scattergun boomed again and Pedro's left arm went away, taken off at the shoulder. The moon, the big eyeball, the whole world went dark. Pedro felt his heart thud to a sudden stop and then the bottom dropped out, the bottom of his life, the bottom of existence itself, and he was falling down a dark shaft, screaming, screaming all the way down. He came to a wrenching halt and realized he was back in his mangled body.

His remaining eye saw things in a different light. A harsher light. Not a new light but an old one. Ancient.

When the man with the raised machete stood over him and

howled in triumph, Pedro recognized that the powerful craving he suddenly felt was ferocious hunger.

Hunger for living flesh. He ached to sink his teeth into the machete man's inviting throat.

Then the machete's blade came down and hacked hacked hacked his head off his neck.

And still he was hungry, snapping his ruined teeth and broken jaw at the man who lifted his head by his sparse hair and held it up to the moon.

# 8
# Dead But Not Gone

Piggy Poop walked the tracks. Not thinking. Just walking. Walking. One foot dragging. Step. Drag. Step. Walking.

Until she saw the fire. Then thoughts formed, flickered, flared against dancing memories. She veered off the tracks and headed toward the firelight, her gait gawky and halting because of the injuries sustained in the fall, the leap and impact. A hitch in her get-along.

A thought leapt into her mind: hobo fire. Then: campfire . . . cookfire . . . food! She was achingly hungry. Hunger kept her going now. Where the impulse toward death had been a driving force in her life, now it was a raw visceral hunger that drove her.

She knew she was something other than alive. She could feel herself swinging like a wobbly pendulum between the poles of Dead and Alive. You didn't do a flip off a bridge like she did and live. No way. Impossible to walk away from that. Yet she had. And was. Walking. Dead. Walking. And oh so hungry. Hungry with a deep carnal lust. Carnivore lust. Stronger than sex. Stronger than death. She wanted, needed bloody meat. Extremely rare. Make that raw. And while you're at it, make it living. *I want blood pumping through my dinner.* Blood. Lots of blood. To sate the terrible thirst on the underbelly of this infernal hunger.

She left the rail bed and shambled up a short weed-choked slope. She saw two men huddled round the fire. What used to be called hobos, bums. Sitting there like they were waiting for her. An existential invitation to dine. Meat on the hoof. She heard the blood pulsing through their veins. She knew the taste would be intoxicating. Even orgasmic. Yes.

One of them was wiping the bottom of a bowl clean of bean juice with a crust of bread and the other was turning up a pint of dark port. A third man lay curled in an army blanket, shivering and groaning.

"Be cold as a bitch tit 'for this night is through," said the bean eater.

"Old Sambo's shivering his ass off already and the bitch ain't even here yet," the other man said between sucks on his bottle.

"I could use me some warm titties 'bout now. Piece of pussy wouldn't hurt none neither. 'Bout as likely as winning a billion-dollar lotto."

"Wouldn't do it no how with that God's Eye up there watching ya."

Then the wine drinker saw Piggy Poop step into the firelight and said, "Jesus God girl!"

"What in hell happened to you?!" Bean Sop said.

"Damn me but what she ain't got a big hole in her head," Wine Suck said.

Piggy Poop said, "Mumph mee" as she stagger-stepped over to the bum in the blanket.

"What'd she say?" Sop asked his bud.

"Fuck if I know," said Suck. "Damned if I didn't just shit myself. *Shit.*"

Piggy went awkwardly to her knees beside the man in the blanket, who had for the moment stopped shivering and groaning.

"Hey," shouted Sop, "he's took sick. Leave him be, little lady."

She bent over and took a big bite out of Sick's face.

Sop shouted.

Suck doubled over and shat himself some more.

Piggy spat and sputtered, sickened a little herself by the mouthful of cooling meat. Just that quick the sick man had died. And dead meat was not at all what she craved. Flesh drizzled with pumping blood was the only thing that would fill the bill.

She craned her head slowly, looking for a bite to eat. Just as her eyes fell on Suck, Sop cracked her across the side of the head with a piece of firewood. The blow dropped her. Her face hit the dirt by the edge of the fire.

"Jesus Christ Almighty," Suck said, agawk and fanning his own foul fumes, "I can't take no more of this crazy shit."

Piggy Poop opened her eyes. She thought she could feel her lips forming a smile. *Crazy shit* had always been her thing. Her forte, her *raison d'être*. (Funny she could remember a French phrase but couldn't remember being anybody other than Piggy Poop. Though she was sure she'd had another name. A real name. Oh well. *Piggy Poop* would do as her *nom de guerre*. Huh? *Merde!* There was another one. Maybe she was French?)

Before she could get up, the guy with the log-turned-cudgel said, "I'm gonna fuck this gimpy bitch sideways" and walloped her again.

Then the dead man in the blanket sat up and eyeballed his former companions with gimlet eyes and a crooked mouth. The gaping wound in his cheek looked like a second mouth, toothless, raw gums shining wetly in the moonlight.

# 9
## Incident At Mo' Tail Motel

". . . also said they are looking for a very tall man in a red hooded sweatshirt. Officials would neither confirm nor deny the possibility of related terrorist acts, saying only that the hooded man is at this time a 'person of interest' in some of these incidents."

"Turn that down, dammit," said Jamie, standing naked at the window and peeping through the curtains as she smoked a Virginia Slim. "I can't hear what they're saying."

"Don't let them see you naked," Thomas cautioned her as he decreased the volume with the remote.

"Why would they give a shit? I'm not breaking any law here. They don't arrest people for adultery. Hell, they'd probably appreciate a peek at my goodies. I do look pretty damn good, ya know."

The only light in the room flickered from the TV screen. Outside, flashing blue light from two cop cruisers lapped at the room's windows as if it wanted in.

"According to the news, weird things are happening all across the border and on into the interior," he said from the bed. "Reports of the rapid spread of an unknown disease, unexplained outbreaks of violence. A health official said the disease appears to mimic death, in some cases."

"You heard all that while I was in the bathroom? Jeez." She reached back and swiped her fingers between her ass cheeks. "And I've *still* got your spunk leaking out of my bum."

"What are they doing out there?"

"Why don't you come look?"

"I don't want anybody to recognize me."

"Don't worry, you're not that famous, Reverend."

"Just tell me."

She exhaled a smoky sigh. "Two cops are talking to the night manager and the other two are still in the room. I could hear them talking through the wall before you turned the TV up so damn loud. Oh goody, here comes the ambulance. Now maybe we'll get a look at what they roll out."

A scream came through the wall from the room next door. A muffled shout, then two loud gunshots.

"Holy shit!" Jamie said. Then she doubled over, clutching her belly.

Thomas jumped out of bed. "What? Are you shot?"

She shook her head. Gasped: "Cramps. Bad ones."

As if a switch had been flipped, she started shivering. Her teeth chattered. Thomas wrapped his arms around her and pressed his nakedness against hers to warm her. "Back to bed and cover up. Whatever you're coming down with, it sure came on fast. It couldn't be any sort of toxic shock, could it? From what we did? The anal thing?"

"No, you idiot," she chattered. "I'll be fine. *You* watch at the window. See what the hell's happening."

"We should get out of here. A bullet could come through the wall."

"I can't, not yet. After these shakes stop maybe. Aspirin. In my bag. Glass of water."

He put her to bed and gave her two aspirin tablets. She gulped them with water out of a plastic cup from the bathroom. Thomas slipped into his boxers and stationed himself at the window.

"See anything?" Jamie asked, huddled and shuddering hard beneath the covers.

"No, just the police cars and ambulance. Whoa, wait. They're bringing out the stretcher. Body's covered up, purple blanket. Head covered too. That means deceased. Guess they had to shoot him, whoever it was."

Jamie grunted. Her teeth kept up their chattering racket.

Thomas suddenly stiffened his spine. "Good Lord! What in the name of . . . ? *Unbelievable.* The guy under the blanket *isn't* dead. He's trying to get up off the stretcher. He's . . . his face. No *way* he could be alive."

Jamie said, "Come. Hold me. I need a warm body. I'm so c-c-c-cold."

"Whoa. They're buckling him down with extra straps. Sweet Jesus, half his face is missing."

"Tommy . . ."

"Yeah, just a sec."

"Cold."

"Oh! A cop just clubbed him. A good one upside the head. Damn!"

"*Tommy . . .*"

"*Now* they'll get him in the ambulance. They subdued the shit out of him. So much for being dead. It must be the mystery disease they were talking about on TV. Said it mimicked death. I hope to God that's not what you have."

"Just a bug. Hold me. I can't seem to get warm."

He stepped out of his shorts and slipped under the covers. He held her tightly and vigorously rubbed her everywhere his hands could reach. "Better?"

"Maybe a little. Don't stop."

"Uh-oh, I'm getting another erection. Sorry. It's just—"

"Fu-fu-fu-fuck me. I feel so empty. I ne-ne-need you inside me."

"You sure you're up to it? Maybe that's not such a good idea."

"Fuck me, d-d-damn you."

He gave her a crooked grin. "Yes ma'am. You're the boss."

He rolled on top of her and she took him in both hands and pushed him inside.

"I think you need a little lubricant this time," he said.

"No. Stay there. Fuck me. Fuck me hard so I can feel it. I want it rough. Are you still in? I can't feel you."

"Yes, I'm in. Don't belittle Mr. Willy. He's sensitive to that kind of thing." His chuckle rang hollow.

"God," she said, her inflection inching closer to the realm of hysteria, "I'm going numb all over. *What's happening?*"

"Shush. It's all right. You'll be fine."

"No I won't be fine. What's happening to me? Tommy?"

"I'm right here. Take it easy. Just rest."

Her shudders became more violent, and then finally subsided. She shut her eyes and drifted toward sleep. He did not shrink inside her. His erection sustained itself through the magic of modern chemistry. He shut his eyes and listened to the low-volume voice on the cable news channel. The anchorman said, "Joining us by phone is Reverend Barry Grayson. Reverend Grayson, I understand you have a different take on the extraordinary events unfolding as we speak. You believe there may be a link between the mysterious outbreak along the southwest border and the unexplained spectacle of the so-called *eye in the sky*."

Grayson said, "That's right, Bret, I do. In fact, I think it's obvious that what we're witnessing is the beginning of End Times. Nonbelievers in the secular world will mock me for saying so and pooh-pooh it on reflex, but I believe with all my heart and soul that the End of Days is upon us. As prophesied in the Abrahamic religions, the doomsday scenario is about to play itself out on the world's stage. Whether Christian, Muslim or Jew, you can't look up at that magnificent eye in the sky and deny that it is the very eye of God. *For these be the days of vengeance, that all things which are written may be fulfilled.* The message couldn't be clearer, Bret. As it is written in scripture, *Men's hearts failing them for fear, and for looking after those things which are coming on the earth: for the powers of heaven shall be shaken. And then shall they see the Son of man coming in a cloud with power and great glory.* God's judgment is at hand. Fall on your knees and pray for forgiveness. I don't believe we have much time."

Thomas whispered, "Amen, brother."

His penis remained stubbornly erect inside his unconscious lover.

He remembered that a possible sideeffect of Cialis was priapism, an erection that would not go away for hours.

Was the little yellow caplet (Jamie had jokingly called it his "hamburger helper") putting *too much* lead in his pencil, he wondered.

But he didn't trouble himself long with worry. Feeling unaccountably fatigued, he fell asleep with his hard-on held firmly within the folds of Jamie's sex.

# 10
## Fuck Me Dead

Piggy Poop stayed on the ground and didn't try to resist as the bum unzipped and stuck his prick into the hole in her head. It was an odd sensation, nothing much sexual about it, but not unpleasant for an erstwhile antichrist and former Goth chick with a death wish. It reminded her vaguely of the recreational cutting she used to do on her flesh with a razor blade, except that the skull-fucking didn't hurt. Come to that, nothing much hurt her now. Weird. As shit. And getting weirder.

The dude's dick made squishing sounds against her exposed brain. "Fucking your brains out, cunt," he said and laughed between ugly grunts of piggish passion.

Piggy smiled, or thought she did, it was hard to tell because she was pretty much numb all over, physical sensations dulled by death—or whatever this was. It was certainly some variation of death because you sure as shit couldn't call this living. But smile she did, or tried to. She'd always wanted her brains fucked out. Not necessarily by a stinking hobo but beggars and dead girls couldn't be choosers. She would let the guy get his nut and then she would have his nuts and his cock too, as appetizers. After that she would make a feast of his choicest parts before he died. The bum with the shitty britches was not on her menu. And for the moment Suck was busy wrestling with Sick, trying to keep him on the ground and wrapped in the blanket. Suck was apparently so dense that he didn't know, as Piggy did, that Sick was like her—some kind of dead.

Sop was on his knees with his loins bridging the back of Piggy's head and his hands resting on the ground as he made short thrusts into her head, the tip of his prick hammering her brain as he worked the narrow fissure in her skull. He made nastier grunting noises and occasionally snorted like a rooting pig as he got closer to getting his nut.

The way Piggy Poop was positioned, she had a good view of Suck and Sick going at each other, shitty Suck having the upper hand because Sick was half swaddled in the blanket and couldn't get clear enough to win the advantage and do what Piggy knew he so wanted to do to his opponent with the beating heart and tantalizing living flesh.

"I don't know why you ain't dead, bitch," the brain-fucker sweet talked her, "but this is the best brain I ever had, haw hee haw."

Getting into the spirit of the crazy-ass moment, Piggy said, "Fuck me dead," or tried to. What came out as a whisper was more like "Uck ee edd."

"I wouldn't touch your skanky pussy," he said, "with Sambo's dick but your skull hole is sweet. Damn!"

"Fuck me dead, cocksucker." Which of course hissed out as "Uck ee edd, ock ucka."

"Here it comes, you retard whore. Yeeeeeeeeeeeeeeeeeehaaaa-aaaaaaa . . ."

# PART II
# AFTERDEATH

*And the sea gave up the dead which were in it; and death and hell delivered up the dead which were in them: and they were judged every man according to their works.*
—Revelation 20:13

## 11
## Terror Man

Nadif Awad was a long way from Somaliland. It was a strange and winding path that brought him from his African homeland to the border of the United States, land of infidels and corrupt kingdom of the Great Satan. It was not until he came to understand that the stoning death of his betrothed Aziza was the will of Allah that Nadif was ready to join the Grand Jihad and to take the attack to America. Now whenever he relived in nightmares the stoning of his beloved Aziza, he turned his resulting anger on all enemies of Islam and blamed them, however indirectly, for her death. Such anger was useful to a warrior.

She was buried up to her neck in the ground and killed by the hurled rocks that turned her beautiful face into a bloody abomination because she had been gang-raped by godless thugs. Nadif didn't precisely see the justice in her punishment, nor understand how it was that she deserved to die for having been raped, but who was he to argue with an imam whose devotion to the laws of sharia was unimpeachable?

Had Aziza not died, Nadif would not have joined Harakat al-Shabaab Mujahideen, Movement of Warrior Youth. Her death had left him ripe for recruitment.

Had Aziza not been stoned to death by the villagers, then Nadif would not be carrying the seeds of Great Satan's destruction in his backpack across the border. He would not have learned to speak flawless Spanish in order to pass himself off as an illegal immigrant from Nicaragua.

Now when he saw Aziza in his mind's eye, he saw her with one eyeball hanging over her cheek by a stem from a ruined socket, hanging like a broken flower. Nadif's rock hadn't knocked her eye out of her head, that much he was sure of. The stone he threw at his beloved's head had struck the delicate bridge of her nose. He hadn't wanted to participate in the stoning but it would have been wrong to go against the dictates of sharia law as well as against the will of the other villagers. Nadif had a responsibility as one of them. So he had mustered enough anger at Aziza, anger for getting herself raped by thugs, to propel the stone with enough brutal force to break her nose.

The image of her once lovely eye hanging like a broken flower over her bloodied cheek would not leave him. And try as he might, he could not absolve himself of the guilt he felt for having had a hand in killing her. He told himself he had no reason to feel guilty but he felt it nonetheless.

He looked up at the unholy eye glowing in the night sky and he shuddered. That unnatural eye terrified him. Others among his party of border crossers speculated that it was the eye of their Christian god come to either judge them or watch over them but Nadif feared that it was the very eye of Great Satan looking down on his cursed continent.

Looking down on him.

Seeing into his heart and reading his murderous intentions.

*Allah protect me*, he silently prayed. *Give me the courage and strength to unleash this plague upon the infidels of this godless country.*

All he had to do was follow the plan mapped out for him by his al-Shabaab handlers. The Mexican "coyote" had been well-paid to see that Nadif got across with no untoward difficulty. He called himself El Lobo and was in effect Nadif's guide and bodyguard. He was a filthy man of slovenly habits and Nadif disliked and distrusted him. But he would follow the plan. As instructed. As he had trained to do. Once across the border, Nadif would rendezvous with a Shabaab brother already in Arizona and would be driven to Los Angeles, California, where he would deliver the canisters of the weaponized plague virus to those brothers who would set it loose upon Great Satan's left coast. They would provide further instructions for him. Nadif was prepared to give his life if necessary. He was ready to earn his place in paradise.

El Lobo spoke harshly to the others in their party, barking hoarsely at them to step lively, to stop dragging, to stop talking, but he said nothing to Nadif. Nadif suspected this was because the man had been very well paid to deliver him to his Shabaab brothers.

But perhaps it was something more as well. Perhaps the coyote was afraid of Nadif. Afraid of what he carried. As well he should be. Yes. It was good to command such respect. Nadif was sure that El Lobo could not know what was in Nadif's backpack but he sensed that something of terrible power was secreted within it.

One of the women stumbled and fell to her knees. El Lobo cursed her and kicked her on the rump to urge her on. Nadif had to bite his tongue until he tasted blood so that he would not rebuke the filthy man. It was not easy to see in the dark, not even with the bright moonlight on the land but Nadif knew the woman had stumbled because she had been keeping her own wary eye on the wicked eye above, looking down on them with searing malevolence.

El Lobo coughed, fitfully at first, then with increasing regularity until he had to bend at the waist in a veritable fit of non-stop coughing. He retched. He cursed. He wiped his mouth with the back of his hand. Coughed some more.

The party of sixteen souls had to halt to wait for El Lobo to recover from his coughing attack. When Nadif saw that the coyote was coughing up blood, he feared that one of the canisters had leaked and that El Lobo was merely the first among them to succumb to the virus. But no, the former Soviet scientists who had genetically manipulated and weaponized the virus would not have been so careless as to improperly seal the air-tight containers.

Nadif warily approached El Lobo, who was now on his knees and still coughing. "Are you all right?" he asked.

El Lobo growled at him and waved him away with a blood-speckled paw. "¡Estancia lejos!" Stay away!

Nadif was going to stand his ground and remind the man that he had been paid handsomely to take him where he needed to go, but then El Lobo fell face-down on the ground and didn't move. Didn't breathe. Nadif reluctantly checked the man's pulse. He didn't have one.

"Él es muerto," he said. Dead. Just that quick. Unnaturally quick, Nadif thought. He glanced up at the fearsome eye above. Then at his traveling companions. Now what? Did anyone else know the way they were supposed to go? A stout man in a baseball cap and dirty overalls said he could get them to the outskirts of Tucson.

The woman who had stumbled and had been punished for it by El Lobo was suddenly seized by a fit of coughing.

Nadif pulled the stout man aside and told him he would pay him two hundred dollars to get him to Tucson. The money was stashed in his sock. He showed it to the man and told him he would pay him upon reaching their destination. The man nodded.

The coughing woman begged them to wait for her to catch her breath, promising that she would be able to keep up with them once she stopped coughing and could catch her breath. Nadif said she would not stop and that she was going to end up like El Lobo. Make peace with your god, he told her. You are already dead.

He swatted a fly buzzing near his face.

She coughed. She pleaded for them not to abandon her.

Some of them said they thought they should give her a chance. Wait awhile.

Nadif shook his head, steeled himself, then pulled his knife, grabbed a handful of her hair and slit her throat. He looked at the others and said, "Vayamos."

The woman died noisily. Blood gurgled in her throat and bubbled and foamed in the raw gash which made Nadif think of female sex organs and how unclean they were. He realized that he was still holding a handful of her hair. He let it go and her head thumped to the ground. She writhed. She clutched at her slit throat, eyes wide with panic and fear. The others silently watched her die, terror engraved in their moonlit faces.

"Vayamos," Nadif repeated. *Let's go.*

As if responding to Nadif's command, El Lobo rose up from the ground.

*Rose from the dead.* Stood there unmoving for a long moment, and then lurched forward, reaching for Nadif.

Nadif's knife-hand shot out to stab the dead man's throat even as his mind whispered to itself that there was no way El Lobo could be up and walking because the dead did not walk. He jerked the blade out and jabbed it back in.

Out, in. Out, in. Jab. Jab Jab.

And still the man stood, still reaching out so that finally Nadif had to take steps backward to avoid the dead man's grasp and the feel of his cold fingers.

"But he was dead," Nadif said. But he said it in his native tongue, not in Spanish. Not that these Mexicans would know Somali when they heard it, but it was a sign that he was losing control.

How could he maintain control when the world no longer made

sense? When the dead walk. When repeated stabs to the throat have no power to stop a dead man's walking.

Nadif tripped over a rock and stumbled backward to the ground.

As he struggled to get up before El Lobo could set upon him, he saw another impossible sight. The woman whose throat he'd only moments ago cut was on her feet and was bearing down on him as well.

Just before he jumped up and started slashing at the ghouls with his knife, Nadif glimpsed the evil eye of Satan gazing down on him and he realized that this was hell on earth and he was already damned.

Allah was not at all pleased.

An abyss of terror opened inside him and threatened to swallow him up.

## 12
## Accidental Necrophilia

Thomas drifted in darkness. This was one of those I'm Dreaming moments when he knew he was dreaming strange pathways through sleep and had arrived at a crossroads—he could go toward the muted light and wake up all the way or he could plumb the depths down dreaming's darker path.

Two things brought him slowly to the light. The cold remoteness of his lover's body and the intimate tones of TV voices. First (*In the beginning was the word*), he focused on the soft and slightly sultry voice of the female newscaster: ". . . because emergency responders are stretched so thin. In related news, the statewide demonstrations and counter demonstrations set for tomorrow will go on as planned, according to spokesmen for both sides of the illegal immigration issue. The embattled Arizona governor says she won't hesitate to call out the National Guard if necessary, in the event the demonstrations turn violent."

Then he realized, much to his horror, that Jamie was cold and lifeless. Her chest did not rise and fall against his. Her skin was clammy and as cold as a cut of meat on a butcher's block. Her eyes were half open, hooded with swollen lids, glazed and death-clouded.

He tried to push himself off her but they were joined at the loins. Stuck! His painful erection refused to come out of her. The cold walls of her vagina held him fast.

"No, no, this can't be," he said, whether to himself or to his deceased lover he couldn't have said.

He tried again to free himself.

No go.

"Please, Jamie, you have to let me go," he said, not caring how crazy it was to say such a thing to a corpse.

He fought the impulse to pummel her to escape the claustrophobic closeness, told himself not to panic. Stay calm. Be rational. He knew he could roll over onto his back, stand up and carry her across the room to get his cell phone from his pants. He could call for an ambulance and hope the paramedics could get him unstuck here in the motel room without having to haul him into the emergency room like *this*. *In flagrante delicto*. That was the *worst* that could happen. And that was if he couldn't get his penis out of her by his own efforts. He'd never heard of this happening to humans. He'd seen dogs stuck together in intercourse and he'd had a good laugh at their doggy dilemma but this was different. Being stuck to a dead woman was not only not funny, it made him an accidental necrophiliac. Having sex with a corpse was against the law. He couldn't prove she was alive when he entered her. Medical personnel could report him to the police. He could go to jail! And even if he wasn't arrested, there would be whispers and rumors and wicked gossip.

He looked about the room as if there might be some answer to his dilemma waiting there. Could he pry himself out of her with something? Like a shoehorn? No, that would damage her and raise terrible questions. And he might damage himself in the process.

His cell phone rang. His ringtone was the ring of an old-fashion phone, a subtle point of rebellion against the high-tech takeover of civilization. It seemed silly now. How civilized was it to be stuck in a dead adulteress's snatch?

It had to be his wife Jean calling. It was almost midnight and she would be worried.

He sat up with Jamie straddling him like a life-size rag doll and scooted to the edge of the bed. Then he stood up and walked with her like a drunken acrobat across the room to slip a hand into his trousers and extract his phone. His wife's name appeared in the LED display. He did not open the phone. He let it ring. And ring. What could he possibly say to her now? *Sure, honey, I know I'm a man of the cloth but I'm also a man of flesh with wicked carnal appetites.* No way would *that* do. He would call her back later, once this pressing situation was resolved. He was confident that he could think up a suitable explanation, as long as he didn't have to come up with a way to explain how he happened to be in a motel room with a dead woman. And the only way to avoid that was to get his dick out of her and slip off into the night. The room was registered in Jamie's name. All he had to do was get *unstuck*. But Jamie was holding him fast, not unlike Bre'r Rabbit and the tar baby.

He had an idea. A cold shower and lathered soap. It was worth a try. Like soaping up to get a ring off your finger, right? "Damned right," he muttered.

He headed toward the bathroom. Walking with a woman attached to his loins was murder on the lower back and thigh muscles. He walked with an exaggerated and contorted swagger, bent backward at the waist, swinging his hips and swinging Jamie as well. He thanked God that she wasn't a large woman. The unusual movement produced novel sensations on and within his swollen penis, sensations not unpleasant, and he realized in horror that he was inching closer to climax. He scolded himself: *If you come in a corpse you'll be damned beyond redemption.*

As he was doing his preposterous walk through the bathroom doorway, Jamie's head banged against the doorframe.

"Oh, sorry," he said, automatically.

*Idiot, talking to a dead woman.* No sooner had the thought run through his mind than the dead woman opened her eyes.

"*Jesus*, Jamie?"

Her dead eyes fixed on him and her mouth went through a swift series of juddering contortions. He thought for a moment that she was trying to say something but then she bared her teeth and he realized too late that she intended to sink them into his neck. Which she did, viciously and with surprising power in her jaws.

In trying to get away from her perfect teeth and evil intentions, Thomas fell backward, banging his head on the floor and knocking himself out. When he came to, he came to a world of pain and hellish suffering.

The woman he'd made an adulteress—a woman dead but in no way departed—was eating him alive, bite by ripping bite.

He fought back in desperation. He pummeled her head and face but they were at such close quarters that he couldn't put much force behind his blows. Between bites, he managed to put a forearm under her chin and jam it into her throat and then rolled over into the missionary position. She snapped her teeth at his face. He bore down now with both his forearms in her throat. Their feet were in the bathroom, the rest of them in the bedroom, where the carpet was collecting his spilled blood. That which wasn't spilled, Jamie had already claimed. And she showed no sign that she would soon be sated.

She snapped. She made guttural sounds in the back of her throat, even as he exerted still more pressure, trying to crush her throat, trying to return her to the everyday realm of the dead.

But she would not give up the fight to remain here in the half-life of living death. Jamie—if it *was* still Jamie inside this ferocious corpse—fought with as much strength as she'd had in life. Maybe more. And now Thomas was having a harder time fending her off because his skin was so slippery with blood. *His* blood. He was losing too much of it and was rapidly growing weaker.

The phone. He had to call for medical help or he wasn't going to survive.

He tried to drag himself (and his zombie attachment) across the carpet with one hand while keeping the other arm on Jamie's throat. But his arm kept slipping off her and she kept biting his forearm, her teeth digging in like big-gauge needles. And the more she bit, the more he bled, the more his arm slipped, the more she bit, the more he bled . . .

(Was that his phone in his hand? His thick thumb tapping 9-1-1?)

It occurred to him that this was hell. God wasn't waiting for him to die to send him to hell. Hell was right here, right now.

Apparently, hell was a porno zombie movie. And Thomas was damned to play out his part. For the moment Zombie Jamie was mostly chewing scenery but if he passed out from losing too much blood, she would freely feast upon his flesh until he was nothing but gnawed bone—or until she exploded like an overfed tick.

*Will I be like her when I die?* No RIP for Zombie Tommy. Tommy Zombie. Tomby. Zero, none, nada. Not for Zommy.

*Mommy?*

Such were his last living thoughts as his bloody arm slipped, slid and slithered off Jamie and he collapsed face-first on the carpet.

At the end (if *the end* it was), her teeth didn't hurt him anymore. They only tickled a little.

# 13
## Postmortem Pedro

Head's in a hatbox.

Stinking to high heaven.

Ranker than a cat box.

This cat with no hat.

Pedro passed his time in the box making bad rhyme, influenced by his love for Dr. Seuss. How his grandkids Juanita and Jorge had loved having him read those stories! But this, this was not a tale for kids.

He had never been sure he could believe in God or trust that there would be an afterlife but he sure as the devil hadn't expected anything like this. His head in a hatbox, his body back there on the prairie by the side of the road, doing God-knows-what?

This was some kind of bad joke. Unless he was dreaming, which he didn't think he was. He wasn't capable of dreaming up anything this wild and crazy. No way. Not bullheaded Pedro, no.

Pedro the Undead Head, maybe.

An hombre could go loco in such close confines.

The worst was this thirst. Or hunger, whichever it was. Thirst, yes. For blood. That he could recognize it for what it was, was some sort of miracle in itself. It was the heart of the curse of being an undying corpse. The Baddest Sheriff in America was no novice at deduction. That this was a curse rather than a gift was a logical conclusion.

He'd also deduced that he was riding in the front seat of the truck, in the hatbox his killers had dropped him into, now resting between the two killers who were arguing over what they should do with his decapitated head. The pickup's radio was on an all-talk station and some nitwit scientist was laying out his theory that the big eye in the sky was there because of global warming (which he used interchangeably with "manmade climate change of the catastrophic kind").

"Put his fucking head on a spike at the border, as a greeting to all crossers," the driver said.

"No, we stick to the plan," said the other guy, "and deliver it to his daughter. That way it hits the media big time. And that's the whole point."

Pedro wanted with all his heart (not the one still in his headless body back there on the side of the road, but the metaphorical one) to break out of this box and chew these two *pendejas* to death. Trouble was, he couldn't move. All he could do was work his broken jaws. And his good eye. He couldn't blink or jaw his way out of the box or jump out and attack anybody. He couldn't talk or yell without working vocal chords in a voice box and lungs full of air. He'd already tried. All he could do was mouth silent curses at his killers.

Yeah, this was hell all right. No doubt about it.

And Pedro was in it for the duration. Didn't need to be Sherlock Holmes to deduce that. He wasn't sure what he might've done to deserve such torment but like they said, God works in mysterious ways. And the Big Guy couldn't get much more mysterious than this hellish horseshit.

The driver said, "I don't care what we do with it as long as we get rid of it quick. Fucking head's haunted, man."

"I told you, that was reflex action," the passenger said. "Like when you cut off a snapping turtle's head, it can still bite the shit out of you. I got the scar to prove that shit."

"No, man, did you see his eye? It was still looking at us. Seeing us, man."

Pedro's heart (not the unbeating one) sank at the thought of his daughter Maria opening up the hatbox and seeing her father's hideous dead head. That he would have to *see* her seeing him filled him with horror. And murderous rage.

He wanted to tear into these assholes so bad he could almost taste it. Taste *them*. Not their assholes, their throats, where rich blood ran in tasty arteries, blood that would pump into his mouth in thick spurts if only he could sink his teeth into their tender flesh.

*Ay yi yi!*

Pedro wasn't sure, but he thought his mouth maybe watered a little.

## 14
## Cruz Control

Bobby Cruz couldn't remember how he got here. Didn't really know where *here* was. Wasn't sure it mattered very much, if at all. Here, there, everywhere. Nowhere.

There were lights. Streetlights. Neon signs. Few cars cruising the streets. Tires hissing over wet pavement.

Damndest thing. He felt like he was in someone else's body. A stranger's body. Walking around in it, taking it for a lazy spin the way punk-teen carjackers used to go joyriding on "borrowed" wheels.

But that wasn't quite right either. There was something else going on here. A strong feeling that he was under the control of someone or some*thing* else. Something was taking *him* for a joyride. But that wasn't right either, because there was no joy here, and there wouldn't be any. He didn't know how he knew this, but he knew that he did. No joy.

He'd been manjacked and he felt certain that he was heading for one hell of a crackup.

And somebody was watching it all happen. Watching *him*. He looked up at the night sky.

When he saw the eye he remembered.

He was on a story. The sacked reporter going undercover and incognito for a border-crossing exposé. Then he remembered being stuck in the back of the old U-haul truck with the monster flies attacking him and his fellow travelers.

And the weird dude in the red hoodie. Lord of Flies.

And that fucking crazy eye up there seeing everything. Maybe even making it all happen. *Was seeing believing?*

And that was where his memory went blank. Whatever happened after that, he had no clue.

No matter. There was a bigger story here. Much bigger than the one he'd set out to do. It didn't take a crackerjack reporter to get that.

And Bobby Cruz felt that he had been chosen to write it. He was to be the scribe who sets it all down for posterity.

All he had to do was sniff it out.

Scare it up and write it down.

*The Real Story* by Bobby Cruz. Or whatever it was to be called. He would be told when the time came. He had faith in that much. Someone or some*thing* would clue him in.

A bar up on the right. Beer lights flashing in the windows.

Yeah, he could use a drink. He had a bitch of a thirst that wouldn't quit.

And who knew? There just might be a lead to his big story waiting for him in there.

Something told him it was.

# 15
# Apparition

Magda Menendez was good and dead. Her flesh was meat-locker cold in this barren land's night winds. Dead. Yet aware of everything. She didn't understand how this could be. How she could be so intensely aware of her surroundings. How could death be such an eye-opener?

The panties on the rape tree fluttered like little pastel ghosts. A coyote yipped in the distance. A scorpion strutted by. A spider skimmed over sand.

It was true: Magda was trapped in a broken and abused body, decay already eating away at the edges of her timid existence. But somehow it did not distress her. Somehow it seemed as if it were meant to be exactly like this. If the vultures came in the morning to do their part in eating Magda out of the world, that would be fine and natural. God put bacteria and buzzards on the earth to clean up the mess death leaves behind. *Life* leaves behind.

There was no pain. Where in life there were aches and pains of every variety, now there was only the sluggish heaviness of gravity and an all-over numbness akin to the effect of Novocain dentists use to deaden your mouth.

It came as a surprise and a revelation that she could move the unbroken parts of her dead body. At first this horrified her. It was ghoulish. It made her an evil instrument of the Devil. But then she found the rosary she had put on like a necklace before she left home, and she lifted it off over her head, kissed the attached crucifix and mouthed her heart's prayer: "Hail-Mary-full-of-grace-the-Lord-is-with-thee-Blessed-art-thou-among-women-and-blessed-is-the-fruit-of-thy-womb-Jesus-Holy-Mary-Mother-of-God-pray-for-us-sinners-now-and-at-the-hour-of-our-death. Amen." Then she amended: "Now *after* the hour of my death. Amen."

She made the sign of the cross with the rosary, fingers brushing the mutilated remains of her chewed-up breasts. The woman who'd done the chewing had apparently eaten her fill and stalked off into the dark. In search of fresher meat?

Magda wondered where she herself would go if she could walk. Where was there to go? If a dead Catholic girl cannot go to Heaven, why go anywhere? No, it was just as well that she could not get up and walk. She believed with certainty that there was no decent destination for the walking dead.

If idle hands were the Devil's playthings then surely the feet of the walking dead were something much worse.

Clutching the rosary's crucifix in both hands, she silently uttered another prayer the nuns had taught her: "O my Jesus, forgive us our sins, save us from the fires of hell and lead all souls to heaven, especially those in most need of thy mercy. Amen."

She avoided looking at the evil eye in the night sky. She closed her eyes and tried to concentrate her thoughts on the Savior but she was finding it more and more difficult to hold thoughts long in her head. Death was eating away at her thought processes.

Fear seized her in its crushing grip. She was all at once terrified by the notion that her soul was doomed to wither with her body.

An explosion of light burned through her eyelids. She gasped, or would have if there had been anything other than dead air in her deflated lungs.

She opened her eyes.

An elongated sphere of blindingly bright white light towered over her. The air hummed with anticipation. Deep blue blossomed in the midst of the white light. The blue of a long, shimmering gown.

"Do not be afraid, little one," the light said.

Magda mouthed the words "¿Madre santa?" *Holy Mother.*

She could just make out the apparition's elegant face in the center of the light as a feeling of peace washed over her like a warm and gentle wave from a holy ocean.

—*Have you come to take me to Heaven?* Magda asked in her mind.

"No, little one," said the Lady of Light, "I have come to tell you to show others the way."

—*But I died. I can't walk. I can't even talk. Except to you. What way?*

"The way to the Kingdom of Heaven. But don't fret, Magdalena, you will move through this land of death in your risen body, immaculate and uninjured. You will be in this world but not of it."

—*Like . . . an illegal?*

The Holy Mother smiled. "More like this," she said and extended a white hand from the blue folds of her gown and held it inches above Magda's head. She did this without having to bend over and it wasn't till then that Magda realized that she was floating in the air. The holy apparition had made her levitate.

An incredible instant later, everything changed.

## 16
## Underground With the Dead

Border Patrol Agent Betty Davis Wolfe knew they were not alone in the tunnel. Something or someone was directly behind her, watching them. She could feel its presence just as surely as if it had reached out and tickled the tiny hairs on the back of her neck. Her partner was on his hands and knees three feet ahead of her, following his flashlight's beam deeper into the inky black tunnel.

Crawling along with her rear end raised and vulnerable was not a position a woman wanted to be in, especially in such a cramped and confining space as this tunnel under Nogales. Especially when she felt such a palpable presence at her back.

She told herself it was her imagination, sparked by her extreme dislike of cramped spaces. A cigarette would calm her wired nerves. She hadn't had one in more than four hours. She had been about to light one up but then they found the trapdoor in the floor of the empty warehouse, opened it up and now here they were, checking out the secret tunnel running from the other side of the fence in Mexico, smack-dab straight into Nogales, Arizona. Underground USA. There were many miners in Mexico, which meant a lot of guys had the know-how to engineer a tunnel like this one, shored up with wooden beams and even air-conditioned by a long plastic tube that resembled a fat green snake. It would've cost a drug cartel a pretty penny to have this tunnel dug but the profits from the product they could run through here would have earned them *prettier* pennies—a hell of a lot of them.

That was, if Border Patrol Agent Betty Davis Wolfe and her partner Alejandro Bravo hadn't found it and already called it in. Betty had wanted to wait for the team to get here before they went down but Bravo Macho (as Betty called him when she wanted to needle the cocky little guy) couldn't wait, so here they were, just the two of them, with backup a long way away.

God but she was dying for a smoke.

Then she smelled it. Whatever the hell was behind her *was* behind her. There was no doubt now. This was not imagination. She smelled the stinking son of a bitch.

She reached back to her right hip and unholstered her Heckler & Koch P 2000 .40 caliber automatic. The only way to turn around to face the rear was to sit and turn. There would be a few seconds of darkness before she would have time to draw and thumb on her flashlight with her left hand. But first she had to alert her partner.

"Hold up, Bravo, I've got somebody on my tail," she said and then turned as fast as she could and shot the flashlight beam into the darkness.

Nothing there. The light played on the wooden beams at the tunnel's ceiling. The beams made her think of the ribs of some giant serpentine beast, as seen from inside the monster. Jonah in the whale. Or was it Pinocchio?

"Where?" Bravo asked. From the sound of his voice behind her, she knew he had also turned around. Which meant he could also see that there was no one there. His beam joined hers and the tunnel looked more like a tunnel and less like the inside of a dragon or giant serpent.

"I smelled it," she said.

"Smelled what?" He didn't disguise his disgust for her rookie-like jumpiness.

"I don't know. Shit."

"You smelled shit?"

"No. I mean, maybe. I don't—"

Bravo Macho screamed. It was a very unmacho scream.

Betty spun on her ass and put her light on a dark-skinned man burying his face in the side of Bravo's neck. And on the blood spilling onto the shoulder of his uniform. Was the guy actually going vampire on Bravo?

Wiry Bravo hit at his attacker with his flashlight, clocked him a good one on top of the head but the guy didn't let go. His thick, hairy arms were wrapped firmly around Bravo's torso, holding him fast.

It was then that Betty saw that the attacker was totally naked. This was almost as shocking as the fact that he was eating her partner's throat. Why should the man's nudity be so deeply disturbing?

She drew a bead on the naked man's head and shouted: "Let him go or I'll shoot you!"

He didn't let go. Didn't acknowledge her at all.

"Hey! I'm not fucking around! I WILL SHOOT YOU."

The naked biter was unimpressed. Or batshit crazy.

"Shoot 'im," Bravo said in a wet, strangled voice.

She reaimed and fired. The slug hit him squarely in the center of the top of his head and he fell backward, taking Bravo back with him.

Betty heard a scraping noise to her rear. She spun back around to see a disfigured man in bloody clothes crawling toward her. The raw-meat stench told her that this was the one she'd smelled earlier.

"Stop!" she yelled. "*Alto!*"

He didn't.

She shot him. His right eyeball disappeared in a splash of blood.

But he did not stop. He merely paused long enough to wipe at his empty eye socket with the back of a filthy hand, then he came on with one crazy eye shining in the light beam.

Betty fired again. And again.

Her weapon held 13 rounds but she wasn't going to get a chance to fire them all. The man was on her as she fired the fifth round.

The sixth ricocheted off the tunnel wall with a whistling whine.

The seventh shot was pointblank to the belly as he fell on top of her, teeth tearing into her throat.

The eighth blew off the tip of Betty's left breast.

There was no ninth.

Betty Davis Wolfe died slowly.

There were no dead relatives waiting to welcome her, no light shining at the end of a tunnel, just her failing flashlight in this drug-runner's tunnel.

She died wishing she'd had a last cigarette.

When she woke to the afterdeath, what she desired was not a smoke.

# 17
# Mystery Train

Piggy was too pooped to pop. She was like the hobo campfire, flamed out and burnt down to dying embers. Lethargic, gorged on hobo blood and meat to the point where she didn't want to move. Warm liquid seeped out of her anus. She reckoned it was the blood she'd imbibed from that silly skull-fucker Sop. Hadn't he been shocked when she chomped his drippy little dick off! One fell snap of the teeth and his limp sausage was in her mouth and he was screaming his ass off, but not for long. By the time she'd chewed the blood out of his cock and spit the thing on the ground, he was flat on his back, passing out. And that was when Piggy made a pig of herself. She took the stump of his dick in her mouth and sucked and sucked and sucked the blood out of him. Couldn't call it cocksucking because his cock was mostly gone. But that was some sweet nub-sucking, right? She drained him nice and slow and didn't stop until his heart did. When she was finally done, she rolled over and saw that Sick had bested Suck by chewing his throat out like a fast-food junkie. Piggy preferred dining at a more leisurely pace and figured that made her a more refined diner than hobo Sick, who must've wandered off to find another snack. Suck was just now stirring to life (or non-life) and would likewise be about the business of finding food with a heartbeat.

Piggy thought this was some weird shit, all right.

Weirder still was how quickly it became second nature to her, this new way of life, or undeath, or whatever the devil you called it. What wasn't so weird was that her suicidal impulse *had* survived her death. Doing away with herself now was a bigger challenge. A harder row to hoe for any ho. But she knew she could do it. And now that her gut was so full of blood that it was leaking out her ass, it seemed the ideal time to end this nasty-ass excuse of an afterlife. And she knew just how to do it.

She rose from the earth. Like a slow shadow, Sop the Dickless Dead rose a moment after her. He looked at her, his blanched face shrivel-wrinkled in death, then he shambled away in shame. Or maybe just to find warm-blooded victuals.

Piggy heard the distant train whistle and hobbled as fast as she could toward the tracks. She slipped and slid down the embankment to the rail bed and then slipped on the gravel thereabouts, but she beat the train to the tracks and stood there with her arms outstretched in a kaput parody of crucifixion.

She looked up at the fabled rosy-fingered dawn, renamed it *bloody-fingered dawn of the dead,* and then looked at the Cyclopean beam of light shining from the mighty engine that would (with any luck at all) turn her already mangled body into mincemeat, and she said (without sound), "I'm not Piggy Poop. I'm Peg Pope and I quit this world of my own free will. God damn it all to hell!"

She couldn't know for certain where this mystery train might take her. But if it wasn't the Oblivion Express, she was going to be appallingly pissed.

# 18
## Paradise Denied

Nadif didn't know how to be dead. Dead in the way the two Mexicans who killed him were. Dead but still going. Going about the business of killing. And eating. Human flesh. Once he was dead, or at least without breath and a heartbeat, the murderous dead left him alone. They—and now he—wanted only living flesh and streaming blood. How could this be?

*What must Allah be thinking to allow such a thing?* But no, this was not Allah's doing. This was Satan's. Allah was simply sitting back and letting it happen as punishment for this crazy-quilt continent of infidels. Was this not right? Nadif didn't know. Could only guess and his guesses were not so good now that his brain was dead and his consciousness was running unknown ethereal circuits, plagued with power surges and brownouts, the brownouts characterized by mindless walking and virtually no mental activity. And beneath it all, the constant craving for warm blood-in-the-flesh.

*Was this a test?* A test of his will to fulfill his mission? The canisters of Black Death remained in his backpack but he was far afield from his jihadi job, and his feet seemed to be going their own way. His feet cared nothing for the Grand Jihad. Was his spirit strong enough to prevail? He wanted to face Mecca, drop to his knees and pray for strength but his feet kept walking the cursed land, in search of the only thing that would satisfy his infernal craving.

The irony was not entirely lost on him that he had been prepared to die hideously of the Black Death, so long as Paradise waited to welcome him on the other side of death, but now here he was stranded in a hellish realm where death itself was a permanent state of being. This was too diabolical for words. This was—

Something slapped his arm.

A moment later came the echoing pop of distant gunfire. Someone was shooting at him.

Up ahead a cluster of three or four other dead walkers also drew fire. The tallest one's head exploded and he went down like a marionette whose strings have been all at once severed.

Another slug slapped into Nadif, this time striking him squarely in the chest and knocking him backward to the ground. As he got slowly to his feet, Nadif's memory lazily looped back to his combat training at various camps in the Horn of Africa and he recalled his abbreviated training with a high-powered Russian sniper rifle. By the time he was standing again his sluggish mind had worked out that right now there were at least two shooters taking pot-shots at him and his . . . kind. Zombies. Zionist zombies?

There would be a big exit wound in his back. One of the backpack canisters containing weaponized plague had most likely been breached. The virus would be wasted here in this wasteland.

He thought he should remove the backpack and note the damage but as soon as the thought came into his head, it evaporated and he walked on into the dawn, thinking single-mindedly of finding bloody sustenance.

Nadif paid little mind to the sniper's slugs snapping past and sometimes slamming into him. They were hardly more annoying than aggressive insects, hungry horseflies or fat mosquitoes.

## 19
## Man Walks Into A Bar

Cruz came to with a shotgun muzzle pressed hard against his forehead, just above the bridge of his nose.

"What'll it be?" the shotgun-wielding bartender asked.

"Uh, shot of tequila," Cruz said. "Make it a double and uh, hold the buckshot."

The bartender pulled the shotgun away. Cruz raised his head off the bar and rubbed the throbbing knot over his left ear. The last thing he remembered was sitting down at the bar and then the bartender swinging a shotgun at his head in the manner of a batter going for a bunt.

"Can't be too careful," the bartender said, "what with all the wild shit coming down."

"Right," Cruz said. Who was he to argue with a psycho strapped with a shotgun?

The bartender set the shotgun down and poured Cruz a shot. "Now that the world's turned into a fucking Romero movie, a guy can't be too careful, ya know?"

"Right."

"Could've just gone ahead and shot you, you know. But I gave you the benefit of the doubt. Little love tap to see if you woke up dead or not. Sometimes you can't tell right off the bat. If a dude's dead or zombied out or normal. One thing that ain't like the movies, a headshot don't put the deaders down. I can prove that shit. You wanna see?"

"Uh, no, that's all right," Cruz said after he downed the shot.

"C'mon, what's it gonna hurt? Ain't like you got something else to do. What with the world gone to shit and dead. Hell, I would've closed up hours ago but I don't wanna have to go home to shoot the wife, you know? Ain't got the heart. It's all over the news. They don't come right out and say all the dead are walking but a little reading between the lines tells the tale. Me, I've seen it for my own damn self. Hadda blow away two dead cocksuckers. One a good customer too. Come on, pal, it ain't gonna kill you. Come meet Joe the Dead."

Cruz didn't move. He said, "How about another shot of tequila?"

"Sure, sure. After you see Joe. Joe the Dead. Ain't got no head but he keeps going and going like that fucking battery-hyped bunny beating a bass drum. He's locked in the ladies room. C'mon, he can't hurt you. He's so shot to shit he just lies there twitching."

"No thanks," Cruz said. "I don't have the stomach for it right now."

The bartender scowled, leaned close and lowered his voice: "You better find it real quick, buddy. Dude in the booth over there's got plans for you. And he don't strike me as somebody you wanna rub the wrong way."

Cruz turned his head as casually as he could to get a look at the dude in the booth.

Blink-click: mental snapshot: man in a red hoodie, hood up to conceal his face. The same guy.

Bad juju coming off him in waves.

*Baad* juju.

"What're you talking about?" Cruz asked as quietly as he could. "What plans?"

"Fuck should I know? Ask him. He's the mystery man on the news. Where he shows up, the shit goes down. They been showing cell-phone pictures of him. They think he's some kinda terrorist but he's something a damn site worse than that."

Cruz stole another glance. It looked like the guy *had* no face.

Bartender whispered, "Get off your ass and come with me. I don't want on this guy's bad side. Let's go. Joe ain't getting no fresher."

"Right," Cruz said, sliding off the stool. "Tell me, what city is this?"

"Jesus Christ. Phoenix. Where the fuck ya think?"

Cruz shrugged. "I have no idea how I got here."

"Yeah, well, that could be the least of your problems, pal."

# 20
# Shoot & Loot

Wyatt put the crosshairs on the guy's forehead and fired again. In the scope it was great the way the wetback drug mule's head came apart.

"That did it," Clint attaboyed him. "Put him down *that* time."

"Dink's dead but won't stay down," Wyatt said, using the term his granddaddy often used for the Vietnamese whenever he told war stories. "Watch. He'll pop back up in a minute. Weird shit happening here, bro."

"End Times, dude. Time to be lewd, crude and screwed."

"Not before we get that dope," Wyatt said.

"We got three backsacks full. That ought to do us dumb awhile."

"We get this one and then haul ass before the Border Patrol's choppers start chopping."

"Whoa, there he goes! He's getting up again. That shit is ill."

Yes, it was, Wyatt had to agree. Yesterday the world was the same old ass-dull place it always was, and now here they were a few hours into the next day and the dead were walking and it was even weirder than the news guys knew or were saying. Maybe it *was* the End Times. Whatever you wanted to call it, it was the perfect time to put their longtime plan in effect.

Shoot & Loot they called it. They had trained themselves with their self-styled sniper school. No actual teachers, just books, videos and related internet sites. It was a short leap from being boys raised on hunting to becoming men skilled in the deadly art of killing with long-range weapons. Once they were proficient in shooting, they worked on refining the Loot part of their plan.

The drug cartels used the Arizona-Mexican border for smuggling dope into the U.S. Everybody knew it, just as most folks knew the Feds did next to nothing to stop it, mostly because of dumb-ass political reasons. The way Wyatt figured it, the drugs were theirs for the taking. The "mule" trains were usually guarded by guys with automatic weapons but a couple of Red White & Blue American boys with sniper rifles could take out the guards at a safe distance, no problem. Then all they had to do was put down as many mules as they could (all you had to do was wing them, not kill them) and go down and collect their dope-crammed backpacks.

Shoot & Loot, baby. Protect the good old U. S. of A. from illegals and get paid in dope. This was a shooting war and the spoils of war went to the best shooters with the best battleplan.

The only wrinkle in the plan was that these walking dead motherfuckers messed up the One Shot, One Kill sniper's credo. Apparently, you couldn't kill these zombies with *any* number of shots. That *Shoot em in the head* shit worked only in the movies, not out here along the fucking border. But that was okay. Wyatt was digging the shit out of shooting dudes who were already dead (or supposed to be). It took any guilt right out of the fucking picture. Even with that freaky eyeball in the sky watching like the eye of some goddamn god.

God had to cut you a little slack for blowing away living dead dudes humping dope.

"That's five mules down," Clint said. "Let's go get us some drugs, dude."

"Hope none of them zombie shooters accidentally gets off a lucky killshot," Wyatt said.

"Nah, man, you can see they ain't even holding their weapons no more. They still kicking but they can't shoot shit. Ain't in their minds to do it."

"Reckon you're right, clit."

"Don't call me that shit," Clint said.

Wyatt chuckled. It felt good after the extreme stress of their first Shoot & Loot. He said, "Let's hike down there and get the shit. Check out these zombie motherfuckers up close and personal, like."

# 21
## Plague Be Upon You

Nadif was more than a little amazed that he could still see even though his eyes and much of his cranium had been destroyed by the last sniper's shot. He didn't know if this was a good thing or a very bad one. That the disembodied soul could still see was not so surprising. That it must witness such abominations was. Where exactly were the soul's eyes located? he wondered. Was he somehow seeing now by the grace (or curse) of the great eye in the sky? (An image of his beloved's eyeball hanging by its stalk over her bloody cheek flashed through his memory, then faded as fast as summer lightning.)

Two young men stood over his spasming body. Infidels. American devils with scoped rifles. His destroyers. Mocking him. Laughing at him.

Nadif's soul smiled. Now he understood. Allah was granting him a divine favor, a blessed boon. Allah was allowing him to see that the exquisitely weaponized plague virus was about to be passed on to these two ignorant devils and carried back into their homes and environs, thence to spread as if on fiery desert winds. The onset of symptoms would be unnaturally rapid and cruelly devastating. Best of all, the organism would remain insidiously virulent as it spread through the population.

Nadif's soul shouted: *God is great!*
*Allahu Akbar.*

# 22
# Joe the Dead

Dude was the Devil.

Bobby Cruz had a nose for news and his news nose told him so: *This dude in the red hoodie is the honest-to-God Devil.*

And unlike most people in the news business, Bobby believed deeply in the Devil, and had done so since he was old enough to grasp the concept of Ultimate Evil Personified. Six, as he recalled. That was how old he was when he actually saw in his mind's eye Satan rising from the ground to grab him and take him down to hell. A childish image now. But was it really? If the dead could rise, then why couldn't the Devil come up from hell? He could. The question now was: Why? And what did the Devil want with Bobby Cruz?

"Go on," said the bartender. "Ask him. If you got the balls. But first you gotta see Joe. I call him Joe the Dead after a character in a book a customer left on the bar one time. By William Burroughs? You heard of him? Faggot addict, dead now. Boy, did he come up with some crazy faggy shit. Anyway, here's Joe."

The bartender threw open the Ladies Room door and the smell of death and deodorizer hit Bobby full force in the face, kicked open his sinuses and blew them out like a teargas bomb. His eyes ran with tears. Runny eyes, runny nose-for-news.

The body was on the floor by the first stall. Its head was completely separated from the hideous blackened stump of its neck. From the looks of things, the bartender had blown the head off with several close-range blasts. The eyes in the head were intact and looked up at Cruz and the bartender with worried puzzlement, as if Joe the Dead were wondering if they were going to play football with his head.

His arms and legs had likewise been blown off and lay twitching several feet from their stumps. One bloody hand was trying to drag itself across the wet tile with its fingers, like a wounded rat seeking to hide in a dark corner.

"See and remember," the bartender said. "I think that's what the man in red wants you to do. Like some sort of reporter for the end of the world. Like the red dude's disciple."

"He told you this?"

"Well, not in so many words. Not in words at all. Guy never speaks. He puts thoughts in your head. Slips em right in there some-fucking-how. That's why I gave you a whack on the head when you sat at my bar. He made me do it, I think, just to knock you off balance, sort of like a master smacking sense into his apprentice. Him being the master, not me. Call me crazy, but I think he's an angel. Not the airy-fairy type. More like the ones God sent to destroy Sodom and Gomorrah."

"Let's get out of here," said Cruz, wiping his eyes. "I've seen and smelled enough of Joe."

"Yeah. Rest in pieces, Joe." The bartender chortled at his own trite joke.

## 23
## Beelzebub

They left the Ladies Room and returned to the bar. The Red Hoodie Devil remained in the booth, his face—if he had one—remained hidden in suggestive shadow.

Bobby wondered what would happen if he took the bartender's shotgun and pumped some slugs into the red-hooded son of a bitch.

The Devil laughed inside Bobby's head. Laughed so hard it rattled Bobby's eyeballs and gave him a splitting headache.

"Okay, okay, I get it," he said, pressing both hands to his head as if to keep it from splitting apart. "So what do you want with me?"

The Devil plopped a leatherbound book on the table in front of him.

Bobby warily approached the booth.

The air changed. It was as if the Devil had brought a little of hell's atmosphere with him. It fairly crackled. It smelled not of brimstone but of cloves and cinnamon and something long dead and mouldering.

The Devil raised a hand and the TV over the bar came to life. A local news anchor who looked like she hadn't bothered with the usual makeup and hairspray was saying: ". . . and demonstrators on both sides of the issue are already gathering in downtown Phoenix in spite of the governor's warning to stay away. Similar demonstrations are also planned for other Arizona cities, but no word yet on what's happening at those locations. We'll be going live to our on-scene reporter shortly."

Then the Devil was in Bobby's head. It was a voice that required neither tongue to speak it nor ears to hear it, yet it was melodiously full and powerfully seductive.

It said, *Go there and record what you see in the book. Report faithfully. Soon there will be no electronic record and no electricity. Your way of life is about to be wiped. Set all you see down in these pages and keep them safe.*

Bobby grew woozy. Blood roared like an ocean in his ears and he thought he was going to faint. He leaned forward to brace himself on the table.

The Devil's hands were long, bloodless and without a trace of hair. They were *delicate*. One of them produced an ornate black pen of a type Bobby Cruz had never seen before, obviously antiquated and adorned with ram's-head horns. He knew without looking that the Devil's fingers would be devoid of fingerprints. Angels had no fingerprints. Neither did a fallen angel. Cruz knew this without knowing precisely how he knew it.

TV voices came back into his ears: "That's right, Janis. Now that the CDC has been called in and the National Guard has been called out, you would expect smaller crowds here in the streets of Phoenix, especially so early in the morning, but as you can see, the crowds on both sides of the illegal immigration issue are large and growing. And tempers are already flaring. The riot squad only moments ago arrived and are beginning to deploy. They're using bullhorns to tell the crowds to disperse but no one is showing any sign of leaving this tense scene. And as you just reported, Janis, the governor has said she won't hesitate to declare martial law if necessary, which it well may be, with emergency response systems all over the state so overloaded as to be virtually nonexistent. Arizona is in a crisis of unimaginable consequences and nobody knows how this bizarre series of events will end or how far the growing chaos will spread. I can tell you, there is a feeling of panic bordering on hysteria out here on the streets and a sense that things are about to explode. Whatever the outcome, we will be here to bring it to our viewers, for as long as possible. But as one riot cop told me just minutes ago, 'When the dead walk, all bets are off.'"

Cruz picked up the pen and the leatherbound book. He thumbed through pages and saw that they were all blank, as he expected. He licked his parched lips, reached down in his gut for the courage to address the red-hooded entity and said, "For the record, who are you?"

*You know who I am. You may call me Bub. But don't call me Nick or Scratch.*

"As in Beelzebub, Lord of Flies?" Cruz all too vividly remembered the attack of the fierce flies in the back of the truck. He couldn't remember much of what happened after that, but he remembered enough to know that it was probably best not to remember too much horror.

*Don't be so pedestrian. Use those qualities for which you were chosen. No scribe of mine should be prosaic. Moreover, I am not the story. The story is the final fall of man.*

Bobby nodded. "Uh, one more question. Where is God in all this?"

*Don't be obtuse, Cruz. He is the author of the entire epic. He wrote it in genetic codes and in the dark matter of the spirit. He should have stopped with the angels and kept it all in the spiritual realm. When you create a material realm and then make flesh self-aware, how else can it end but badly? Now go, scribe, once more into the breach.*

He snugged the book under his arm, pocketed the ram's-head pen, turned on his heels and started away. Then he stopped, half turned and said, "Why me? Would you mind telling me that?"

Bub gave a slight shrug. *Because you were ripe for it. And you're not a complete moron. I'm the only thing between you and a life of zombie bloodlust.*

Bobby Cruz nodded and then headed out into the wild streets.

## 24
## When The Dead Walk, All Bets Are Off

Nuts. Everybody was. The whole scene was soup-to-nuts insane and getting crazier by the minute. By the second. How the hell he was supposed to capture this bedlam-hits-the-streets shit on paper was beyond him.

Cruz didn't know this city very well, but it wasn't hard to find the heart of the action. All he had to do was follow the howling sounds of mass destruction, madness and violent death. Downtown Phoenix had indeed become an extended scene from a George Romero zombie movie-turned-reality-TV-show on steroids, on crack, on crystal meth and mad mushrooms. In the highest fevers of his imagination, Romero had never dreamt anything to rival what Bobby Cruz saw unfolding like the giant wings of a fallen phoenix struggling mightily to rise from this ashes-to-ashes nightmare necropolis.

The dead walked.

The dead ran.

The dead took down the living and feasted on their yummy bleeding flesh.

The living fought back. With whatever makeshift weapons they could find, including severed body parts and heads.

What had started as a sprawling rumble between opposing groups of demonstrators quickly deteriorated into an out-for-blood free-for-all when ravenous zombies began popping up on both sides and even within the ranks of the riot squad. It seemed to Bobby that a disproportionate number of zombies wore the purple shirts of union thugs. One such unlucky ghoul stumbled along the sidewalk with a teargas canister spewing acrid fog from a big hole in his belly.

Fires broke out. Streets became hellishly fogged with smoke and teargas.

Streets ran with blood. With bile. With urine. Feces. Phlegm. Pus. With every kind of bodily fluid there was, including semen spilled during various instances of rape, gang-rape and all manner of rock-out-with-your-cock-out buggery. It was a veritable orgy of carnal degradation and neo-death. *Death is the new life*, Bobby mused.

He saw it all from the relatively safe remove of the arched balcony of a church tower, one tier below the bell tower. He stood transfixed. Unable to stop watching the carnage. Writing anything in the Devil's

Book was impossible. His job now was to witness and remember. Later, he would set it down on unholy paper. What he was seeing now he would never forget, so long as he lived, and probably longer.

A helicopter fell out of the sky and crashed into the side of an apartment building just before noon. There was no fiery explosion, as there most certainly would've been in the movies. Just the impact, and then the flying machine tumbled lazily to the pavement below, crushing a handful of rioters or demonstrators or whatever the hell you wanted to call them now.

Cruz figured *demon*strators had it about right. *Demon*strators at the end of the world. As we know it. And love it. So . . . Goodbye to All That. You Can't Go Home Again. But It's All Right Ma, I'm Only Bleedin'. Look Homeward, Angel, but you can't get there because of this Idiot Wind so all you can do is Ring Them Bells down on Desolation Row and forget those Subterranean Homesick Blues 'cause When The Deal goes Down It's A Hard Rain's A-gonna Fall. Bob Dylan and Thomas Wolfe warred in his head, and that seemed to Bobby to be about right, given what was going on round about him.

To remain sane you had to go a little mad.

At noon a U-haul truck came barreling up a street that was supposed to be closed to traffic and slammed into a gaggle of street fighters interspersed with blood-crazed dead.

It was at this moment that the cartoon lightbulb went on in Bobby's head: The ranks of the living-dead crazies were growing exponentially. At this rate, the dead undoubtedly would triumph in the end. It was a mathematical certainty, short of divine intervention, which Cruz didn't expect, not after his tête-à-tête with Satan. The dead had the numbers advantage and it wouldn't take long for this zombie *craze* (what else could you call it?) to break out of Arizona and spread to other states, even other countries as long as planes remained flying. For all he knew, it could've started in other states as well, if Beelzebub or his minions had gone there with his zombie-making flies.

On the other hand, it seemed fitting that the original outbreak was at the Arizona-Mexico border, the site of so much hostility, hate, fear, envy, violence and specific depravity related to drug cartels, human trafficking and political huckstering. Surely hell's dark forces were drawn to such places like flies to shit. Surely Satan (Old Nick 'Beelzebub' Scratch himself) loved such sinful symmetry. And if Big Red

Riding Hood wasn't lying about God being the author of civilization's crazy clusterfuck entire, then *there it was* in a God-given nutshell.

Zombies Gone Wild. Mankind mostly gone.

In the distance, about a mile from where he stood on the church-tower balcony, a jetliner came screaming out of the sky and crashed into a tall building.

Jet-fuel fireball.

Cruz could easily imagine the sort of onboard zombie drama that likely brought down the plane. How could he not?

He yawned. He was very tired. He could quite easily curl up right here for a catnap.

*What's the matter, old man, is this end-of-the-world action boring you?*

Was the voice asking the question his or Satan's. In the end, Bobby Cruz didn't figure there was that much difference.

# 25
## Virulence

Clint was sick as a dog. Sick as a mangy coyote with half its guts hanging out and dragging the ground. Sicker than cancer-ward shit. He felt like he was sure as shit dying. He said so to Wyatt. But Wyatt didn't hear him. Wyatt was on the floor, delirious and puking his guts up. And from the smell of him, shitting his britches.

The world was made of shit.

Clint wanted to get up off the bed and look again in the mirror to see what those sores under his armpits and on his neck looked like now. He was afraid to look at the ones he felt in his groin. He sat up, got dizzy and fell back onto the bed. He had already stripped down to his Joe Boxers so all he had to do to check out the sores in his pits was turn his head, lift his arm a little and look. He got up the nerve and looked.

"Jesus fuck! Gah!" The sores were hideously swollen and leaking bloody pus like big infected blisters. And the leakage stank to high heaven. The ugly sores had gone from red, to purple and now to black. Oozing that vile shit. Clint retched but didn't hurl, not yet. The steak & eggs breakfast he and Wyatt had had at the Waffle House after they'd stashed the dope was not agreeing with his stomach, and in fact it felt like the breakfast was eating *him*.

Feverish, aching, coughing.

"Dying," he said in a terrifying rasp. Because of that fucking zombie mule with those silver cylinders in his backpack that looked like hardware from a sci-fi movie, the cold shiny ones that always contained Very Deadly Shit.

Fucking terrorist!

Clint clumsily grabbed his cell phone off the nightstand, flipped it open and touched up his mother's number. His thumb made a bloody smear on the touchpad. *Fuck that. Call 9-1-1. No! You can't do that. Not with that bag of dope in your room. Shit! Oh shit, I just did. Shit myself. Mom!*

He hit SEND. No answer. She *always* answered. Where the hell was she? Her car was still in the driveway. Here he was, still living in the little cinderblock bunkhouse in his mother's backyard, a grown man of twenty-one fucking years.

*And that's all the years you get, numb nuts.* All because you and jerkoff over there on the floor decided to cowboy up and go outlaw on the border. *Fuck me!*

He wanted to get in the shower and wash this oozing shit-blood-pus off himself. Escape the stench if he could. But he knew he couldn't. Couldn't make it, not even if he crawled to the shower stall, which was no more than a hearty fart's distance away. As a fucking crow flies. Or farts. Crowfart. *Losing my mind. Call mind-one-one. Fuck-me-momma-it-hurts!*

Someone at the door. Mom? He managed to call out: "Ma!"

The doorknob rattled. Had he locked it? No. It was swinging open. Somebody just standing there. Mom! Thank God. She shuffled into the room. *Shuffled?* Mom didn't shuffle, unless she was soused on Johnnie Walker Black Label. This was not good.

Clint said, "Mom, I'm sick."

She said nothing. Just shuffled forward, coming toward his bed.

"Take me to the hospital," he said. "Bad sick."

He retched. Vomit gushed from his mouth and nose. He rolled onto his side, coughing to keep from choking on his lumpy puke.

Mom shuffled.

Clint puked.

Mom shuffled.

Clint panicked when he saw her face. It was pasty white, her smoker's wrinkles deepened in shadow, her eyes cloudy with dead-dog fogginess. There was a blood smear across her mouth, skewed like lipstick applied by a drunken hand.

Mom was a fucking zombie.

"Mombie," he said, giggling stupidly, deliriously.

The rifle. In the corner of the room. If he could make it all the way over there . . .

He scooted to the edge of the befouled bed but he was too slow and it was already too late. His mother fell upon him with all of her two hundred pounds and sank her teeth into his painfully inflamed groin.

He screamed.

She ripped and tore with her teeth. She chewed his flesh and slurped the brackish bloody stew pouring out of him.

Black blood. Black Death. Dead mother.

"Wyatt!" he screamed. Clint was too weak to fight off the mombie, and all he could think to do was call on his friend to help him. *Save him.* But Wyatt was probably weaker than he was.

*God it hurts! Killing me.*

But wait.

Wait, what?

Wyatt was getting up. Thank you Jesus, he was up on his feet. Shuffling toward the bed.

Wyatt elbowed Clint's mother aside, bent down and chomped into Clint's throat with his picture-perfect teeth, devouring his friend's final scream.

## 26
## Out of the Box

Pedro felt the world turn upside down and rolled with it because that was all he *could* do. Over and over the truck tumbled, finally crashing into something big enough to stop it.

And Pedro was out of the hatbox, his mouth ending up miraculously close to the neck of the hombre who'd hacked off his head with the machete.

There was a God after all!

Pedro worked his wrecked jaw just enough to inch his head closer to paydirt. He didn't know if the crash had killed the dude or not. He didn't care. He was going to eat out his throat. He worked his mangled jaw. Snapped his teeth, though they were badly out of alignment. His lips brushed the man's jugular. A pulse!

Pedro bit into the warm flesh and drank deep.

It didn't matter that the blood he imbibed immediately dribbled out of his neck by way of his dissected esophagus. It was the sweetest drink he'd ever had.

# 27
## Jake Moon Snake Rides Again

Jake Moon Snake took a hit of tequila, set the bottle between his legs and then gunned the Mustang down a stretch of Oklahoma highway not far from Anadarko, steering with his right hand while drawing a bead with his left on the sudden target of opportunity. He wasn't a natural lefty but he was getting pretty damn good at picking off deadheads with the .357 S&W Magnum snugged in his left fist.

Few things in life were more important to Jake than keeping his Magnum and his Mustang in good working order, well-oiled and loaded.

His *new* thing in life was shooting deadheads in the face. Maybe you couldn't kill these zomboys and zombabes with headshots like in all the horror flicks but if you blew their jawbones apart they wouldn't be eating anybody. Jake figured he was doing his civic duty with his drive-by roadkill shooting.

Wasn't like he was actually killing anybody. The deadmeat dickheads were already dead. No harm, no foul. Still, he worried sometimes that he was enjoying it too much. But tequila kept his worries at bay and kept him as well-oiled as his Magnum and Mustang. Even so though, he could never quite shake the feeling that that creepoid eye up in the sky was watching him extra close. *Keeping an eye* on him. Judging him.

The Mustang was a vintage 1965 red beauty with a rebuilt engine. The Magnum was a monster with a scary-long Dirty Harry barrel. The tequila wasn't top-shelf but it did the job just the same.

He glided over into the opposite lane and fired when he was less than ten yards from the target.

It was a good hit. The zomboy's face blew apart, the lower jaw suddenly just gone. The dead dude kept on walking. Jake saw this in the rearview and gave a little salute with the smoking barrel to the brow. "Walk on, freakoid," he said.

Several miles later he came upon a couple of hitchhikers. Boy, girl. Young, scared. Scared to death the zomboids would find them and eat them. Jake wouldn't have stopped for them but for his soft heart. You grow up soft when your Mom and Pop are hippies who have their kid (namely Jake) too late in life and give you a groovy name like Jake Moon Snake and proceed to fill your head with every counterculture cliché in the book. Peace, Love & Fuck the Man! Kick out the jams! Up against the wall! And while you're at it, how about some of that far-out free love and some trippy-dippy acid.

When he was old enough to figure out the contradictions, Jake called Bullshit! *How can you be into peace and love while you're starting the revolution? Besides that, you're both too late. All this hippie shit ended when the war in Nam did. The revolution went undercover into the heart of America and now the radicals are running the government. Congrats on that. Now we're all fucked, the whole freaking world. God is dead and the dead are on the move, taking over and looking to eat us for fast food.*

Still and all, Jake didn't hold any of that too harshly against them now that he was grown and they were dead (*really* dead). He dug the nomadic life and staying mostly on the road. And his name was pretty cool most of the time, like now with these two young hitchhikers.

Amanda and Todd. They wanted to know if Moon Snake was an Indian name.

"Native American," Jake corrected them, pretending to be PC. "And yeah, it is." Thinking: *naïve American*. He might have a little Hopi in his blood, but he doubted it.

He laughed to himself. He gave them the romanticized version of his personal story. He left his home in Tombstone when the world went into Dead & Gone mode, took his act on the road and became a road warrior for the Truth, Justice and the American Way. Right, like Superman. No way to stay in Arizona, not unless you were dead.

Arizona was Ground Zero. Arizona was Arizombie. Zomboid Central. Stick a giant fork in it, it's done.

Jake was making his way back east, back to his Florida roots (his roots never went that deep anywhere, but he figured that when the powergrids failed he would fair best in a warm clime). Gasoline was going to be a problem too. Staying on constant move like a shark took a lot of gas. His badass 'Tang was a thirsty guzzler. He would need an out-of-the-way homebase, a place to keep a shitload of full canned gas and guns and ammo. Not to even mention dried and canned food and bottled water out the yin-yang. There was going to be a lot of gasoline left in underground tanks after the power dried up and Jake was going to have to figure out how to get it out of the ground and into the 'Tang's tank.

"Got anything to eat?" Amanda asked. "We're starving."

Jake didn't answer right away. He was wondering if he should share his newfound source.

"I'll suck your dick for food," she said, dropping her voice just a tad.

"Jeez, Manda," said Todd.

"You ain't gotta suck nobody's dick," Jake said. "I'll get you something to eat. There's a place a few miles ahead where I've got a stash. Barbecue joint, owners dead and gone off to find food that ain't dead yet. Lost their taste for barbecue. I been on this stretch of road since yesterday, popping deadheads quick as they pop up. Shoot em in the mouth so that they can't eat nobody. Only reason I hung around is 'cause that barbecue is so good. I coulda been in Florida by now."

"We saw a few of those back there, with messed-up mouths," Todd said. "Wonder if they can starve to death."

"Seeing as how they're already dead, I'd say no," Jake said.

"You sure you don't want me to suck your dick?" Amanda put a hand on his thigh.

"God a'mighty, girl, I'm sure. Okay? How old are you anyway?"

"Seventeen and a half."

"Six months short of legal."

"What's the difference?" Todd asked. "Laws ain't shit anymore."

"You got a point there, I reckon," Jake said. "What that means though, is that you got to have your own moral code to live by. Know what's right and wrong and try to do the right thing whenever you can."

"What's wrong with sucking somebody's dick?"

Jake gave her a look. "Damn, girl. You get your teeth in something you don't let go, do you?"

"I wouldn't *bite* it."

"That ain't what I mean. You can't go around offering to suck strange dick. No telling what you might catch. Radio said the plague is coming out of Arizona now. Folks that ain't zomboids are just as likely to be carrying the Black Death if they ain't already dead from it."

"If you die of the plague do you turn zombie?" Todd wondered aloud.

"I don't see why not," Jake said. "I sure wouldn't want to meet up with one of them bad boys. That's got to be some nasty shit. Still and all, I reckon they could be carrying the plague, spreading it everywhere they go. Radio didn't say. Hell, they don't know. Nobody does. Government can't do shit no how. Whole shebang's gonna come crashing down. I'll drink to that." He turned up the tequila. Didn't offer the kids any.

Todd seemed to shrink into the seat a little. "I don't see how we can survive all this stuff. Don't hardly seem worth it. The zombies don't get you, the plague will. And that's if you don't starve first or get murdered by bad guys who're alive."

"Sad words of wisdom, little bro," Jake said. "But as long as I can ride and shoot, I'll keep plugging away. If the Good Lord put me on earth for a reason, I reckon this must be it. Beats any damn video game."

"We met a man who said he saw an angel," Amanda said.

"Is that right," Jake said, thankful that she'd stopped talking about dicksucking.

"Him and his wife. Back in Amarillo. They said she glowed with heavenly light and swore she could show them the way to salvation. Her name was Magdalena and she was a cripple. Or had been."

"Ain't that a whore in the Bible?" Todd said. "Magdalena?"

"Nah," Jake said, "that's Mary Magdalene and she wasn't no whore. She was possessed by devils until Jesus called em out. Then she became a disciple."

"You know a lot about the Bible, Mr. Snake," Todd observed.

"A little. And just call me Jake." Before his hippie parents turned godless Marxist, they went through a Jesus-freak phase and he'd learned a lot of scripture then.

"Anyways," Amanda went on, "they said she died and came back from the dead, but not as a zombie. The Holy Mother brought her back and told her she's supposed to lead the people that aren't damned through the Tribulation. That's what all this mess is, and that's where we're going. To find her. They said she'll be by the sea in Savannah, Georgia, because that's holy ground. Todd don't believe in any of it but I do. I *have* to."

Jake slowed and turned off the highway at Tewey's Okie Barbecue. He said, "Sounds like a plan, Miss Amanda, but if you do hook up with them holy folks, don't offer nobody a blowjob. That'd be what you call shooting yourself in the foot."

He killed the engine and shoved the keys in his jeans. "Let's have lunch," he said as he stepped out of the car with the Magnum in his hand. "Stay close and keep your eyes peeled. Deadheads pop up when you least expect em to."

# 28
## Little Sister by the Sea

Magda stands in the sand to receive the dead from the sea.

Her followers have taken to calling her Little Sister because she is small and because they each feel a special kinship with her. One by one they fell in with her growing band of ragtag pilgrims as they made their way to the seacoast, drawn by something none could name. (Magda named it for them: the Holy Spirit.) One by one they were in some way healed or spiritually reconstituted.

Now they are gathered on the shore behind her to witness her welcoming the dead as the sea gives them up.

She glances over her shoulder at Randy Riggins, who is standing immediately behind her and a few feet to her left. He wears denim overalls and no shirt and he is holding a very old scythe in his hands. On the way here Magda spent a night in his barn and he has been with her since then, stubbornly devoted to her. The ever-present scythe has earned him the nickname, Randy the Reaper.

Just behind and to her right is Levy Cohen, bushy-bearded and wearing a black hat with a round crown and a wide brim. When she feels the need to consult scripture, she turns to Levy. He is a self-taught scholar of the Old Testament, though he calls it the Hebrew Bible, or more often the Torah. Levy stops short of calling himself a Jew for Jesus, but Magda knows that his heart has been opened to Christ.

She stands barefoot in the waves that lap the sand and her ankles. The sun is pleasantly hot on her skin. Her disfiguring wounds have all but healed, steadily and miraculously, by virtue of her single encounter with the Holy Mother.

"My God," Randy says, "look at that thing."

The sea gives up the first of its dead. It comes crawling out of the waves on seaweed-green bones wearing the mottled leather of old skin rotted or eaten away in spots. Once human and now long dead, it crawls forward, new musculature forming on facial bones and everywhere beneath the old skin as it comes. Another miracle.

It rises on two legs as flesh fills out its manly form.

"Holy shit," Randy Riggins says. Then: "Sorry, ma'am."

Little Sister holds out her welcoming arms. By the time the walking dead man reaches her, his skin has been renewed and his face is an animated mask of confused emotions. She takes both his hands in hers. "God bless you, brother," she says in her charmingly accented English. Then she passes him off to Levy, who leads him to join the others.

"Here comes another un," Randy says as a second figure comes walking out of the waves.

This one is a badly bloated woman, her skin gone greenish black. Not so long dead. She is completely naked. Chunks of flesh have been nibbled away by sea creatures. She plods out of the water, her fat feet stiffly thumping the sand.

Magda tries to tamp down the repulsion she feels as the hideous creature comes close enough to smell.

The drowned woman reaches out with stubby fingers and swollen arms as she bares her greenish teeth. Her eyes resemble cloudy-gray pustules surrounding beady blackheads: zit eyes.

Randy swings his scythe. It sings against the wind and slices off the corpse's head as smoothly as if it were slashing through rotten fruit.

Magda looks at Randy with raised brows.

He gives a slight shrug and says, "Wheat from the chaff. She meant to hurt you."

Levy quotes scripture: "'His winnowing fork is in His hand to thoroughly clear His threshing floor, and to gather the wheat into His barn; but He will burn up the chaff with unquenchable fire.'"

Randy ponders this a moment, then barks an order to the others to gather wood for a big fire there on the beach.

"Here come two more," Levy says.

Magda says a silent prayer to the Holy Mother, asking for the strength to do her Son's bidding. Then she steps forward to receive more of the sea's rising dead.

## 29
## Meat and Greet

"Mmm," Amanda said.

"Um-hm," Todd said.

Their mouths were bright red with dripping sauce.

"Y'all look like a couple of fresh zomboids feeding," Jake said as he wiped his lips with a napkin. "Use your napkins. Just 'cause the world's gone to hell don't mean we have to eat like pigs. It's up to us to maintain good manners and such. If we're lucky enough to live through these times, we'll need to make a good restart."

"Reboot," Amanda said, belching into her hand.

"There you go." Jake took a swig from his bottle of pop. "We're not in Kansas anymore but we're still in America. It'll be up to folks like us to keep it someways alive."

"We ain't been to Kansas," Todd said with a mouthful of barbecue.

"He means like in The Wizard of Oz, dummy," said Amanda, delicately dabbing her lips with her napkin.

Jake winked at her. He dropped his napkin in his plate, leaned back in his chair, took his pistol off the table and stuck it in the hand-tooled leather holster on his right hip. He sucked on his teeth with a whistling noise and said, "What we'll do is put the rest of the meat in a cooler and head east. Ain't that much left no way. If I hadn't found that deepfreeze in their basement next door, we wouldn't a had any. Joints like this get looted right quick with so many survivors on the move."

"We ain't seen that many," Todd said, finally using his napkin.

Jake nodded. "Me neither. Not really. But enough to where restaurants get raided right off the bat. Everybody left alive knows what's coming. And it ain't gonna be pretty. Only the strong will make it. And the lucky. So, children, be strong and make your own luck. And don't forget to say your prayers."

Amanda smiled for the first time since Jake had met her. It was a pretty thing to see. "So," he said, lacing his fingers over his flat belly, "you kids hooked up for the duration or what?"

"What now?" Todd said.

"You in love?"

Amanda quickly said, "No."

"Hey," Todd said, jerking backward and making his chair legs screech on the floor.

"Whoa," Jake said. "That ain't no reason to—"

Todd raised his arm and pointed his finger like it was a gun. "Dead guys walking."

Jake turned his head and looked out the eatery's storefront window. Three men in suits and ties were crossing the street, coming toward the entrance. He stood, drew his Magnum and said, "Stay here." Then he went outside to wait on the sidewalk for the well-dressed trio to get close enough to shoot without wasting ammo.

The tall man in the middle raised his hand and said, "Hold on there, friend, we ain't dead. We're Christians."

Jake kept his gun out. He said, "Reckon you must be pretty pissed you didn't get raptured up to heaven already."

"There's no reason to be insulting," the tall man said. "We come to thank you for the work you've been doing and to ask you to join our church. Right down the street there. Church of the Holy Ghost."

"The work I've been doing?" Jake cocked his head.

"Disabling the dead. So they're not so dangerous."

"Hell, that ain't work. That's too much fun to be work. Besides, I just stayed for the barbecue. Fixing to move on. But thanks for the invite. How many you got holed up in that church?"

"Ain't but thirteen of us," said the short guy with tinted glasses.

"Lucky you," said Jake. "If it was me, I'd be moving on. Get as far from Arizona and her bordering states as possible. No offense but this little town ain't no more than a bump in the road. Got to be greener pastures somewhere else."

"Not according to what we heard on Luther's shortwave radio," the tall one said. "That's why there's not any more TV. Things went bad fast all over. We heard that even the president turned zombie. And the plague virus is spreading like wildfire. Ain't nowhere to hide. Only thing to do is pray and get right with God."

Jake was about to make an unkind comment about the president turning zombie when Amanda screamed inside the eatery.

It was a gut-wrenching scream that shook Jake's toughguy persona to his boots. He stood frozen with the three churchmen watching him as if withholding harsh judgment.

Her second scream set him in motion. He spun on his heels and ran back into the brick barbecue joint with the Magnum up like a steel boner and ready to rock.

Amanda was crouched in a corner, using a chair like a lion tamer to fend off the biggest, scariest zombie Jake had ever seen. The ghoul was a ginormous nightmare, going on seven feet tall in his stocking feet (with several fungus-encrusted toes sticking out of a hole in his sock) and with well over three hundred pounds filling out his stout bloodstained overalls.

Then Jake saw what had ripped the terrible screams from Amanda. Her boyfriend's head rested in a plate of leftover barbecue pork, while his body lay on the floor on the other side of the table, blood still leaking from the stump of his neck. Todd's left eye looked at Jake over the mushy pile of red-sauced pork.

It blinked.

Whether it was a knowing wink or a dying reflex, Jake didn't take time to contemplate. He yelled, "Hey!" and put a .357 slug in the center of the giant zombie's face, making a crooked-toothed mush of his mouth, as well as taking off the tip of his long nose. The back of his head came off and decorated the wall behind his hulking bulk with brain bits and skull chips and black blood.

Amanda took advantage of the zomboid giant's distraction and dashed from the corner to the doorway, where she stopped and turned to see what would happen next.

Jake fired again and took out the monster's right eyeball. Even though his mouth was no longer much of a threat, he was big enough to crush Jake in a bear hug and obviously strong enough to tear off his head (as evidenced by Exibit A, Todd's bodiless noggin), but if Jake blinded the sonofabitch, they could avoid his clutches and disable his arms and legs at their leisure. Or just leave him to go bump in the eternal night.

Jake put the gun's muzzle in the zombie's face and blew out the other eyeball, taking off most of the rest of the back of the head and turning the wall behind him into as fine a piece of zombie art as could be found anywhere, in Jake's less than humble opinion.

The mammoth zombie shambled and shuffled with arms outstretched as if in a bizarre burlesque of Karloff's most famous monster. Now he was about as scary as a slow-moving mummy in one of those old black & white flicks from the 1940s.

Jake left him to his blind ramble and escorted Amanda outside.

"Sorry about your boyfriend," he said with his arm around her shoulder.

"He wasn't really my boyfriend."

"Yeah, well . . ."

Jake removed the empty shells from the Magnum's cylinder and replaced them with live rounds as he addressed the three men in suits. "He's big but I blinded him and blew out his mouth. You could chop him down with an axe or cut him down to size with a chainsaw, if you're of a mind to. Me and the lady here are heading out for Savannah, Georgia. Good luck to you." Just like that it was decided. What the hell, he couldn't let her go alone, could he?

"We heard pilgrims were gathering in Savannah," said the short churchman, getting a sour look on his face. "Something about a female savior?"

"Something wrong with that?" Amanda said with her hands on her hips and fire in her eyes. Jake was glad to see the flash of angry defiance in her. She was going to need that kind of fire to get through what was coming. They all would.

"Uh, no ma'am," said Shorty, casting an uneasy glance up at the mystic eye in the sky.

"There ya go," Jake said, saluting them with the Magnum's muzzle. Then he holstered it and offered Amanda his arm.

"Miss Amanda," he said.

She locked her arm in his and they walked with as much dignity as they could muster to the waiting Mustang.

"Godspeed," somebody said.

Jake opened the passenger door for her and said, "Whatever the world's got waiting for us, we'll greet it with a grin and a big goddamn gun. And if that ain't good enough, then fuck it. We'll go out in a blaze."

Amanda said, "Amen, Jake Moon Snake."

Jake said, "Amen."

"My God, look at that!"

Jake turned to see the three churchmen looking up, the tall one pointing to the sky.

Jake looked up in time to see the great eye blink again.

Then it winked out, leaving only the big empty sky.

# ZEE BEE & BEE
## (a.k.a. Propeller Hats For The Dead)

### By David James Keaton

David James Keaton's short fiction has recently appeared in the Red Room Press dark crime anthology *The Death Panel*, as well as *Plots With Guns, Thuglit, Espresso Stories, Big Pulp, Six Sentences, Pulp Pusher*, and *Crooked*. He is a contributor to *The College Rag* and the University of Pittsburgh's online journal *Hot Metal Bridge*. A graduate student in the MFA program at Pitt, he is also a full-time closed captioner and the ill-fated founder of a Bed & Breakfast where staff would be encouraged to attack the guests. Investors balked. He considers apocalyptic survival scenarios more than most, hopefully.

"Follow me, and let the dead bury their dead."
—Matt 8:22

We aren't supposed to start moaning and pounding on the house until the sun goes down, but we're taking our jobs real serious these days. Over by the fake gas pump, I can see a shadow crouching down, and know he's finally going to shit in the football helmet. I can just make out the Steelers logo as I watch him fill it up to the ear holes. There is no chance of it being worn this time, even if it's hosed out again.

Another shadow takes a swat at the one squatting, but the first shadow just hunches over and keeps concentrating, kind of like a cat still trying to get the ham off someone's sandwich after it's been busted. He just gets lower and lower and lower with each blow, but never moves to pull up his pants. I hear the second shadow demanding an explanation, and I sigh. I don't have to see their faces to know who they are. We've played this game too many times already.

"It's my love letter to the city that gave birth to us," the first shadow explains, now deciding it's a good time to run.

Our instructions were to display precisely one character trait. This, we were told, was because it is both the most efficient way to make a memory in the allotted time, and because it was so hysterical in *Dawn of the Dead* when they wandered over the hill inexplicably wearing baseball uniforms and ballerina outfits. Most of the boys just want to wear their favorite jersey though, and that means there's almost always too many sports fans to be bumping shoulders among our small band of the undead.

"I'm just saying," the first shadow laughs as it backpedals and falls down under a rain of backhands and elbows, "If we already have a Baseball Zombie, we probably don't need a Football Zombie. But we definitely don't need *two* Football Zombies."

"Said the Football Zombie."

The fight escalates and someone hustles them behind the shed and out of sight. Tonight, everyone's tired of them already, but I have to admit one thing. The first shadow was right. Pittsburgh was the city that started it all, and it was the reason we were here, if you got right down to it. But it was also hard to see any love in that gesture, and it wasn't even my helmet. As handy as one of those might be during an actual siege, two helmets were obviously one helmet too many.

"Why would that one be wearing a catcher's mitt?" we used to complain during our end-of-season, zombie-movie marathon. "Come on, did he get bit during a game?" But our previous Baseball Zombie was ready to defend any criticism:

"It's not that complicated, man. He put the glove on later, just like me, right after he died. He's just pretending."

"Then why can't I have roller skates with this catcher's mitt?"

Because we were told very sternly by our employers never to mix and match. You couldn't wear a cowboy hat and carry a hockey stick, for example. You couldn't wear a Hawaiian shirt and a Santa Claus cap. You couldn't fumble around with a book while wearing a KKK cloak, not just because books are like Kryptonite to the Klan, but because, obviously, what the fuck would a Library Zombie wield? And you couldn't stand outside a window slowly and comically figuring out how to aim your gun all over again if you were a Face-Painted Big Game Zombie. Yes, it would be hard with a giant foam finger anyway, but that was the Cop Zombie's job, always would be. This rule was particularly hard to follow for our own Cop Zombie, since it was always so tempting for him to make fun of my nervous cough, something I've been afflicted with all my life, but also a trait that makes little sense for him or me.

Especially me, the Truck Zombie.

"Shouldn't it be 'Hit-By-A-Truck Zombie?'" someone's always asking.

At one morning meeting, I tried to explain that it was a result of the impact of the grill of that imaginary 18-wheeler that crushed my chest. I even showed them the cookie-cutter impression, Jesus on the cross, that I'd pressed deep into my skin to simulate a hood ornament. But everyone just scoffed and said that coughing was for the Cigarette Zombie, not me, and I should just continue to hold mine in. As if I could.

I suppress my first cough of the day as my earphone informs me the first couple is already heading for the basement. This means that they will be confronting our first "plant," the hysterical yet tyrannical businessman, followed soon after by a reveal of his wife and their injured daughter. This is about an hour ahead of schedule. The sun isn't even down yet.

I pound harder, furious that they've never seen *Night of the Living Dead*, or the hundreds of imitators like us, or they would know that running to the basement always means doom. At the very least, they should remember that the trip to the basement comes at the end of the goddamn movie. Even *Day of the Dead*, despite that deceptive title, only displays approximately nine minutes and seventeen seconds of total sunlight throughout its entire running time. Almost that whole movie takes place in a basement. It's no accident that it's considered the logical end of the series.

I let my legs give out, start crawling toward the next open window, then snap back up. Sometimes I play it like my legs are broken. Sometimes I even put my pants and shoes on backwards to pretend my body has been turned around completely below the waist from some sort of massive impact. But tonight I decide that backwards shoes won't be enough of a hindrance. I turn them back around when no one is looking.

Here's some trivia. I actually knew the actor who got hit by the truck in the '90s remake of *Night of the Living Dead*. Okay, he was a friend of a friend, but I heard that he had no sweat glands and, legend has it, had to smear chap stick all over his head if he was stuck out in the sun too long during filming. I wish he could play this game with us, because, with that kind of dedication, I know he would probably take it just as seriously as I do, maybe even shame me into turning my shoes back around for good.

I punch through the window and everyone squints as glass showers faces, forearms, and chests. Cowboy Zombie stops moaning for a second to hold the eye up off his cheek and glare at me. Then he flicks a glass shard from behind a sticky blue ear and starts to pound again, face slack, all business. Baseball Zombie shakes his head, brushes his jersey with his catcher's mitt, and waits patiently for me to notice him. Then he gives me a shrug under his perpetual slouch, jaw still swinging, but the assault momentarily forgotten. I shrug back, then turn away to grab a pink and panicked hand before the wood covers the hole and a deafening burst of hammering finally displays some respect for their situation.

Beyond the hand, I catch a glimpse of some weary eyes inside the house, and I'm glad to see they're finally realizing how long this game might last.

They got the idea by trying to be the last bed and breakfast in the phone book. Mags came up with the name "Z B & B" specifically to trump Youngstown's Country Inn. And it was this name and the meaningless "Z" that started her boyfriend, now husband, Davey Jones, thinking about zombies, of course. Soon after, as an experiment, they were involved in an altercation at an Italian dinner theater/fake wedding combo that was touring the Midwest, "Tony Baloney's Reception." It was a gimmick that Mags called, "vaguely racist bullshit," although she did eventually admit that getting shoved into a ten-tier cake while Mafioso caricatures staged a fist fight might be a good story to tell a party after enough time had passed.

"Tragedy plus time equals comedy and all that," she reminded Davey the morning after his headfirst Pete Rose cake slide.

"But wait!" he exploded over corn flakes, bloody twist of toilet paper popping from his nostril. "What if zombies were trashing the shit out of that wedding reception? Would you pay to see that? I'd pay to see that! Hell, I'd pay to *do* that." And *pow!* they suddenly found themselves with an untapped gold mine of couples who would rather spend the night of their honeymoons pretending they were hiding from zombies instead of tapping glasses with forks to encourage some failed actors to stage a kiss.

"Zee Bee & Bee?" Davey Jones mumbled. "Sounds German."

Whether it was a new groom wanting to posture and protect his woman during a life-threatening emergency or the blushing bride wanting to demonstrate how she would, much to his surprise, bloom in an apocalyptic crisis, business was good right out of the gate.

And when they hired me (their second cousin and initiator of years of Sunday night zombie film festivals) to amp up the threat level of the scenario, word spread fast. I helped hand-pick a crew, and by the next fall, we had things up and running.

Two years after we'd started making enough money to think about our first 4:00 a.m. commercial spot, a movie popped up in the video stores called *Dead and Breakfast*. Everyone panicked a little. But, luckily, it bore no resemblance to our original idea. This movie was just another attack on a house, their storyline treating everything as if it was actually happening, something even the occasional survivalist couple rarely considered for long. Clever title though, we all had to admit.

And it was my idea to have the evening start with Mags and Davey Jones meeting two couples at the bottom of the long driveway leading up to the house. This is where they would sign the waiver. And it was also my brainstorm for the two couples to arrive about an hour apart. This gave one couple a chance to get settled a bit and locked in before the other couple came banging on the door. See, now the door was *their* door, just because of that extra hour. And there was always only one bed between the two couples to encourage competition and arguments, another good reason to keep the arrivals staggered. It was surprising how much controversy was caused by one couple getting an unfair opportunity to toss a suitcase onto a bed first. Mags chalked that up to the influence of reality television.

She eventually started profiling them carefully to choose which couple was most likely to not want to give up that bed without a fight. We were never sure how she figured this out. There was talk of Mags going through trash cans and peeking through windows of potential applicants. But she always seemed to pick the right couple to go into the house first. Sometimes I pretended she picked me.

"What the hell is going on?! Where did *you* come from?!"

Inside the house, someone is screaming, and I don't need my earphone to hear it. It's a Plant, not a Camel. That's what we called the guests, "Camels." Cigarette Zombie sort of made it up. Something about the title of Albert Camus' short story "The Guest" being a translation of the French word "L'Hôte," meaning both guest and host. According to her, this was "precisely" what we were asking them to be. She tried to get us to call them that for awhile, but we couldn't pronounce it *and* we had no idea what she was talking about. But they did become "Camus" for awhile, and that made her smile. At least that's what somebody told me. I've never actually seen her do this myself. Smile I mean. Then the word got changed to "Camels" for good, and she has scowled ever since. Even though we tried to convince her it was based on Aesop's Fable about "familiarity breeding contempt," the one where the Arabs first see a camel and are all terrified, but by the third sighting they're putting saddles on it (because, hey, wasn't that "precisely" what we were doing?), it didn't matter. She never got on board with the term.

But it isn't a Camel that's screaming. I can tell by the level of acting ability. And it can't be Tom. Not yet. He should still be in his locked room, waiting to be discovered if and when they find the key in the bucket of nails under the sink. For now, he should simply be happily rustling some aluminum foil, maybe scratching at the door or floor every so often, maybe making just enough noise for someone to start wondering what's in there, mouse or monster.

For a second it's silent, then I hear that girl, the newlywed, making her "tisk" noise at something that disgusts her. I heard her doing it an hour earlier when I was hiding in the bushes watching her new husband sign the waiver. I remember thinking that if there was some fine print in that contract that she missed and was having second thoughts about, it was too late now.

I always hated those noises, those impatient clicks and hisses people always do when they're annoyed. I had a girlfriend once who ruined every movie by sucking her bottom lip and making a sharp snap, sorta like gum popping, whenever something dramatic happened on screen. It was especially excruciating in the theater, and I found myself taking her to more comedies than I ever wanted to see. And at a zombie movie, she would "tisk" so many times that one nearby theatergoer actually asked if she was shuffling a deck of cards. I start thinking this particular little noise might screw up our game, maybe make some other zombie out here, a zombie with less patience than me, try a little harder to make her stop, maybe by pulling her tongue out from its root slow and steady as a flower you don't want to break off too soon.

In my earpiece, I can hear the honeymooners talking about a shower curtain. They are exchanging the kinds of details you'd guess should have already surfaced before their marriage.

". . . well, *my* dad used to flip out if we messed up the bathroom. With two boys, it got real messy real quick . . ."

"See, I told you it wasn't blood. Somebody dyed their hair in here recently, that's all."

". . . and then when my little sister came along, she was one of those vacation babies by the way, that's why there's that age gap, she'd trash the place and dad never said peep. She'd change her hair from black to red to green and get it all over the walls and he'd just sigh . . ."

"This sure looks like blood though."

". . . and when I tried to tell her how he used to lose his mind if we got one drop of urine behind the toilet seat, she wouldn't believe us. I mean, a little yellow on the toilet is a lot more understandable than a green bathtub . . ."

"You know what? If they try too hard to scare us, I might call their bluff."

Bad things happen sometimes. Not often, but sometimes. It comes with the territory when things really start rolling and the emotions spike: Overly aggressive behavior, minor theft and vandalism, a general disrespect for the situation. But to discourage these shenanigans, we discovered early on a few simple things we could do. We didn't want to hurt anyone, but we did need to convince people we were really trying to get a hold of them.

So Davey Jones told us to always go for the meat.

"Avoid the bones," he said. "If you look for spots that an actual zombie would prefer to bite into and instead grab with your fingers, you will usually hit a spot less likely to inflict pain."

He was right. The skulls and elbows and knees were a lot of trouble in our hands, just as they would disappoint a hungry mouth. But nothing caused as much trouble as an agitated Camel. Therefore, in the wavier, it clearly stated that they could be expelled from the house by any staff or Camel ("For the sake of the human race!" our Plants would declare to the rest of the survivors) the minute they crossed that line into purposeful injury or, as described more explicitly in the contract, "catching a zombie's finger under your hammer more than three times."

That part was easiest to remember. Three fingers and they were out.

And it wasn't fun to get kicked out. Since they would have already turned in their car keys, they'd quickly understand that they could either sit in a ditch all night and watch their girl or boyfriend have all the fun *or* they could allow themselves to be gently steered along the path of our reasonable and satisfying story line. However, if they were really ornery (like that little fucker last fall with the cherry bombs), they would be held down and forced to take a slathering of blue paint to the face and, if they wanted to, attack the house with the rest of our staff. We called it "getting bit," and it always surprised us how many decided to join in on the pounding. Probably because it was a choice between either punching a door or walking aimlessly around the woods, two things a real zombie would probably be doing with his Saturday night anyway.

"Why the need to give everyone advice all the time? You get that from your uncle."

"Just trying to help you make the most of that wood. And why bring my uncle into . . ."

"Tell everyone the advice he gave you the first time you got on the bus to Kindergarten."

"He said, 'Be careful.'"

"Uh, no. What else did he say?"

"Yeah, tell us."

"He said, 'If you stick your hand down a girl's pants and it feels like you're feeding a horse, you're in trouble.'"

Tell "everyone?" Yep, between laughter, hammer strikes, and another "tisk," I finally recognize the voices of our Plants and that old joke. It's our Irritable Couple Hiding In The Basement, Jeff and Amy. Apparently, they were forced to join the game early since the Plants already opened their door. They seem to be ad-libbing a little more than usual to fill the gaps and expected questions. I cup my ear, listening to the banter. The rest of the zombies would be doing the same thing. After another couple seconds of listening, we could safely assume the couple haven't seen the injured daughter yet and we should stick to the plan. Up until a couple seasons ago, this particular stage of the game would have been alerted by barking because the injured daughter had been an injured Blue Labrador (more hairless than "blue" really) for awhile instead, a wonderfully irritating, half-domesticated, very snappy little monster we referred to as "shark dog." Now we just use the earphones to synchronize the plot without animal noises.

An animal is sorely missed though. Having one around changed the way we all acted. Critters never doubt the sincerity of our acting, not for one second. But any twist on the timeless Zombie Attack story usually turned out to be a mistake, and this was no exception. There was a reason they kept dogs out of most of those movies. And what happened to our dog was something we zombies rarely talk about. And, as always, we worried Amy would bring up the incident by the end of the night.

I'm pulling at a window frame when someone nicks some skin off the side of my thumb with the claw end of the hammer. It's the same set of eyes from earlier. I frown and count "strike two" in my head.

At least Jeff is laughing tonight, having more fun. See, back in the day, Jeff used to date Amy. Davey Jones encouraged this, thinking it would be great motivation since he'd puff out a little more around her, and maybe that would help sell his role to the Camels. And he let them keep their real names to help stay in character, too.

It worked for awhile.

The problem was that it quickly made some emotions bleed over into real life in increasingly dangerous ways. It didn't help that one season Amy cheated on Jeff with Jerry, a.k.a. "Baseball Zombie." That made Jeff target the big number 3 on Jerry's back a bit too aggressively sometimes. During one seemingly endless barrage, Jeff broke character and mercilessly ridiculed Amy for liking athletes, even though Jerry had never thrown a pitch or hit a ball in his life. This, in return, caused Jerry to punch one Camel in the face last year ("barely a swat," he finally admitted), a very solid and un-undead-looking right hook that plowed through some bottom teeth like the Garden Weasel and cost the equivalent of a dozen of them (not cheap, we used one after each attack to fix the landscaping), plus shipping and handling, to settle out of court. A lot of "dead baby mama drama," Mags called it. Now, Tom, our military Plant, and part of our locked room mystery during the climax, was very quick to freestyle through the awkwardness of any bloody nose by coming up with his own story off the cuff about their platoon reporting zombies imitating what they'd seen on the screen at a drive-in *Rocky* festival ("could happen," he shrugged) then stood humming nervously in a dogpile of corpses as he held a toy phone over his head desperately searching for a signal.

But besides that recent love triangle, this year there was also a new power struggle in our ranks. The two Bobbys, Bobby Z and Bobby B, had both developed a strange impulse to lead us on the attack at all times. Each of them wanted to be the head zombie, standing on point, the first to use tools, first to snarl, et cetera, sort of like the "Gas" character in *Land of the Dead*. You know, leading assaults, making decisions, very slowly of course, it all became quite a nuisance, more and more important to each of them every siege. It made for low, slurring but serious arguments over cold barbecue chicken, over who broke what window. And even though we all guessed it was mostly because they had the bad luck of both being named "Bobby," there was also some talk about one of them wanting to be the first zombie to drive a Camel's car. This was inexcusable. Not just because it wasn't in the contract, but because this would be a scene that is not in *any* of the movies, remakes included.

But tonight they are just fighting about that helmet nonstop.

"I don't know why you even like the Steelers. It goes against our philosophy."

"The fuck you talking about?"

"That Polamalu-malu-lu's girly-ass hair would be a serious liability during a zombie uprising. I can't believe none of the announcers ever bring that up, to be honest."

"No, he's way too fast to get caught."

"Maybe with a ball in his hands. Without it, he's lunch. In fact, I saw him take a hit so hard once that the ref yelled, 'Fatality!' instead of 'Offsides' . . ."

"Bullshit."

". . . got hit so hard he left his multiplication tables on the 50 yard line, along with memories of three Christmases ago . . ."

"Never happened."

". . . so hard his helmet rolled into the end zone and his head was still in it."

"Unlikely."

"I was there, man. And I couldn't believe they played such an inappropriate song in the stadium while they gathered up the pieces. If he ever did wake up, he'd have thought he was in Maroon 5 . . ."

"A level of exaggeration I've sadly grown accustomed to . . ."

"Shhh!" A zombie tries to get them to keep it down.

"Anyway. You owe me a helmet, asshole."

"Yes, my asshole owes you a helmet."

"You guys seem to forget your roles," I interrupt. "Mags didn't give you two those shirts to represent the Army and Navy football teams for no reason . . ."

"Fuck off," they tell me in stereo. Then the weight goes out of their arms, and they get into character. Just in time, too, as the second couple comes bounding up the driveway, laughing and zigzagging past the Bobbys as they make half-ass swipes at their shoulders. I'm closest to the house and the only one that sees what the Camel drops near the front door.

It's a paper towel. My heart would have jumped if it still pumped. As the brother of a child with OCD, I suddenly suspect this might change some things. A guest like this might not be ready for prime time, not ready for the trials and tribulations of our particular game, not ready to fiddle while Rome burns. This might be one of those guys who doesn't want to get dirty enough to convince himself it's really happening. Well, then he shouldn't have signed up, should he? This should make me angry, even angrier than the Bobbys' constant nonsense, but for the first time since I started shuffling up the driveway tonight, this Truck Zombie is scared.

"*I Bite,*" someone says.

"Nice work. Hold on. Bite what?" someone asks.

"No, I'm just saying that would be the perfect name for a zombie movie. It's even better than *I, Zombie* because it's like the shortest sentence in the history of the English language."

"Actually, 'I bite' is not the shortest possible sentence. 'I am' will always hold that title."

"*I Bite Therefore I Am!*"

"Sounds like Dr. Seuss."

Turning back to our mob, I see her keeping to the rear, head down farther than anyone's. At some point tonight, I will have to tell her how I feel. It is expected, of course, end of the world confessions are almost required. But this is only half the reason. The other half is the perfect advice I'd heard her giving to another zombie about something entirely different. Whether or not to eat some expired eggs was the original subject of the debate, I believe, but the answer was universal.

"If not now, when?" she said.

✳   ✳   ✳

The smoke break was probably her idea, our Cigarette Zombie (a.k.a. Coffee and Cigarettes Zombie, a.k.a. Term-Paper-Grading Zombie), whose one character trait was, once she broke into the house, trying to smoke every cigarette and drink as much coffee as she could. But doing it really, really slow. This was all a result of trying to relive her previous existence as a grad student, according to Mags. I never thought it was fair that she was the only one claiming to be a Grad Student Zombie as we were all, without exception, University of Pittsburgh drop-outs, kicked-outs, and failed-outs, every cursed one of us.

We usually took the smoke break behind The Joshua Bush, the squat and lonely shrub in the middle of the field near the fake gas pump. This was where most of our debates occurred. It was *not* named after the U2 album. You'll see.

The break was usually scheduled for the reveal of the Plants in the basement, since that should occupy all the Camels' for a good half hour. But the timing was off tonight, and the second couple had just arrived, so we decided to eat our lunch fast. We were always tired of barbecue chicken and entrails by the end of the night (the best meat to simulate zombie feasting), so most of us usually stuck to fruit or vegetables to balance our diets. Ever see a zombie with rickets? It's not pretty. Looks just like me.

Since we're out of earshot, we don't have to whisper or moan. Passing around a box of fig bars, our discussion turns to the word "zombie" and how hard it is to not acknowledge exactly what we are every time we play the game, how the existence of zombies has to be a new discovery every single time. I agree, but don't say so. Just like my small-brained cat used to think every day was her first day on Earth, it's taboo to ever say the word "zombie" out loud, a strict rule that the British comedy *Shaun of the Dead* mocked quite effectively. Contrary to popular belief, the much revered 1978 *Dawn of the Dead* was actually the first movie to break this law. But the worst infraction was, of course, in the more recent *Land of the Dead* where a visibly bored Dennis Hopper seems to be speaking not just directly to the audience, but directly to the movie's goddamn *trailer*, "Zombies, man, they creep me out." I still cringe thinking about it. You'd think he would have been thankful to have a script written for his complete comfort and indifference. He has to be the only villain, zombie movie or otherwise, ever to spend 90% of his screen time in a luxury hotel sipping whiskey. He probably thought he was doing a buddy-cop flick the whole time.

Waiting for the fig bars to come back around, it's just a matter of time before someone's stirring the pot of discord, as usual.

"Then why are you, say, 'Lumberjack Zombie?'" Baseball Zombie asks, pointing over the bush and talking through a mouthful of masticated mush. "We're always encouraging the word, too, you know?"

"We don't count, asshole," he scoffs. "And I'm Seattle Zombie now. Don't forget it."

"And don't let them see you guys kissing this time, Jack."

"I ain't Jack. Seattle Zombie, damn it! Recognize!"

"Who was kissing?" I ask, heart pounding, way too interested in the answer.

"Cigarette Zombie and one of the Bobbys," someone mutters.

"Why not?" Cigarette Zombie laughs. "Zombies should want to do that just as much as they'd want to find a catcher's mitt. Hell, they're actually fucking in *Dead Alive.*"

"You mean *Braindead?*" someone corrects her.

"Whatever."

"No. Not *whatever.* That's the original title."

"Whatever."

"Ha! I schooled your ass."

"Yes," admits Cigarette Zombie. "You have indeed taken me to Ass School."

Cigarette Zombie turns away, but Josh, the instigator, a kid who was technically supposed to be Sushi Chef Zombie but we liked to call "Sour Towel" Zombie because he smelled like a ripe bath towel at all times (as if he never heard of a dryer even *before* the Apocalypse) plopped down next to me and kept inching closer and closer to my shoulder. He was always way too into these debates. And surprisingly unfunny for a kid named "Josh."

"That's right, baby," he laughs. "You have definitely been taken where asses are regularly schooled."

"Dude, take a step back," I hiss. "They don't make toothpaste strong enough for the undead."

I elbow him toward Cigarette Zombie, and she elbows him right back.

"You know what Sour Towel Zombie reminds me of?" asks Cigarette Zombie, looking up from the rotting parts of the apple she was eating around, "He's like *Night of the Living Bread.*"

"How's that?" Sour Towel Zombie sneers, ready to jump on any inaccuracies of an obscure parody.

"Like the bread on the lawn, dude! Every time we look away, you get a little closer."

"Yeah, seriously," I agree, then cough. "Back up, man. You're in my bubble."

Somewhere, the conversation takes an inevitable turn.

"Okay, sure, they may hope it'll be like trying to deep-throat an old splintered baseball bat. But that's just wishful thinking. It's more like trying to inflate a decade-old New Year's noisemaker by sucking instead of blowing."

"Hold up. Does it even count as a 'deep throat' if there's a convenient exit wound?"

"Those days are over. As we dry up, don't tell me I'm the only one who noticed his balls are on the wrong side of things lately."

"What do you mean?"

"You ever smack one of your Hot Wheels too hard and the wheels ended up near the windows?"

"Que?"

"The wheels on the cock go 'round and 'round . . ."

"Quiet!" snaps the other Bobby, and we hunch lower around the bush instinctively as Cigarette Zombie lights up, signaling the break is almost over. I look around the circle.

Besides the Plants, Jeff, Amy, and their dog or daughter (and, of course, Mags and Davey Jones, who were supposed to burst into the house later tonight) there are about, what, a dozen of us these days? Yeah, that's got to be right. I remember the number because of a carton of rotten eggs where Mags drew every one of our faces on the yellow shells to remind us not to eat them.

First there's Jerry, a.k.a. Baseball Zombie, a.k.a. somebody's little brother. Then there's the kid with the unlikely name of We Ma, a.k.a. Cowboy Zombie, a.k.a. We "None" Ma, the result of filling out a driver's license application, putting "none" in the space for a middle name, and the clerk mistaking it for just another crazy Asian moniker. (To show her own cultural sensitivity, Mags once vetoed Davey Jones' attempt to make him the cleaver-wielding Sushi Chef Zombie.) Then there's Lumberjack Zombie, a.k.a. Seattle Zombie, a.k.a. Steve? I don't think I ever met that guy, actually, and probably couldn't "recognize!" no matter how many times he said it. He's been known to wear two shirts to try to look bigger, I'm told. At least that's the only possible explanation for a nickname like "Zombie Two-Shirts." He was also Sensible Shoes Zombie for awhile, and he shuffled ever so comfortably. Then there's Matt, a.k.a. Security Guard Zombie, a.k.a. Rent-A-Cop Zombie. His title doesn't really fit as he sports a huge beard like a surfboard hanging off his face that he could hide half a chicken in. We're still petitioning to make him Shoplifter Zombie instead (would have been Sticky Fingers Zombie if we didn't all have sticky fingers) and fire Glen, a.k.a Midlife Crisis Zombie, who's balls-deep in exactly that.

Then there are Michael and Rachel, a.k.a. Indian Zombie and Indian Zombie, one Native American with the feather behind his ear, one European with the dot on her forehead that sometimes doubles as a bullet hole. Michael loves his one characteristic, never showing emotion, and says it suits him perfect as, supposedly, he has never shed a tear in his entire life. "And now, of course," he likes to tell us, "it's way too late." And Rachel, she doesn't just stick to citing various Eastern religions. She's also been known to ironically quote the Bible to us when the Camels aren't in earshot (Matt, too, of course, in honor of his namesake, both always in a deep, movie narrator voice). And Mark, a.k.a. Fast-Talking '50s Newspaper Man Zombie (who never really fit at all), he walked off the set one day and never came back. Said our plots were predictable, our jokes stale, our lifestyles unhealthy, and he just didn't have the stomach for it anymore.

And then there's Nate, a.k.a. Third Stage Zombie, the slippery, oily, decaying ghoul you'd see toward the end of the film that's having an even tougher time putting one foot in front of the other. He's one of those zombies who's swimming in that limbo right before his muscles stop working entirely. Nate actually walked awkwardly on the tips of his toes back when he was alive, back when we used to call him Obsessive Compulsive Zombie, a.k.a. The O.C.Z., so his adopted role here is a no-brainer.

We try not to look at him. He reminds us the game can end.

And then there are the wild cards, sitting directly across from each other, as always, the two Bobbys, Bobby Zelienople and Bobby Balldinger, a.k.a. Bobby Z and Bobby B. They aren't zombies, not yet. At this point during the game, we aren't even supposed to see them. They are supposed to represent the military that always show up in the third act to screw everything up and dash any hopes of rescue or civilization. But they can never get this right. They like to pretend they already got bit, got turned, always way too early. They want to be both, neither, apparently. A tradition in most zombie films is that the military is never to be trusted under any circumstances, and they do relish these roles. Too bad they can never wait for their cue. Sometimes, they play Army, sometimes Navy, sometimes Air Force. But their rivalry started when, after we started making the big bucks, Mags brought them Armed Forces football jerseys instead of just T-shirts so they'd be more visible at night. Then someone brought a Steelers helmet. Big mistake. Now their competition regularly comes to blows.

Tonight, however, neither Bobby wears a jersey. They claim they're playing the roles of National Guard volunteers and are sick of the uniforms. Nobody bothers to argue. Rumor has it among the two higher-ups this is gonna be their last season if there are any more problems. And defecating in the football helmet probably sealed the deal, even though they tried to pin their behavior on some shocking news from the real world, the untimely motorcycle, train, Segway, hot-air balloon collision (and subsequent final decapitation) of their favorite Fantasy Football father figure, beloved number 7 but number 1 in their hearts, cereal endorser and serial rapist, Big Ben "Has Been" Roethlisberger, a.k.a. Hand-off Burger, a.k.a. Rapist Burger, a.k.a. Roethlisraper. But now and forever Headless Road Burger Zombie. Some say you can still see him lurking around bathrooms.

They glare at each other, arms crossed, pinched mouths and smirks crawling like caterpillars around their faces. We all know it will be a long night for us, but they won't disappoint anybody just tuning in.

Cigarette Zombie? I never got her name. And I can't remember when I first noticed she was stumbling alongside of me as I sighed and pounded the house embarrassingly limp-wristed.

And, finally, there is the "live" staff inside the house. Mags and Davey Jones, long-suffering proprietors, our secret bosses, both buried so deep in the plot that they rarely come out at all. And Jeff and Amy, our Plants in the basement. I don't know who is playing Jeff and Amy's daughter this time, whether it's the scarecrow, the tackling dummy we borrow from the 6th graders practice field on occasion, or the cowboy silhouette we took off the neighbor's barn and cut down to toddler size. But I am hoping Amy doesn't bring another dog. This is always a concern.

One of the Bobbys is mocking me by clearing his throat, so I try to distract him with a question that's been on my mind.

"Did either of you notice anything weird about that guy?"

"Which guy?" asks Bobby B, never looking up from Bobby Z. We used to call Bobby B "Cloverfield" because of his freakish height and tendency to destroy any beer can or small village he's squeezing. But he was less effective attacking a house that you might guess, so the "Cloverfield" thing was dropped. No one could have anticipated his rivalry with Bobby Z, who carried at least a foot and 50 pounds less than him.

"The Camel," I whisper. "He was moving a little shaky, looking around too much. I don't know."

"Well, maybe they're getting more cynical," Sour Towel Zombie offers. "We've got to be famous by now."

"Yeah, but . . ."

"The Camels shouldn't know too much if they want to play the game right," Sour Towel Zombie interrupts. "But they shouldn't know too little either."

"They need to be the porridge that's just right, is what you're saying," Bobby B scoffs. He's Rembrant in the art of the scoff.

"Exactly!" Sour Towel Zombie actually holds up one finger. "With so many movies showing the usual pattern of behavior in a house under siege . . ."

"I know, I know," I say impatiently. "And this is why the puzzle pieces have to be juggled sometimes. I understand all this. But there was something about that guy that just . . ."

"See," Sour Towel Zombie goes on, "these movies are basically just home invasion stories. It is the *house* that is most important. The Camels could just run away, and it would all be over, the movie, the game, everything. But by protecting the house, things escalate nicely. It's the most natural thing in the world to protect a house. And we're all doing this, even by tearing it down . . ."

"So, technically," Cigarette Zombie jumps in, "the first zombie movie was that book about the two guys that kill that family for a silver dollar. If a book was a movie, of course."

"What?" asks Rachel, a.k.a. European Indian Zombie. "No, no, no. That was technically the first true-crime novel you're thinking of."

"*Bed and Breakfast at Tiffany's?*" Cigarette Zombie laughs. Clearly Rachel was in her *house,* daring anyone to challenge her book knowledge. "No, I meant his other book."

"*In Cold Blood,* right?" Sour Towel Zombie laughs. "No, that was technically the first pop-up book. You open it up . . . Foomp! There's the house. Turn the page . . . Foomp! There's the basement where they killed the dad. Turn the page . . . Foomp! There's the crime scene upstairs where they raped the daughter. Open up the little flap . . . and you tore the page. Good job, kid, you fucked up your book already. Children will love your gift when they aren't crying."

"The girl wasn't raped," Cigarette Zombie corrects. "That's why she was shot."

"Lucky her," European Indian Zombie mutters.

"Never mind," I sigh.

"Wait, if you think this Camel might potentially take things too far," says Bobby B as he stands up, "maybe we should introduce the military presence a little early."

"Here we go . . ."

"Yeah," Bobby Z agrees. "Maybe you can shit in his lunchbox and give him a heart attack."

"Wait," Bobby B laughs. "Did you just say 'hard' attack?"

"No," says Bobby Z, standing up too, trying to be the one to signal our break is over. "You fuckin' heard me."

"Sorry. Just trying to figure out what a 'hard attack' is and how I can make sure you don't give me one, faggot," Bobby B says, smile slipping as Sour Towel Zombie steps between them.

I don't even know whose turn it is to shove our poor Sour Towel into the bush when he gets close enough, but, for some reason, I jump on the opportunity. I push him so hard, he almost flips over twice. I don't even wait for a Bobby to get on all fours behind him, the usual drill, and I can tell both of them are a little disappointed. This is very uncharacteristic of me, and I cough nervously to let everyone know it. No one says anything, even though they've done their share of flipping that kid turtle-like into that bush at least once apiece. But the worst is when Cigarette Zombie quietly helps a dour Sour Towel Zombie out of the broken branches and back to his feet.

Then we all crack some knuckles and put on our game faces and start lumbering back toward the house. I'm the last one standing up straight as I think about what I did and who I did it for.

\* \* \*

Someone is sick, coughing instead of moaning. Coughing for real. And Sour Towel Zombie is telling anyone who will listen about the movie *Gates of Hell* and how that poor actress had to swallow still-warm sheep entrails for the effect of vomiting up her entire intestinal tract. Cigarette Zombie stops coughing, then lights another cigarette off the orange nub of her last one before she drops it.

"Now *that's* a chain smoker," Sour Towel Zombie laughs. "When you light one off one and they're both yours? Time to quit! And why don't you ever flick 'em for dramatic effect?"

I leave them crouched down next to the porch and navigate the gas meters and gutters. It's my turn on recon and psychological warfare. I scratch around the aluminum siding until I find a good window to peek inside. I can see the good bed, the made bed, the bed with the big, pink, fluffy comforter and someone's shiny, new suitcase dead center in the middle of it. Then two Camels appear, the women, arms flailing away and gesturing to the bed, both apparently explaining why it should be hers. I snicker. They must have already located the damp mattress in the corner of the unfinished family room (or "Tetanusville," as Mags calls it. "Or Spiderville to the locals.")

One of the Camels eventually leaves, defeated, and the other walks to the bathroom and clicks on the light over the mirror. She checks the lines of her face, then places a sickly green Tupperware bowl of something on the edge of the tub to soak. I blink a few extra times as I realize what it is. Then the other Camel storms back in, still yelling and I take off. When I come back down to the Joshua Bush, everyone is shuffling in a circle, killing time between attacks, and Cigarette and Sour Towel Zombie are still arguing.

"I've seen that movie!" Cigarette Zombie almost yells. "There's way worse."

"Like what exactly?"

"Like *Beyond Re-Animator,* zombie schlong vs. rat during the end credits. Or even like your precious *Braindead,* uh, I mean, *Dead Alive,* where the dude's rectum flops out and then runs amok around the house. Hell, it even tries to groom itself in a mirror at one point, like comb its head with little bladders."

"Yeah, that scene's okay," Sour Towel Zombie admits. "But everything in that movie is overshadowed by the Greatest Moment Of All Time."

"Which is?"

"Sigh. I shouldn't even have to say it. Do I have to say it? I won't. Okay, I will. The lawnmower scene, fuckers. If my own death came at that moment, I would be okay with that."

"Next time just sigh instead of saying the word, douche bag."

I try to get their attention by shuffling the wrong way against the flow of traffic.

They dodge me easily, mostly keeping game faces glued. Not like the summer when there was a hornets nest under the porch, angrily activated every time more than two limp-wristed feet hit the steps, an extra obstacle that made us dance around in a seriously comic, quite un-undead-like fashion. We almost changed our name to the Zee Bee & Bee & Bee & Bee & Bee. It took at least three smoke bombs to get rid of it for good, but every so often a sting will still surprise a thin-skinned zombie into breaking character with a high-stepping wince at the most serious of times.

"Hey, guys?" I whisper. "There's a suitcase on a bed now."

"Good," says Bobby B. "Are they fighting over it in a beautiful passive-aggressive way?"

"No, more like actually fighting."

"Sweet. What are the men up to? Have they found the key to the closet yet?"

"No, just the nails, obviously. But they may have run out already. There's no more hammering."

"Great. Good job," Bobby Z says sarcastically as he grabs my shoulders. "Now turn around. You're going the wrong way, fucknuts."

"But, uh, I did notice a couple things that were kind of weird . . ."

"Yeah, you already said that. Something about a paper towel. So the Camel washes his hands too much. It's just habit."

"No, it's the female. One of them has a pair of bloody underwear soaking in the tub."

Everyone stops shuffling.

"And?" Bobby Z asks.

"What do you mean 'and'?" about three zombies say at the same time.

"So, what, you think she'll be more on edge, more likely to defend her personal space?" Bobby B wonders.

"No." I speak slow like a child, seeing that some of them don't know what I'm getting at or are just pretending to ignore it. "What

I'm saying is that she must still be . . ."

Bobby Z shoves me over before I can finish.

"Dude, don't fuck this up. It's the only job I've ever liked."

"Hey, that reminds me!" Bobby B laughs. "What do you call a zombie melting in your bathtub?"

"What?"

"Duane! Get it?"

Bobby Z smiles a big blue smile and starts to stumble around next to Cigarette Zombie so he can put his arm around her. I start to grit the last of my teeth. I've never seen a season with so many love triangles, dead, undead, or otherwise.

Bobby B keeps telling jokes, trying to break the tension with some oldies but goodies.

"What do you call a zombie with no arms and no legs?"

"Matt."

"What do you call that same zombie in the pool?"

"Bob."

"What do you call that *same* zombie hanging on a meat hook?"

"Chuck!" Bobby Z is trying hard to answer them all before he finished the set-up.

"Or it could be 'Art!'" Baseball Zombie interrupts it. "That works, too."

"Shut the fuck up and watch the house." Bobby Z has his arm around Baseball Zombie's shoulders instead. "Go on."

"What do you call a zombie stuck under your car?"

"Jack. Go faster."

"What do you call a zombie head stuck in your mailbox?"

"Bill."

"What do you call a zombie with one leg?"

"Eileen. Come on, don't you have any new ones?"

"What do you call a zombie with no arms or legs in a pile of leaves?"

"Russell."

"What do you call a zombie with no feet?"

"Neil."

"What do you call a zombie in the middle of a baseball field?"

We know them all backwards and forward, but even Baseball Zombie isn't fast enough for that one.

"Second base."

"I like it better when Davey Jones does them," says Cigarette

Zombie. "He's always so serious about it."

She's right. He used to fire them off as a sort of calisthenics before the game, something to get our minds right, get us down to that "just . . . one . . . thing" he was always babbling about. Rumor had it that Davey tried to be one of us at first, back when it all started. Supposedly he would attack the house all by himself. And he was a miserable failure. Refunds were demanded. But that didn't stop us from calling him "The O.G.Z." sometimes to fuck with him.

It's quiet for a while, until Bobby B starts cracking knuckles for another siege. I point to the Camels' car at the bottom of the hill, still trying to initiate my discussion.

"Look at that. What kind of vanity plate says MARCH-7?"

"Is that today? How tempting would it be to fuck with that car if that was today?"

"Did anything important happen on that day? I mean, besides . . ."

"We all know what happened on that day."

"It's telling us what to do." Bobby Z shoves me again and suddenly we are all running toward the house. "It says 'get moving.' That's a fucking order, soldier."

Ironically, it's hard to be a good zombie in Pittsburgh with all the hills. Much too tempting to run. Cigarette Zombie is from here originally, and she says she smokes so much because the coughing reminds her of home, mostly the buildings still stained black from the dead factories.

One afternoon when we were the first two to get to work, she swore to me that there was a little bit of Steeltown in all of us now, then she turned and spit a little splash of black onto a nearby butterfly.

It was beautiful.

"And one more thing!" Bobby Z yells out, running harder to get in front of Bobby B. "No one says that word again tonight! We're over the limit! Now march!"

Sour Towel Zombie catches up with him thirteen steps before the porch.

"You know, I thought I was watching a *zombie* movie the other night, but it just turned out to be that one about the lame-ass rapper getting shot nine times. But he's *got* to be a zombie, right? Ain't everybody?"

"Fuck him," Bobby B answers him before Bobby Z can get mad about the word. "That guy's a pussy. All rappers get shot. Doesn't mean shit. Bullet holes? It takes more than that to prove you're a tough guy. You can't even see a bullet hole. You usually just have to take their word for it, especially when they tattoo over them. Now, if he'd been shot with nine *arrows*, that would be a different story. That would be impressive. Can you imagine him stumbling past the DJ, crashing through the turntable at the party, nine arrows sticking out of his body? Maybe one in his face? Now that's tough."

The house is about five feet away, and we can hear the hammers again. They can probably hear us, too, and we still aren't in character. Davey Jones would flip out.

"Less like a rapper," I offer, "and more like the cowboy in the western who stumbles into the camp fire after an ambush . . ."

That's when Bobby Z punches me in the mouth, and I feel two of my bottom teeth tip a little toward my tongue. I jab him in the throat before I can talk myself out of it, and we both tumble into the porch. The other zombies dogpile on us to pull us apart just as Davey Jones' furious mug appears from behind a cracked flap of wood in the door.

"What the hell?" he barks. "Knock that shit off! And why the fuck were you guys running? Real zombies don't run! Wrong movie, assholes!"

Sour Towel Zombie steps up behind me and sarcastically flexes where his bicep would have been, an ironic tattoo of the character Tattoo from "Fantasy Island" renting the space instead.

But Davey Jones is right. We've always chosen to emulate the shambling, drunken interpretations of the walking dead and not subscribe to the latest, more popular, run-amok versions in, for example, *28 Days, Weeks, and Months Later* and the latest *Dawn of the Dead* remake. We usually followed this code religiously, but sometimes we had to remind a few extra-excitable staff, like our very first, now deceased, Cowboy Zombie, not to howl "Brains!", a war cry first heard in *Return of the Living Dead.* It was almost irresistible sometimes, and mostly we successfully fought the urge. Mostly.

The angry face of our boss is gone before we can respond. I stand up, wiggle my tooth, wipe my nose, and turn to find a Bobby scratching at the door, already forgetting what he did to me. I join him reluctantly.

Yes, "no running" was an old rule, but a necessary one. First, there's the indisputable fact that when it's dark, trees are a real danger. Like Sour Towel Zombie always said, "Run too fast through the trees and you can lose your virginity" (just like the poor girl who was spread-eagled and penetrated by a stop-motion spruce in *Evil Dead*), but the biggest problem was it also got people too excited about crashing into that house by the time they got to it. Tempers were always too short when people moved too fast. That's why the walking dead could boast such a snowball of new memberships every weekend the world ended.

I scratch harder even though it's all wood instead of windows now, and at least three splinters slip under my fingernails. I count each one as it goes in and feel nothing.

Most of the game never changes.

The hammer is under the sink. They usually don't find it right away. And when the windows run out of glass from our fists, there's a stack of replacement wooden doors (an interrupted renovation) upstairs for them to find. And under the other sink, of course, the bucket of nails. But to get the power going, they have to use the car battery in the cupboard. And when the TV's up and running, they'll see our eight-hour videotape of fake news broadcasts (a VCR hides in the wall). First is the newscaster in denial, expertly played by my father. Then comes the interview with the scientist, Mags' uncle Mike actually. Finally, my sister interrupts the broadcast with her Casio keyboard rendition of an extra creepy Emergency Broadcast Signal. She cried when I said she couldn't do the theme for the news, too. "Sometimes too much music ruins a movie," I said.

Once the real arguing starts in the house, there are two choices. Basement or roof. Okay, three, actually. There's always that mysterious locked door and whatever's rustling inside. One of our Plants, usually Mags, will argue hard for the basement.

But the basement is doom. The basement has always been doom, and not just when we were scared of the dark as kids. And if the couple chooses the basement, come morning, everyone in the house will greet them at the door all zombied up with a resounding, "You lose!"

But they should know this. Remember, *Day of the Dead* was just one big basement. That movie should have taught them all they needed to know. Wait, maybe that was *Alien 3*. Which movie was it where someone said, "But this whole place is a basement"? Sour Towel Zombie tried to argue that this line was from the movie *Dog Soldiers* when the girl reveals to the platoon stranded in the farmhouse that the monsters were never in the barn out back, but simply hiding in the basement the whole time.

"They were always here," she explains as her foster family of werewolves slowly rises up behind her. "I just unlocked the door, and it's that time of the month."

Hearing this theory, Davey Jones grabbed Sour Towel Zombie by his damp, wrinkled collar, the maddest we'd seen him up till then, which was no joke. Must have had something to do with that dog we had. Always the dog.

"You're not werewolves, fuckface," he spat. "You can never change back."

But before those basement debates begin, there's the TV. One time, I saw a scowling newlywed click past our fake news and click on the real news instead. Just for a second, right before a Plant slapped his hand away, but long enough to catch the real news anchor sniffling:

"They're calling it the end of . . ."

You could see the question in his eyes. The end of what? The end of something, anything. That's all he needed to know.

Then the show was back on my dad in the anchor seat, reading his script in his best solemn smirk, but accidentally correcting the real news he also couldn't help but sneakily watch off-camera, "Actually, they're calling it Judgment Day, not to be confused with *Judgment Night,* a fine film and cautionary tale about a siege on a *mobile* home . . ."

That particular night, I slumped down by the gas meter to giggle through our break, and one of the dead, I thought it was Cowboy Zombie at the time (although later he denied the entire conversation), plopped down wearily next to me. He was wearing the Pittsburgh Steelers football helmet, which was crushing his ten-gallon hat (a direct violation of the "one characteristic" rule) that shadowed his face more than usual. I noticed he had one of his shoes off and a bloody fish hook stuck in the ball of his foot.

He wiggled it free and held it up in the moonlight.

"Can you imagine what this must look like to one of them?" he asked me in a voice unfamiliar. "That wiggling bait with the line stretching up to infinity, catching the sun every so often like a lightning bolt. If you were swimming by, you would know something was wrong, but there is just no way you could resist taking a bite."

\*    \*    \*

The puzzle is called "The Executioner and the Four Hats," and it's new this year. Apparently, Mags got it from a kids' book, a bush-league knockoff of the *Encyclopedia Brown Mysteries* series called *Dictionary Blue's Bafflers*. A day earlier, Mags and Davey Jones had us all get together for a brainstorming session on how to apply it to our job. We started the meeting in the house on the loosely-screwed, breakaway dining room table, but we all felt so creatively stagnant in there that we moved the meeting to our home away from home away from home, the Joshua Bush.

Our bosses told us they wanted to "kick things up a notch" because the state of the world had them worried this might be the last season. At the table, Mags had ineffectually tried to explain this complicated puzzle with a pen, paper, and a saltshaker, but we'd just stared at her, mouths agape, of course, but more agape than usual. But outside huddled around the Bush, when Davey Jones tried acting everything out with some Halfway Homeys (imitations of the popular but racially-insensitive Hispanic bubblegum machine toys, costing half as much as the actual Homeys and coming with feeding-and-caring instructions for when the child took one into their home, a.k.a. their "Halfway House"), that was when the puzzle *finally* made sense. At least we closed our mouths a little.

"See, we got three little dudes in a line and a fourth one behind a wall no one can see."

Luckily, he used the bigger Halfway Homeys (the ones from the 75-cent machines, almost a Whole Homey) for his demonstration or class would have been ridiculous. According to the boss, Halfway Homeys represented the infiltration of the fake Hispanic gang members into the giant, beautiful mall of the '78 film, the actors' faces spray-painted brown instead of blue, making them a much more serious threat to the heroes. Or something.

"Now, look close," he went on. "They're all wearing a hat . . ."

"Uh, no they're not," someone laughed.

"Well, the salt shaker is. Sort of," someone added.

"Just bear with me," Davey Jones grinned as he patted a dusty back. "In the puzzle, the 'prisoners,' they're all wearing a hat. Here, if you look real close, you'll notice I've grass-stained two of the Half-way Homeys green but left the other two brown. The green prisoners represent zombies, or 'red hats.' The brown prisoners, just pretend they have blue hats on for now. On the other side of this wall, or 'pine cone,' is the salt shaker, which is actually another prisoner wearing a blue hat, even though it's silver."

"What the fuck are you talking about?"

"Yeah, when did they become prisoners?"

"He means us, I think."

"It's the salt shaker that's fucking me up. I've never gotten past it."

"Now, if it was the original puzzle," explained Davey Jones, ignoring the grumblings, "then you'd say, 'An executioner is gonna shoot all four of them unless a prisoner can declare with certainty what color hat he's wearing . . . '"

"What hat? There's no hats!"

"Bobby, please, get your head out of your ass," Mags sneered. "He just told you that the green ones represent red hats, and the brown and silver hats are actually blue. So, one more time, how do they know what color hat they're wearing?"

"You mean the hat on their own head?"

"Yes. Sort of. All the hats, really."

"You could just take off your hat and look."

"No. They're tied up."

"I'd just shout out 'blue' or 'red.' You got a 50/50 chance."

"That's not an option."

"I'm confused. That salt shaker mocks me . . ."

"Can they talk to each other?"

"No."

"Why can't they look around?"

"They're tied *up*."

"That one isn't tied up." A finger flicked over a Halfway Homey holding a bundle of oranges. "It's selling tiny fruit at intersections to support its tiny crack habit. Look."

"Fuck it."

"Please don't screw the lid on that salt shaker anymore. The grinding of salt in metal makes me crazy."

"We give up."

"Okay. The answer is the guy second from the end because he knows that if the guy behind him doesn't say anything, then that means that he sees one of each color hat on the guys in front of him and therefore knows by the process of elimination that his own hat is the opposite of the one he can see."

"Uh . . . okay?" someone said through a lip-flapping sigh, repre-senting all of us.

"So, here's the million-dollar question. How can we play this same game with zombies instead?"

"We can't," Cigarette Zombie said, standing up tall in the light of her matchbook. "You'd still need something like a hat. That's the only reason the puzzle works. A hat or, at the very least, something that you can see on the others but they can't see on themselves. Like that poker game where you stick one card to your forehead."

"Maybe if everyone had been bitten?" Sour Towel Zombie offered, standing up too. "Like they're zombies but don't know it? But, like, the others know?

Pause.

"Never mind. This shit makes no sense."

"What if one of the guys in the line was blind?" asked Baseball Zombie.

"Yeah! Wait, no. That doesn't work either," Davey Jones said, clicking his teeth impatiently.

"You only need one prisoner or zombie or whatever tied up, right?" Cowboy Zombie asked as he tipped the first Halfway Homey, the one with the tiny spray can and skateboard, so its face was in the dirt. "The first one can be a corpse *or* a zombie. Only the one with the answer, the Camel, or the *prisoner,* would need to be immobilized."

"I got it!" shouted Bobby B. "Bury them up to their necks!"

"In the house?" asked Mags, eyebrow up.

"Maybe," Bobby Z went on for him, snickering now, too. "What if we rig the floor so that they fall in up to their chests and can't turn around."

"What if one of them was mute instead?" European Indian Zombie asked, quite sincerely. "You know, so they could see who's a zombie but can't say anything?" She reached down to make a Halfway Homey jump up and down like it had something urgent to say. It was palming a tiny basketball.

"No, no, no, then there's no puzzle!" Davey Jones clicked his teeth harder. "The last Camel in the line has to be unable to answer the question because he or she sees one of each, zombie and human."

"Maybe we should just stick with hats," Bobby Z laughed. "Have ones that say 'zombie' on them or some shit."

"That's a horrible idea," Cigarette Zombie scoffed. More like coughed. "Why not just give everyone propellers instead?"

"Yeah," I agreed, scoffing nervously with her.

"Maybe it's just not gonna . . ." Mags started to say.

"Fuckin' forget it." Davey Jones gathered up his toys, stood up over everyone a second, then stomped away.

"Whoa, O.G.Z.," someone snickered. "Chill."

"He should understand that if there's a chance of something happening, no matter how remote, then it has already happened to someone else," European Indian Zombie said to us all, palms out and all wise. "And if you think you have a great idea, someone is already doing it somewhere."

"Did Zombie Rama tell you that?" asked Bobby B, kicking dirt in her direction.

"Zombie-O-Rama. Get it straight."

We all got up and followed Davey Jones up to the house. Inside, he was pouting cross-legged in front of the TV, staring at the Emergency Broadcast graphic. Seeing us, he turned off the television in disgust and stomped to the refrigerator.

"You guys don't get it!" he practically shouted. "Any of you ever see the movie *Things Change?* Well, things change."

"Uh, isn't that a movie about a shoe shiner for the mob?" asked Sour Towel Zombie.

"What's your point?" Davey said, opening up some orange juice.

"I don't see how that applies to us. I mean, the title is cool and all, and I get what you're trying to say, but . . ."

The 'fridge door slammed, and that shut him up. Our boss said this "Things Change" line a lot. In fact, he said it so much we expected to see it on a T-shirt some day soon. He tipped his juice toward all of us like a disappointed dad.

"Pulpier, people, that's the key. Like this," he said, holding up his O.J. "This? See this? This is us. If there's gonna be zombies everywhere playing this game like us, we're gonna have to step it up. We're gonna have to do it with more pulp."

"What's us?" Bobby Z laughed. "That? That missing kid on the side of the carton?"

"Exactly!" Bobby B agreed. It was the happiest we'd ever seen them, both smiling at the same time.

"But orange juice is hell on us zombies to drink," one of them went on. "Maybe it's the fake zombie's diet of cold barbecue to stain our faces, but the heartburn is ridiculous."

"Totally!"

"Maybe we just need weapons again," Davey Jones said ominously. "Like the old days."

The room got quiet. We used to have Laser Tag gear on our chests, then some gear on our heads. Then we moved to paintball for awhile. Then after the incident forever referred to as "The Blinding of Zombie Seventeen, a.k.a. Gamblers Anonymous Zombie" we got everybody goggles. We looked just like those Underwater Nazi Corps in *Shockwave*, according to Sour Towel Zombie.

"Wasn't that called *Deadcorps?*"

"What? Like *Dead Corpse*? Kinda redundant, home boy."

"No, 'corps,' like the military."

"Never heard of it. There's lots where they come up slow-mo out of the water though."

"Or like the movie *Zombie*," someone made the mistake of suggesting.

"What do you mean?"

"You know, that scene with the splinter through that chick's eyeball?"

"It's *Zombi* with an 'I,' not *Zombie* with an 'I-E'" Sour Towel Zombie shouted.

"How do you know I wasn't saying it with an 'I'?" whoever it was asked him.

"And it's *Zombi 2*, not *Zombie*."

"With an 'I,' right?" Bobby Z taunted him. "I mean, I hate to bring it up, but you forgot to say it with the 'I' just now."

"I was saying it with an 'eye.' Get it?"

"I can't wait to kill you."

"Hey, remember that cute eyeball finger monster the mad scientists made in *Bride of Re-Animator*?" I smiled, playing peacemaker. More like pacemaker.

"Don't remember."

"Didn't your dad take us both to see it in Junior High?"

"I don't know," Bobby Z snapped. "I'm not my dad's mom."

And with a statement as confusing as that, the subject of eye injuries and bush-league Italian George Romero imitators was dropped for good.

But there were more problems than that with the Laser Tag Days.

For example, in the fog, it took away all the suspense of aiming at anything. You'd just line up the red line until it was touching their face, like you were slowly stretching out a tape measure to see how long you could get it before it finally collapses (the record being 23 feet, by the way), so we abandoned the whole "shooting Zombies in the head" thing forever. Plus, it made us seem more like zombies from *Return of the Living Dead* instead of the original movies.

"However, at least one of the writers of that particular parody was involved in the making of the original classic," Sour Towel Zombie reminded us. "So maybe a shot to the brain not being enough to stop them was *always* part of a plan."

Right then, Davey Jones kicked open the door and stepped outside onto the porch. He had the orange juice in one hand and a very real Spencer repeating rifle in the other. Later we would always mistakenly remember this weapon as an "AKA-47."

"Whoa, boss," Bobby B said. "You ever see *Do The Right Thing?*"

"You guys better start taking this a little more seriously."

He let this sink in.

"Because I'm gonna hide this gun in the house. And tomorrow, if someone can find it, it'll be fair game."

"Uh, that is not a 'fair game,'" Bobby B said.

But Davey Jones was done talking. He stood ominously in the background, sulking and sipping his orange juice, glaring at us occasionally, while Mags handed out paychecks and W-2s and told us not to be late tomorrow. Which is today.

Before the meeting officially adjourned, I decided to climb the antenna and check the roof for loose tiles, figuring it was safer up there anyway. The object of the game was, will be, and always has been to be on the roof come sunrise. Just like *Dawn of the Dead*, the roof was life. Never shopping malls, like reviewers, film students, and historians insist. They have always made the mistake of thinking more about those movies than the writers did. Or the zombies.

There are always some Easter eggs sprinkled throughout the game. We changed them around sometimes, but one staple is always the footlocker stenciled "U.S. Army" (my sister did the decoupage) that rattles nice and provocative, as if it contains some sort of answer. There's just a broken TV remote inside, however, if they do manage to get it open.

Right then, we hear Amy, our Plant, in our earphones, steering them back to the subject at hand. Looking for the key.

"Remember that embarrassing night when some Camel's kid found the porn stash in the mirror," Cowboy Zombie whispers in my other ear.

"Found what?"

"There was a hidden recess behind an old mirror in there that had a ratty pile of old Super-8 John Holmes videos and *Oui* magazines."

"Oh, I thought you meant porn 'stache,' in the mirror." Cigarette Zombie snickers. "Like a giant mustache in the kid's reflection? That would have scared the shit out of anybody."

"I found my dad's snuff porn and rape movies once," I offer. "Mom flipped out on him."

"What did he say?" Cowboy Zombie asks, taking the bait.

"He said, 'Don't worry, I hide the rough stuff much better than those, baby.'"

We're suddenly distracted by another scuffle behind us. It's the Bobbys, of course. One of them is yelling something about a difference in the paychecks we got the night before. Cowboy Zombie doesn't even bother to break them up anymore, but Cigarette Zombie always *always* tries real hard to make the peace, especially when a certain Swaggering Cowboy Zombie was watching her, sometimes a Baseball Zombie, often just a Forearm Flexing Zombie.

Not necessarily a Nervous Cough Zombie like myself, of course. Sounds like a lot of zombies, doesn't it? It is.

"See, you Bobbys are frustrated because, back home somewhere, you each have a brother who acts just like the other Bobby," she explains, eyes uncharacteristically wide. Arms, too.

"One more time, Psychoanalysis Zombie?" Bobby B mutters, back-peddling from Bobby Z.

"Hey, one semester of psychology is no joke. But it's just like my step-brother situation," Cigarette Zombie goes on. "I'm the same age as the one that acts like my older brother, my blood brother, and he's the same age as a step-brother that acts just like me. But we were forced to pair off because of our age, and we always wished we could switch until we realized, guess what, it makes perfect sense."

"What's your point?" Bobby Z asks, five fingers now around Bobby B's throat, the other five fluttering near his mouth, still adding up taxes deducted from his check.

"It's because you're *brothers*," Cigarette Zombie huffs. "You were meant to argue like this. Think about it, stupid."

"It's like that movie . . ."

Bobby Z quickly closes another throat before Sour Towel Zombie can finish.

"Enough with the *Dead of the Dead of the Dead* movies, motherfucker."

"Wow, that's the original title for *Diary of the Dead*, actually," Sour Towel Zombie squeaks, then, "Sorry."

"You're not allowed to talk the rest of the day, S.F.B."

Sour Towel Zombie's fingers tighten around the handle of his cleaver, then relax. He'd long since grown used to Bobby Z laying hands on him daily. Most of us had. And that's what we used to call him, by the way, the "S.F.B.T.," as in "Sour Fucking Bath (Towel)," previously "Serial Finger Banger," to mock the limit of his sexual experience.

"You know how most people comb their hair before a date?" Bobby Z would ask everyone real loud. "Well, he clips his fingernails."

I'd like to say he deserved the endless abuse, but Bobby had attacked all of us at least once by the time we were picking those nicknames. And whenever Mags would tell Sour Towel Zombie that he was "this close" (fingers about an inch apart) from being fired because of his mouth, I thought about my first lunch with Sour Towel Zombie (a.k.a. S.F.B., a.k.a. S.T.Z., formally Sushi Chef Zombie, officially Josh) and his finest moment.

It was when we both were working at that video store and he went back to Burger King to complain about there being no crust on his Hershey's pie. They gave him a whole one, a whole goddamn pie, not just the little chocolate sliver in the triangle box you usually got, and he happily shared that pie with me. When I asked him why he did it, he said, simply, "The crust is the best part." He was right, and he felt like a friend of mine that day.

But it's been all downhill from there.

The thing people forget about taking off your jacket before a fight is that you're not doing it because it's a throwback to an 18th Century duel or something. It's simply because it makes it far easier to punch someone in the face.

At the end of the night, with all the zombies winding down behind the barn, things always seemed so calm and content. No one ever anticipates that bloody jackets are going to be dramatically removed before our shift is over. And it happens every goddamn time. Even Sour Towel Zombie's endless movie trivia seems oddly soothing at these moments.

"So, I finally watched *Day of the Dead*. Way better than *Land*, which is ironic since rumor has it that *Day's* script resembles *Land* before the funding was pulled . . ."

". . . yeah, that's a man who needs his vision limited or else he would eagerly populate any apocalypse with noble retards . . ."

". . . speaking of . . ."

". . . you're funny . . ."

". . . or populate his world with strange Middle Easterners being called 'spics' . . ."

". . . yeah, that poor Arab in the opening scene was, apparently, doing an alligator call by mistake, judging by what came running anyway. Helloooooooo . . ."

". . . you know Gorillaz sampled that on their debut . . ."

". . . Florida's got plenty of gators, dude, so it wasn't that strange to see one . . ."

". . . think you're getting your racial slurs confused . . ."

". . . no, I think the director was since I distinctly remember a Mexican Army sergeant calling the Middle Eastern dude a 'spic' . . ."

". . . and a 'jungle bunny' at one point . . ."

". . . clearly he was in such a hurry to load that merry band of survivors with every crayon in the box, he got a little confused . . ."

". . . no shit, I think the mad scientist was an Inuit . . ."

". . . and that evil Sarge was screaming more than *Braveheart*, 'Fuck youse, Frankenstein!' cut to drunken Irish helicopter pilot singing theme song from the Lucky Charms commercial . . ."

"Wait, are you trying to say that the filmmakers used these broad strokes as a short cut to characterization?"

Silence.

"Moving on . . ."

That's when Bobby Z takes a swing at Sour Towel Zombie and loses his watch in the process. At least we think it's his watch. Then someone materializes between them wearing the Steelers football helmet, and Bobby Z wrinkles his nose and takes a swing at the logo instead. The helmet takes the blow easily, but the zombie wearing it spits out its mouthpiece to let it dangle on the guard anyway.

"Who the fuck is in there?" Bobby Z asks, making a grab for the chinstrap. Then the helmet headbutts Bobby Z back onto his ass into a blinking daze and blessed silence.

In our ears, Amy is talking about the dog and everyone is groaning. Groaning more than usual, I mean, and not getting paid for it. The dog again. Always the dog with her. Once, Cigarette Zombie called that dog our "Sword of Damocles," then called it our "Gun Over Chekov's Fireplace" twice, and we all had to agree with that description. All except Sour Towel Zombie who settled on "Dog Over The Fireplace," arguing that if you ever saw a fucking dog over a fireplace in a movie, that would be even more of a bomb waiting to go off.

Back in the day, Amy used to be outside, but she couldn't narrow down her personality to just one character trait. So Davey Jones moved her to the basement instead. Originally, he wanted to call her Invisible Shower Zombie because of her tendency to tip her head back and run her fingers through her hair, eyes half closed, at the most inappropriate of times, but that didn't translate well to a horror movie, at least not the ones we preferred to pattern our lives after. So, when she first brought the dog into the game, it seemed like a great idea, a good one for her to focus on anyway. Maybe Dog Whisperer Zombie? But after a couple of weekends, everyone agreed that having an animal around a situation like this negated the mood we were after. And while it *did* help cause some of the anxiety we worked toward, it was the wrong kind. Much like the doomed canine in the novel *I Am Legend* (vampires that acted like zombies), it took our Camels out of the story.

They just worried about it too much.

It was like they didn't want the dog to think anything bad was really happening and tried to protect the animal from the thumping outside that was making it shiver and pinning its ears back. It comes down to this. It's too emotional. A dog has no reasonable place in any self-respecting horror movie. Or this game. It just never seemed like the end of the world around one.

I can hear Amy barking in my ear. Mags is real close to her, so we can all hear what's happening clearly. Amy is telling a somber tale of how the dog was cruelly trained to fight by using battleship chains on its collar, how it made its head and neck so strong that it could walk through walls without flinching.

Then, between sobs, she's suddenly comparing the dog to Vonnegut's short story "Harrison Bergeron," a story that is *not* about zombies, making it a completely unacceptable tangent. Amy's weeping sounds more authentic than usual, and the Bobbys stop putting shredded leather jackets over shredded arms so they can listen, too.

". . . then it ate one of the nails, and Matt tried to coax the nail through its body and out its ass with a powerful magnet, resulting in a perforation of the groin, then the bucket of tools upended, and nails peppered the makeshift operating table between its legs, narrowly missing everything but the testicles, of course . . ."

Mags must have started glaring at her, because she trails off, then adds cheerfully:

"But that's a whole other movie! Don't worry. The dog's fine and much happier living with my uncle. He's got a farm where he can run and dig. But some say that dog still roams these woods . . ."

"That is the worst ghost story I have ever heard in my life."

It'll be the last time we will hear Amy's voice, a ridiculously sentimental but fitting moment.

"I've got it!" Sour Towel Zombie bleats from behind me. "The last name of a zombie movie that hasn't been used yet."

"And what is it?"

"*The Dog of the Dead.*"

"Already been done. *Pet Semetary.* I'm saying that with an 'S,' by the way."

"Hey, is *Weekend At Bernie's* technically a zombie movie?"

"Nope!" Sour Towel Zombie is an inch away from Cowboy Zombie's nose before he even closes his mouth.

"Well, he really was a zombie in the second one. Remember? The sequel with the voodoo music?"

I'm pulling back a strip of particle board to peek inside the house when I smell a sour towel breathing down my neck instead.

"You got your earphone in?" the Towel asks. "What's going on in there?"

"I don't know," I whisper. "But they're clearly having way too much fun. Look in there. Are they playing Twister or what?"

"Dude, zombies would dominate at Twister."

Sour Towel Zombie stops breathing down necks and suddenly stands up straight.

"'Perry, I've been keeping track of the lights,'" S.T.Z. tells us, voice cracking a bit as he attempts to be creepy. "'The way I calculate it, when you turned off the upstairs light, that left the house completely dark.'"

No one looks at him. He's done this before.

"Come on! Nobody? No one recognizes that?! It's from the original home invasion story. No, no, no, not *Night of the Living Dead,* like everybody thinks, we're talkin' *In Cold Blood.* That's where it all began."

"I'm sure there were plenty of home invasions or zombies before that one."

"Sure. William Seabrook's 1926 classic on Haiti, *The Magic Island,* had a chapter entitled, 'Dead Men Working In The Cane Fields.' They dug up some poor fuckers and resurrected their sorry asses for cheap labor."

"Just like us!"

"Voodoo zombies shouldn't count."

"Stop. No one can deny our proud heritage began in 1932 with *White Zombie.*"

"Whoa, 'white zombies?' Fuckin' racist . . ."

"Nope, sorry. Lovecraft's "Herbert West: Reanimator" serial was written way earlier than Seabrook's union-busting manifesto. It was completed at 5:37 a.m., six days before Christmas during the strangely warm winter of 1921. Approximately."

"Speaking of racists, you ever read that thing . . ."

"Enough already!" Cigarette Zombie bellows. "The first zombie was, of course, Mary Shelley's *Frankenstein.* Mary Shelley's Frankenstein's *monster,* I mean. 1818, bitches."

"Don't you mean, *Frankenstein (a.k.a. The Modern Polyphemus)?*" Someone sniffles.

"Okay, maybe it wasn't the first, but it was sure the worst."

I look around, suddenly worried. Whoever was wearing the football helmet has vanished into the dark, and the Bobbys suddenly remember they need to fight and go back to dramatically taking off their jackets again. But the skin of their forearms sloughs completely off with their sleeves this time, so they put them right back on.

If and when they open the upstairs closet door, if they've done things in a certain order, there will be a man hiding in there who is afraid to come out.

He might have a stash of beer and some delicious, honeymoon-type foods, or maybe some wine, cheese or fruit, or, hell, maybe even a vending machine bag of pork rinds and Sterno. It all depends on Mags' profiling earlier in the week. But once they let him out, he'll happily lead everyone through a hole in the attic, up onto the roof, and watch the sunrise while bouncing apple cores and beer cans off our heads below.

So when we stand back and look to the top of the B&B and see nothing but crows, we know the Camels are doing it wrong.

See, if they've done things in the wrong order, as we suspect they have tonight, the man inside that closet will have stuck the Hillbilly Heaven brand bubble-gum machine teeth into his mouth and milky contact lenses into his eyes and will proceed to scare the living shit out of them when they open the door. Yes, the living shit.

And if they've done things *really* wrong, or if Mags or Davey Jones are just feeling spiteful, the Plant in the closet will be wearing a police uniform. This is because everyone, *everyone*, even those with just a passing knowledge of the films, knows you never trust police, fireman, security guards, military (especially the military), or any authority figure for that matter, during a garden-variety siege of the undead.

But some people don't know the movies at all, and most people don't know them as well as they think they do. Just like that guy who played one of our first Plants ever. He insisted on yelling, "It's the end of the world" with an exaggerated Irish accent, quoting the drunk in the diner from Hitchcock's classic *The Birds*. Mags was like, "Dude, birds aren't zombies. Even those birds." Okay, it was an end of the world movie, sure, and maybe Tippi Hedren had a look in her eyes by the end that most corpses would find familiar and comforting, but come on. So, yeah, they had to start jamming fake rotten teeth in the Closet Plant's mouth to discourage any more creativity.

All of a sudden, Sour Towel Zombie is grumbling and sputtering like he's never done before. He's showing a level of commitment to his role that we've never seen, and some of us are getting nervous. Bobby Z starts putting his jacket on again, more skin flaking off his arms, leaving a nasty pink halo around his shoes. If he does this one more time, I'm convinced his arms will stay in the sleeves forever.

"What's up, Halfway Homey?" Bobby Z belches. "You trying for an Oscar?"

Bobby B lurches closer to get a better look, too, and his eyes widen.

"Hey, I think he's really hurt."

We all stumble over and suddenly notice a red dot over his fluttering left eye.

"Uh, I think he's been shot."

"What?"

"Are you serious?"

"I didn't hear nothin'. What the fuck."

As we watch, Sour Towel Zombie begins to wind down, creaky foot over foot over foot like a weary toy robot. Then one knee is on the ground. Then the other. Then he's clutching a handful of grass like it's the answer. I remember something Cigarette Zombie said once when she was sticking up for him. That his nonstop movie references were just his way of hanging on by his fingernails to a world long gone. Maybe she was right, and we all did it, too. But no one ever seemed to need a savage headlock as often as he did.

He looks up to us all one last time, his left eye now closed completely, the other one dilated 8-ball black, as red fingers of brain and burger spiderweb down the side of his neck. He points up to his beloved European Indian Zombie to quote one final movie before his arms hang limp like balloon strings a week after your birthday.

"It should have been you," he croaks.

His face hits the ground so hard it disappears up to the ears.

"Our hearts have stopped," the news anchor sighs. "But our brains just keep going."

Right before we break through all the half-ass defenses and into the house for good, I hear a strange voice on the television. One I'm not related to. A Camel must have found the real news broadcast and left it on. They would have already known that hearts were stopping everywhere, of course, as most of theirs had, too. But seeing the real news, hearing it out loud, as well as all of us pounding on each other instead of the walls, must have empowered them to accept everything as real enough to finally fight for the house.

But I am still convinced that one of the Camels has a pulse, that one of them came into our game alive as hell. I'm sure of this. The towel he dropped when he compulsively avoided the door handle was my first clue. And now, judging by the gasping and bubbling in my ear, this man is probably upstairs with Underwater Zombie's head in the toilet, trying in vain to drown him.

I already miss Sour Towel Zombie. At a moment like this, he would name-drop the Nazi Zombie movie *Shock Waves* again. Just like I did. We loved that flick to death though, huge fans of the tasteless ending where hapless victims were forced to hide in ovens to escape.

To my right, Bobby Z has broken into the living room, and now he's choking out one of the other Camels who's trying desperately to warn his new bride through coughs and sputters. When his eyes roll back, Bobby Z helpfully moves the Camel's mouth and plays ventriloquist as the bridge gets low and tries to hide.

"Hey, baby!" Bobby Z shouts. "Ain't got no heart, but I love you! You ever hear that song that goes 'Stars are dying in my chest until I see you again?' That's our song! Wait, where are you going?"

Bobby Z gets the Camel down and out for good with a knee in his windpipe, cartilage crackling kinda like bubble wrap, but maybe a little more satisfying, judging by Bobby's smile. And popping bubble wrap was pretty goddamn satisfying for our crew, especially when we got big orders of fake teeth and barbecue sauce.

Then Bobby starts turning over furniture to find the bride. When he gives the Camel a heel to the temple as an afterthought, I hear a "Tisk!" from the corner and suddenly remember that newlywed's familiar but annoying habit. Bobby Z seems ready to find her with the next chair he'll flip, but he's having a lot of trouble with one of his hands, now flapping alarmingly at the wrist. If Sour Towel Zombie was here, he'd tell him:

"It's just like Dr. Frankenstein said in *Day of the Dead*, 'We are them, just functioning less perfectly.'"

With some extra effort he upends the couch, and there she is tucked behind it, deep under some red cushions, burrowing like a tick. More like a "tisk." I watch her reach out to her husband on the floor, fingers tickling the knee-shaped crater in his throat, seemingly trying to coax it to inflate. Some air hisses from him as if her fingernail finds a tire valve, and over a gurgle he points a quivering wedding ring toward her.

I suddenly remember that sinking feeling you always get when you find out a girl you're into has a boyfriend, that feeling when you can tell something changed her mind about having the best conversation with you, and they decide to bring up their relationship out of the blue with a sneaky, off-hand comment like, "Yeah, my boyfriend likes cold chicken and barbecue sauce, too." A feeling that spent most of your adolescence hidden in your stomach under your shirt like a dead animal you were trying to sneak into the house.

When I say I "remember" this feeling rather than feeling it, it's because, without a pulse, I'm long past actually feeling anything.

Then a dripping Camel starts stomping down the stairs, rifle slung over his shoulder, dragging another dead bride behind him, her head tracing her path like the train on her wedding dress probably did the night before. I'm not sure what he just did to Underwater Zombie, but it's clear we're losing staff quickly. Right as I begin to suspect I'm being watched, I suddenly notice Davey Jones sitting in the one upright chair, watching us all in amusement. He's clapping his hands slow and sarcastic.

"You guys did awesome," he laughs. "By that, I mean you *died* awesome."

Fuck him, always playing disappointed dad. How many times can you disappoint someone before you begin to look forward to doing it? About nine.

Davey Jones hands me an orange juice to snap me out of it. Always an orange juice with him with alcohol being recently outlawed. For awhile, we had even tried one of those popular Zombie Cliché Drinking Games (was that really Third Stage Zombie's idea?), but we won't be doing that again any time soon. Among the complications of such a game when applied to our production . . .

First off, "Do A Shot When Arm Reaches Through Window" was problematic because it made lightweights hesitate to push through when needed. Next, "Knock Drink Out Of Nearest Gnarly Hand If Martyrdom Slows Down Flick" caused too many instances of fights, brooding, then more fights, not to mention wasted alcohol. Oh, yeah, "Shotgun Beer If/When Motherfucker in Uniform Pulls Double-Cross, Shotgun Two If Motherfucker Is Carrying Shotgun." That included Army and Navy T-shirts, so we were faced as soon as the Bobbys punched the time clock. And, of course, "Claim Beer of Closest Corpse if Character Shows Confusion About Living or Dead

Status Of Approaching Loved One" just caused severe depression as we pondered our own situation.

Oh, yeah, it was "Drink Ninety Beers If Hero Displays Cowardice Or Pussy Saves The Day," but no one ever did, so don't worry. Because crazy shit like that only happened in the movies.

And who knew we were asking for trouble with the staple "Drink Nonstop For Duration of Tom Savini Cameos?" Well, try it when the man himself visits one weekend with a cease-and-desist order about copyright infringement.

We were so hammered after chugging until he stumbled off that we almost had to change everyone's name to Fetal Alcohol Syndrome Zombie in the morning.

Me and Cigarette Zombie still watch one together every night. In front of our own TVs though, miles apart. Synchronized start times are exactly 9:00. Even though, as of today, it was likely we had finally seen them all, I was hoping we could start at the beginning of the pile all over again. It was the perfect way to watch them, hundreds of videotapes we'd stockpiled from every dusty, out-of-business video store in the state, cover art bleached white by decades of sunlight cooking them through the windows, not a single title left to read. We didn't have to talk about the movie before, during, or after either. It was enough just to know she was watching the movie at the same time I was so that I could imagine what parts would make her laugh. I was sure she laughed a lot when there was no one there to verify it.

Still weaving my way through corpses, I see a zombie wearing the brown, crusty football helmet again, stiff-arming everyone in its path. Picking up speed, it lowers a shoulder and puts American Indian Zombie backwards through a boarded-up window before he can react. Then it dips his head, crashes through a door and is gone, leaving a piece of shredded tube sock and skin in the teeth of the door frame left behind.

Suddenly surrounded by unfamiliar faces, pink and blue alike, I recklessly reach to grab someone even though I know this would break the rules and end the game. Mags sits next to Davey Jones, and I notice both her feet are facing the wrong way and think, "Hey, that's *my* job!" She's singing the Rolling Stones and giggling.

"You make a dead man come . . ."

American Indian Zombie is sobbing and climbing outside, then back inside. I turn to offer a sympathetic hand, and he shoves me away. He points to the clutter of the room as if to explain that's why he's crying. "The pollution . . ." he mutters like the old commercial before the Camel's next shot brings him down, ragged jawbone and pinwheeling ear riding the bullet and half his dreamcatcher necklace out the door.

Then the Camel squeezes an eye to take aim at me, and I hold up my hands in surrender.

"Whoa, hey, wait a second," I say as he opens his squint. "Uh, so, did you know there are zombies in the Bible?"

I keep trying to distract him as I back up.

"I mean, besides Jesus? No, I'm telling you, it's true. Where's Matt? He'll tell ya. I can't remember the exact passage. Let me go find a Bible. Should be easy to locate. This *is* a hotel, right?"

The Camel lowers the rifle, eager to debate.

"Did *you* know that the reliability of the Bible rests on 5,300 manuscripts, source material, and eye-witness accounts?" he asks me. "Therefore, if discrediting the Good Book is your goal, there are more facts behind it than any other classic history or literature, including Homer and Aristotle."

"Dude," I shrug. "Zombies in the Bible though. I'm just saying."

The barrel of the gun taps the floor as he ponders this, and it gives me enough time to get out of the room. Behind me, I hear the rifle shot, and I know without looking back that European Indian Zombie, a.k.a. Second-Year Cultural Studies Drop-Out Zombie, a.k.a. Rachel, has just taken a bullet through the red dot on her forehead. Right where it belongs.

And at this time, I make the mistake of running for the basement door.

The stairs turn left at the bottom. So, in theory, you could stand on the top step and not be seen by anyone hiding in the dark. So that's where I wait, counting to a hundred. I think back to one time I shared an apartment with this girl and how I used to come home late from work and stand outside my own door, key in my hand, waiting forever to go in. I had no logical reason for my actions that I could reasonably explain to anyone if they were to walk up and see me frozen there, especially if she were to open the door before I did. I just couldn't face her sometimes. I think that must be it. I just needed to be alone on the steps for as long as I could. Five hours was the record, and I don't break it tonight.

Cigarette Zombie is sprawled out on the basement floor, her eyeglasses two jagged rings of blood and shards. Seeing this is worse than if her skull had been shattered, because I'm reminded of a story she told me about her father first realizing she couldn't see clearly. She had been skiing with her dad, and they were standing at the snack counter between slopes. He asked her what she wanted, and she couldn't see any of the choices on the giant menu behind the clerk's head. Cigarette Zombie confessed to me that she had tried to be sly and get her dad to read the menu for her, trying to make a joke out of it. But he saw right through the ruse and took her to the eye doctor soon after. She said she was ashamed of her lie until she wore the Coke bottles to school and the kids started picking on her, just like she knew they would. She said she'd rather lie, or stumble around blind bumping into things any day of the week, than relive that first day of 3rd grade.

And when she saw the call for zombies in the "help wanted" pages decades later, well, that had nothing to do with anything. Except the stumbling part.

"The job just sounded hilarious," she said.

Reaching for her broken glasses, I see another Camel curled up against the far basement wall, another bride, eyes watching me close. How many fucking brides were there? I must have looked past her when I first came down, possibly mistaking her for part of the house, something that used to happen to Cigarette Zombie all the time back in school. She said she wouldn't see anybody at all until the second or third day of class, even after she got her glasses.

The Camel in the corner has found the car battery, but I can see that she didn't use it to power the portable radio like she was supposed to. From the looks of things, she seems to have been trying to cook the chicken we stored down there for fake entrails. Either that or bring a chicken back to life. I imagine her down here in the dark before she died, sparking the jumper cables over a pile of barbecue. Sour Towel Zombie would have loved that shit. He definitely would have warned her of the dangers of zombie poultry, as detailed in the buddy-cop zombie film *Dead Heat*. Then he would have warned her to watch her feet because of the horrific consequences of reanimating anything more than once, as demonstrated in the same film. And witnessed here every weekend for about 300 bucks a head.

I creep closer and raise her chin out of the shadows. She allows me to do this, and I see that she is striking. I knew a girl once who defined love at first sight as, simply, "The Whoosh," something about the rush of blood from the brain to places on your body you need it less. She admitted this didn't translate well out loud from the definition in her head. I remember Sour Towel Zombie scoping this girl out on the driveway when she was signing the waiver, but I guess I forgot to really look at her until now. The end of the world will do that to you every time.

"Check her out," he had whispered. "A sable hat? What, is she Russian or something? 'Cause if she is, I'd fuck her all the way to *Gorky Park . . .*"

"You do that," I'd said.

". . . I'd leave a stain on her head like Gorbachev . . ."

"Sounds more threatening than romantic."

". . . she'd call my cock *Glasnost . . .*" and on and on and on until someone finally told him that "Glasnost" wasn't the name of the movie he was thinking of.

"You need more salt," the Camel bride whispers to me, her dead eyes milky and staring right past.

"The chicken needs more salt?" I ask her.

"No, the driveway," she answers softly. "We almost slipped when we ran up to the house. There was nothing about that in the contract. We could sue you, you know."

"You know what you can use instead of salt? Kitty litter."

"Does that mean instead of kitty litter you can use salt?" She smiles, maybe seeing me.

"Yeah, if you want your cat to poof out like a pine cone and run around with a red ass." I smile back.

"More salt." She's looking past me again. "Just tell someone you need more salt. Someone could slip." She punctuates this with one weary "tisk" then slumps. I put my head to her chest. No heartbeat, nothing. But it doesn't mean a thing. I should have checked while she was talking.

As I pull her arm up to my mouth, I fight the urge to tell her that she already slipped, and that we don't need salt. We don't need anything.

She'll taste perfect just the way she is. And blood on her wedding night is expected.

I grab both her feet in one hand and raise them high, crossing her legs at the ankles and holding them above my head. With my other hand, I pull off her jeans. I imagine her lifting up to make it easier. I look around the basement nervously, knowing that, these days, being surrounded by an audience of the dead doesn't necessarily mean you're alone. Greedily burying my nose like a puppy in its first bowl, I root around for any other sign of life. It's all very scientific. And I find it, something I noticed earlier when I tried desperately to convince everyone there was someone alive playing our game tonight instead of just corpses pretending they were married.

A white string trails from between her legs, and I think of the tiny strip that pops the batteries out of a remote control. This makes me worry. I sure as hell don't want four double-A's flying out and bouncing off my nose. It would completely ruin any chance of her moving for me again.

But I pull the string out with my teeth anyway, looking for the ring on the end with my tongue, hoping it activates her like a doll. But all I hear is a hiss, and I don't know which end it's coming from. The tip of the string is stained red, bright red, the kind of red they warn you about in First Aid class, full of oxygen, close to the heart, in need of immediate attention.

Coming right up.

I bury my nose deeper, work the last of my teeth, drink her deep. Alive. Because blood *is* delicious, that sharp copper and electric charge, like sucking a handful of pennies when you're a child, almost crying because you can't bite down. Except these pennies let you chew, let you split them open like hard candy.

An urge to cough builds in my chest, and I swallow her some more, thick and soothing nectar rolling down my throat, convincing me that I've finally suppressed my nervous hack forever, this barking reflex that once ruined the mood when I tried this in high school, a sneeze even thrown in that night to utterly guarantee disgrace. A reflex actually diagnosed as a *reflux,* now, of course, worsened by our diet of too much orange juice and barbecue chicken. Yes, always chicken. Yes, it looks like blood, skin, and we gobbled that shit for the sake of the game. But don't believe what they say. Only chicken tastes like chicken. Not this.

And, yeah, blood looks like barbecue, too, but it isn't.

I drink deeper. Blood is the goddamn cure for anything. I know I will never cough again.

Cough gone, confidence building, I move up to solve a mystery. I don't even glance around this time, as I know this bride is mine. Hell, technically, in most countries, we'd be married at this point. Blood this bright is legally binding. That's what Leviticus tells us anyway, right?

I push some skin back with my cleanest fingernail and watch it creep out into the light. Not a bean or a grain of rice or a tiny gold BB like they always claimed. No, it's actually a claw. A cat's claw has been hiding under that hood all along.

"Under the hood?" She said that to me once, that one night I tried this. And I made the mistake of saying, "Well, then it needs driven," and she laughed at me for forgetting the "to be" in that sentence, a grammatical mistake common in and around the Pittsburgh area that she would forever christen the "Hamlet" (just one of many crippling conditions afflicting a typical conversation-addled Yinzer Zombie). After that, I could do nothing right.

After that, I could do nothing right.

My bride slides away from my mouth, and I take this as more evidence of life, and, for a crazy second, I consider putting some salt under her ass for traction, maybe more for flavor. Of course, cat litter works just as well.

Tonight reminds me of my most misguided attempt ever to prove I was worried about my girlfriend losing control if she ever got too drunk at a party. She passed out on my birthday, and I methodically, robotically fucked her while unconscious. The fact that I photographed myself holding a clipboard somehow made it even creepier even though I was sure I could excuse it all in the name of science. Nope.

I'm telling you though, it's a claw I'm chasing. It doesn't just *look* like a claw, pop out, then retract like a claw. It is a claw. I know shit is weird out there in the world lately, but right now I'm sure it's always been a claw under there. Push hard enough on any part of a girl and a claw might just come out.

My sandpaper tongue starts working this shard of rock-hard flint. Do this long enough and it would *have* to ignite. No need to blow the gas pump for a climax.

I knew someone once who had a cat with thumbs, which wasn't

*that* strange, she told me. But when she took a paw in her hand and pushed in all the secret spots, nine more claws curled out into her palm, making, what, about ninety claws total? I actually screamed. So did the cat. Then we both ran. But no one went after me.

Inspired by these memories, maybe more out of habit, I chase this claw around a tiny circle awhile. It does laps around my tongue, proving to me that even if she isn't alive, this part of her has to be. I chase that claw around, feel the point sharpened to infinity stabbing hard into my tongue, feel my own blood mixing with hers, and I gasp as I swallow to keep up. The claw grows longer, and I flick and grind it harder with a man's only visible, glistening muscle, ripping long lines through any tastebuds that remain, right between sweet and sour like a gardener, gouging out the last one that sensed bitterness for good.

*Cunnilingus on a corpse? Sure, that sounds nasty out loud. But only if you don't know what a romantic coming-of-age moment this is.*

I want to bite. How can anyone not want to bite this? Something this small, the way it slips behind your teeth? It fucking *tries* to get bit. Wanna bite. Can't bite. Gotta bite. Don't bite. Impossible. It's like the commercial for that cherry sucker you get down to a tiny nub on the end of the stick. It's way way past licking at that point. It's simply begging to detonate between your teeth.

My tongue licked and leaped like fire. Yes, this is how they invented fire. I'm sure of it. Whoosh.

But you know how I know she is alive? Because just like the other girl I tried this on, I know I will never get her off. Which is fine with me because it means I'll never have to stop.

Maybe we were always supposed to bite.

I'm moving up, my tongue tracing a line of sweat and salt down her wrist when three muffled gunshots upstairs stop me cold.

*There aren't enough of us left*, I realize. *Or enough time.*

Then the Camel bursts in with the rifle and bounds down the stairs, taking them two at a time. When I see what he's wearing, I suddenly understand that he's been outside the whole time, even stumbling in circles with us sometimes without anyone noticing. Once pulling a fishhook from his lip and being all wise. He's been coming and going at will, which is the most disrespect for this movie genre than I've ever seen. But it's okay. I'm still smiling because the Pittsburgh Steelers football helmet finally fits someone perfect.

When he reaches the bottom, the Camel targets me again. The firing pin clicks. And clicks. Empty. Clicks again. Still empty. He drops the rifle and scrubs his palms against his pants.

I drop the bride's ankles and stand. Then I walk towards him and gently put my hand on his back. He's cold, colder than us. And not because he's dead. He's cold because he's been sneaking outside all night, listening to our conversations, discovering our weaknesses, or, at least, our shitty taste in movies. He's been cheating, is my point.

And that's when he turns my arm around at least three times and starts to pull it free from my shoulder.

But Bobby B is crashing down the stairs now, too, with Bobby Z stomping close behind. The Camel quickly and correctly recognizes two assholes united as a more significant threat and releases me. Bobby B leaps quite unzombie-like, and the Camel catches him in mid-flight off the second-to-last step and takes him down hard to the concrete floor, ribs popping in both of them like knuckles under a desk. The Camel begins to punch Bobby B like a jackhammer, just like Dirty Harry did to that motorcycle cop in *Magnum Force*, something that usually happened to Cop Zombie at some point during the game. "The only way to punch someone," according to Davey Jones' dad, Barney, a.k.a. "Barnaby," a.k.a. "Basketball" Jones, or so we were told. It's looking bad for Bobby B, at least until Bobby Z catches the Camel's fist between punches in a very cinematic pose and then wrestles him onto his back instead. I step closer to the dogpile. I don't know how I ever thought the Camel was cold. I can now feel the heat coming off him in waves as he struggles for his life. I decide Bobby B must feel this, too, as I watch him crawl towards the pile of flailing fists, elbows, and "motherfuckers!" as if it's a bonfire, his palms out to soak up the warmth.

Bobby B actually looks up at Bobby Z in gratitude, and I'm glad I'm there to see it. Looking from one dirty mug to the other, I can no longer tell them apart, and it's not just the decay or the blue paint smeared on their faces. The Bobbys used to alternate painting their faces black as a shout-out to the racial overtones of the original trilogy and a misguided guarantee of survival.

Clearly, they didn't remember the first movie very well.

"Bobby . . . Bobby," I say, and I have the attention of both of them for the first time in our short lives. I try not to waste it. "Like she said outside, you two *are* brothers, you know?"

Everyone stops the killing for now, so I keep trying to make this count.

"Okay, you know how doctors ask everyone, the very first thing when you get to your appointment, if there's a history of cancer in the family? There's a good reason. It's not just because bad shit and diseases are more likely for you if your uncle had one. It is because you are actually the same creature. Your mother? Your father? Everything you are came from them. You are not just a relative. You are another one. That's what you are. Everyone knows this but you. And you."

They both look at each other, then down to where the Camel's shirt has been yanked up.

Sometimes in the film circle, there will be a few grumblings about zombie movies and how easily they always seem to tear apart a human body, how hard that would really be and how zombies should never have some kind of super strength. Not just because they're dead, either. Now, I would agree with this. Up to a point. Because what zombie scholars have never understood until recently is that it is relatively easy to reach into a man's stomach and turn him inside out, even easier when a group of us are pulling in all directions, but easiest of all when there's simply one more pair of hands to help push in the place you are.

Bobby B punches deep into the Camel's gut, and Bobby Z's fist follows right behind. They both open their hands to point their fingers at the same time, and of course the skin splits and stretches like taffy and they tumble forward and they're suddenly swimming in that shit like ducks in a pond, heads darting under, blowing bubbles more like two brother in a tub.

I rub my eyes, watching them splash around, looking for blood that never comes.

Turns out our name was perfect. Everyone knows camels are full of water.

"I believe it," a dripping, sputtering Bobby says from the soup. "Even crime scene investigators are confused between a dead man's and a dead monkey's blood. At least for a day. You ever watch them scratch their heads bald when there's a murder at a zoo? We're all brothers . . ."

✳   ✳   ✳

The three of us are back outside and rounding the shed when a Bobby's head opens up like a Thanksgiving turkey and a gunshot echo swirls around the sky. I fall backwards, then look over to see Cigarette Zombie stumbling with the rifle rocking on her small shoulder, broken glasses back but askew on a broken nose. She's talking to herself and seems to be finishing a debate with someone from earlier in the night, probably with one of those Super Bowl fans that sometimes wandered over from a neighboring motel, The Whole Year Inn (third to last in the phone book), a joint that was under attack daily instead of just on weekends.

". . . something about those girls in jerseys disgusts me . . . I mean, I'm all for subverting gender norms but . . . I just don't buy that she actually liked football . . . maybe should have called them 'The Stealers' instead of, huh . . . no, really, that's what spell checker wants to do with the name of that team every time you type it . . ."

Then she flicks the cigarette to ignite the fake cardboard gas pump, sorta the climax to our show when it goes right. The Bobby that remains can't help but smile, and I wonder if he started that argument when he was wearing his helmet. No one is sure which Bobby is left standing or even where their Army or Navy T-shirts have gone. These things don't matter anymore. Never did. However, I do recognize this grin as likely belonging to Cloverfield, a.k.a. Bobby B, since this zombie apparently has the balls to bust out the forbidden Steelers' number 22, black home jersey of cornerback William Gay and official NFL gear. I couldn't tell he was wearing it down in the basement.

It was a very passive-aggressive engagement present from his best friend years ago, Bobby Z, who brought with it the unspoken dare that even the most rabid football fan might not have the guts to wear a "Gay" jersey in public. But whichever Bobby this is that's smiling at us, I think it's telling that he waited until the end of the world to finally put on this uniform.

I reach out with my good hand to see if Cigarette Zombie will accept it. Once, she showed me her chapped, flaking fingers and told me about a problem that followed her all her life, not just since she'd been dead. She said that her knuckles started to crack and bleed in kindergarten, and that her mom made her wear oven mitts filled with Vaseline to school sometimes. Before the glasses, luckily. "It's a good thing kids aren't cruel or anything," she had scoffed.

I try to move slowly towards her, but I'm sure, to the untrained eye, it must seem like the desperate lurch of a monstrosity, arms out, fingers flexing as it growls, "Remember the mittens?" I ask her as she prepares to run. "Where are you going? I know how you feel! Trying to build a house of cards, you must have crushed everything you loved!"

"I wish," she laughs, finally recognizing me after all, right before she falls. It's the first time she has ever laughed, I swear. If I told you she did before this, I was lying.

The Last Bobby is carrying the radio. It still holds a charge. There's nothing but static popping the speakers, and I think of Sour Towel Zombie overanalyzing his thirteenth favorite zombie movie, *The Beyond*. In that film, it was a static from some giant red radio that first called the ants. Then the monsters. Then us.

"Brains!" someone screams in the distance.

"Wrong movie, cocksucker!" the Last Bobby screams back.

There's no denying that we all miss him. We're sounding just like him. Yeah, we'll miss him right up until he stands back up.

One time when I was a boy, I brought a record to Show And Tell, an authentic vinyl 45, and I played Sweet's song "Fox on the Run" in its entirety for a roomful of 3rd graders. Watching their eyes when the guitars kicked in made this the single most triumphant moment of my life. Then the next kid unveiled a toy shark based on the movie *Jaws* where you stacked body parts in its rubber-band hinged lower jaw and gently tried to pull them off until it snapped up and bit your hand. As we gathered around to play with it, they'd already forgotten about my song. And so did I. But later, I knew exactly why they ignored me that day. It was because they wanted to be scared, not sing. That's why we always keep the radio between stations.

I turn up the static as loud as it goes, our dog whistle to call everyone together for the last scene.

The sun is coming up, and The Executioner and the Four Hats is being acted out by whoever's left. We are seven zombies now, unrecognizable from each other in voice and appearance, with no discerning characteristics, except maybe for the cowboy hat that's still being passed around when someone falls.

Now there's five. Whoops, back to six. Nope, back to five.

I think it's Cop Zombie who is now getting his dome unceremoniously bashed into Brunswick stew when he turns his back on us one too many times. "Friendly fire," they call this. We're gonna have to change his name to Fratricide Zombie, if and when he reassembles the purple puzzle that is his skull. Cop Zombies get it worst every time.

Speaking of puzzles, now that we have the perfect number, I set it up as accurately as I can remember. I drag a corpse in the closet, another corpse onto the floor in front of that one, and two more corpses into kitchen chairs to be securely strapped, hair affectionately ruffled if they got any left.

I hold the rifle to it's stone-cold forehead and whisper that it has ten seconds to live unless it can tell me whether it's alive or not. Someone behind me protests that we never found a way to make this game actually work. So I explain, mostly to myself, that the solution is written on our faces. I tap the words I've scrawled in blood, soot, and magic marker above the eyes of these three bodies to illustrate my point:

"Zombie," "Not Zombie," and "Propeller."

But with everyone dead, there's no answer to my question, of course. But this has happened before, and we've always played through it. The dead can talk about movies, sign waivers, do their taxes, take smoke breaks, even need glasses to glare at you sometimes. But sometimes you have to move their hand for them, you know?

See that? Watch me do it. Oh, yeah, remember how I said we were all unrecognizable? That's true. Except for the smell.

I make Sour Towel Zombie wave goodbye to the body hog-tied in front of him, then I click the gun against his ear. He doesn't blink. I study his fingers. Dry as bone. That's because they are bone.

I put the gun to another head and ask it the million-dollar question.

"Are you alive or dead?"

But I know I won't get an answer. Remember in art class when they taught you that a person's eyes are exactly halfway up, right down the equator of the face? Not high on the forehead like you'd expect? This helps us understand exactly how much of a head can be missing on a zombie before it can't work any more. If you see that half's gone, so is the part of the brain behind the eyes that keeps shit moving.

So I can tell already, even from behind, that I'm not getting an answer. Half is bad. Half is over. Half is halfway home. And when it comes to the brain, if you loose that much, your cup is always half empty. We'll need to put the "Zombie Help Wanted!" sign back in the window.

I eat some cold barbecue chicken, a.k.a. "hand in a baseball glove." This is a detail that was never accurate in the movies either.

We eat anything we can, even each other.

I turn Sour Towel Zombie's head toward me and tell him that the only time I agreed with him without question is when he declared the best zombie movie ending of all time as the finale of *Dellamorte Dellamore*. At the end of that film, the camera pulls back, and it turns out that the hero and his idiot manservant were just tiny sculptures in a snow globe all along. It wasn't the image of the heroes as toys and the giant plastic snowflakes coating their heads so much as the tiny piece of broken highway rising at their feet and the edge of the cliff that dropped off into the dark. This ending always made perfect sense to me, and I never considered it a cheat, like the bullshit equivalent of it all being a dream or something. My dad disagreed though, before he died for the last time, ejecting the movie immediately after that coda and breaking the videotape across his knee. And his knee off with it.

We climb onto the roof. Tonight, there are two of us still able to walk. In the distance, the fields are full of stick figures marching across the pumpkin orange horizon. They're a couple miles away yet, but they're moving so slow, just like they're supposed to. It'll take them the rest of the day to get here.

But these zombies aren't playing the game. They don't seem to have any respect, or love, for their predicament. I can tell by their gait. It's too slow. I can tell by those heads that hang lower than they need to.

They want to pretend they're us playing the game, which isn't the same thing at all, I swear.

I just don't understand them. This lack of love for the genre. It's like Romero's last zombie pumping invisible gas for invisible cars. Why did it bother? I'll tell you why.

Because this place really *was* a good idea, even before shit went down. Ask anybody. Then move their mouth to answer you.

I hear wood crack and pop. Splinters. A zombie's worst enemy. Looking over the edge, I watch a dog walk through our house, straight through the wall under me as if it's made of smoke. A dog. Not a zombie's worst enemy, but certainly not our best friend.

It exits the other side, crashing through another wall weakened by a decade of pounding, moaning, and the weight of slumped, tired shoulders. The entire west side of the house explodes all around the dog's path, filling the sunshine with dust and drywall snow. We can't rebuild that.

You ever leave a snow globe in the sun by accident? The water turns to piss. But it's a beautiful color really, especially when the sky overflows with it.

But the dog could give a fuck about these things. It just shakes the shards and nails off its back without missing a step or slowing down.

A shadow will sit down next to me, and I will block the sunrise with my good hand to see. I won't know who it is, but I will decide it's her this time.

Even at the end of everything again, both together on the roof like we're supposed to be, I will clear my throat to ask her a question.

"Let's just wait and see what happens," she will tell me.

I will sigh and take this to mean that, apparently, another dead man with a better character trait than my nervous cough could be shuffling down the hill any second.

"Let's take things slow," she will say.

"Any slower and we'll stop," I will laugh, helping her move her jaw on the word "slow," so I know she means it. I will move in close to her lips and remember her telling me about a game called Zombie Kisses she played back in school. It was just like Spin The Bottle except when she was slouching in that circle, she was hiding an ice cube under her tongue.

Back on the field, I won't be able to tell if they're moving anymore. The sun even moves faster than us these days, so they may not be here for days. Plenty of time to clean up, maybe play another game before the world ends again.

Then everyone will be coming out of the house, cheering and applause if they're able, squinting up high to see who won, not even bothering to gather up any parts of themselves that they will lose again and again. Then they will start to walk in a circle if they can, talking about movies, hands and heads be damned. I will turn to her.

I bite.

# NIGHT OF THE JIKININKI

## By Edward M. Erdelac

Edward M. Erdelac was born in Indiana, educated in Chicago, and lives in the Los Angeles area with his family. He is an award winning screenwriter, an independent filmmaker, and sometime contributor to Star Wars canon. Author of the *Merkabah Rider* series, his weird westerns have seen print on both sides of the pond, but he's way pleased for the opportunity to take a left turn and give rein to his rabid admiration for old school *chanbara* movies, Romero, and the great Kazuo Koike here.

*In the 11th month of the second year of* genbun (1737), *a comet was observed in the western sky . . .*
—from *The Annals of the Emperors of Japan*, Isaac Titsingh

The first time Kumada Sadahiko ever cut off a man's head was when he was twelve years old. His father took him to the execution ground at Kozukaparra and commanded him to behead four condemned men, one after the other. His skinny arms had shaken so badly at first he had feared he would not sever the neck, or else that he would send the head spiraling into the lap of the observing official. His father's long hours of instruction had pulled him through though, and he had delivered a nearly perfect *dakikubi* cut, leaving the head dangling by the requisite scrap of flesh. The shock of the strike traveling up his arms had driven all hesitancy from him forever and enamored him to the art of decapitation.

Even the commissioner of swords had remarked at his skill, so remarkable in a beginner.

"He will be sought after as a *kaishaku*," the commissioner predicted, and it was so.

Over the years he acted as second in eleven state sanctioned suicides, performing the traditional decapitation, including that of his own father, ordered by the *bakufu* government to cut his stomach open after han investigators discovered he had committed serious bookkeeping infractions.

"Do not think I ask this of you because you are a model samurai," his father had told him the day he received the order. "I do it because

I know you will perform the duty flawlessly and I will not linger; because I am a coward and a failure as a samurai and a father. You are a butchering fiend, Sadahiko—a blood splashed dog. You would lap at the stumps of your victims if it were permitted. I have raised a monster. And the time for monsters is ending."

It was true that Sadahiko loved killing and cutting more than anything. He thrilled to see a blade slice flesh and bone, to hear the singular sound of a sword parting a head from its shoulders, to see that head bounce upon the breast and hang as the body stiffened a second before tumbling forward to spill into the blood pit. A decapitation gave him the same sort of satisfaction as the *shodo* brush strokes gave a master calligrapher. He had come into some renown as a *suemono-shi*, an itinerant sword tester whose services were much requested. His customers held him up against even the shogun's own Yamada testers.

Cutting the bodies of executed criminals thrilled him too. A body could be essentially mutilated under the eyes of an appreciative audience, all in the name of gauging the edge and durability of a blade. The office suited him. He took supreme enjoyment in his work.

It was what had brought him here to the Fukuyama han prison on this chill morning, to test a sword for Lord Abe.

He watched the two *eta* corpse handlers set down the stretcher bearing the naked cadaver of a man. They removed the staring head from where it rested in the crook of its own arm. They lifted the body and lay it across the waiting sand mound, arranging it on its back between up thrust stalks of bamboo. This criminal had been beheaded early this morning by the prison's executioner. Sadahiko regretted not having arrived soon enough to volunteer for the duty himself.

Lord Abe sat on the examiner's mat in a handsome kimono bearing the oak leaf badges of his clan. He was flanked by the consultant inspector, the sword appraiser, and the young prison warden. The sandy execution ground was white with snow. Sadahiko stood out like a dark stain in his black clothes.

One of the assistants removed a bright sword from a long, lacquered box and presented it to him. It was of Kanenobu make. Very fine, though not so fine to him as his own blade, *Tasogare*.

He placed the cold steel to his forehead and snapped its naked tang into a plain wooden handle he kept for that purpose. Shrugging out of his *haori* jacket, he touched the back of the sword to the dead man's chest, just under the breastbone (a *suritsuke* cut through the middle of the torso had been requested) and touched the sand and snow covered ground with his left hand, saluting Lord Abe.

Lord Abe nodded his assent to proceed.

Sadahiko rose to his feet. Grasping the sword in both hands, he planted his feet and drew it back behind his head, so that the flat nearly touched his posterior. He stared down at the headless body, focusing on the pale torso, already bisecting it with his eyes. Bodies retained fat in the winter, so the cut would not be easy. He contracted his hard muscles, and when all was in readiness, he dropped to a crouch, flinging the blade down before him with all the momentum of his body and a loud *kiai* yell.

The corpse collapsed inward at the torso like a broken board as the sword cut it in two. There was a satisfying 'whack' as the blade split the spine and buried itself a few inches into the sand below.

Sadahiko stifled a smile and withdrew the blade, wiping the blood from it and handing it to an assistant.

"A very fine sword," he said. "My compliments."

The corpse handlers each took a half of the body and hauled it to the litter where its head had waited impassively throughout the demonstration.

The officials moved forward and inspected the bloodstained mound while the assistant measured the depth of the cut.

"Very impressive, Kumada," Lord Abe said. "It's always a pleasure to see you work."

Sadahiko bowed low.

"You do me honor, Lord."

The assistant handed him a scroll and ink and he stooped to write his official report of the sword, which an engraver would later emblazon on its *nakago*.

"I should think that was a difficult stroke," said the prison warden, obviously excited. "But you made it look easy."

"It's fairly easy," said Sadahiko off handedly.

"What's the most difficult cut to make? I've heard to sever the breastbone itself takes a lot of power."

"Yes," said Sadahiko, signing and dating his report and returning it to the assistant. "But to bisect a corpse at the waist is the most difficult."

"Have you ever cut a man down in a fight, Kumada-sama?"

It was an impetuous question, and Lord Abe smirked. His expression said the warden was young and could be forgiven, but Sadahiko did not smile. The question stabbed him as surely as a spear point. For all his lauded skill, he had never cut a man standing in a life and death situation. The knowledge of it nagged him. There had never been an opportunity, he told himself. This was a peaceful time and except for the occasional drunken brawl or peasant uprising, there were no duels to be fought, no battles in which to test himself. He knew the whispers too—that his profession, for all its artistry, was not honorable. Some said the *suemono-shi* had only come about because the nobles themselves looked down on the practice of cutting corpses and hired men like him to do their testing as a rich man might hire the services of an *eta* butcher to slaughter an ox for his dinner.

"With his skill, you can be assured a man like Kumada has seen his fare share of fights, warden," said Lord Abe, deflecting the warden's query.

"Of course," said the warden, sensing his mistake. He nodded to Sadahiko. "If I've offended you, I'm sorry."

"There was no offense," Sadahiko assured him tersely.

"Please, if you will, have tea with me at my residence," the warden offered. "Have you eaten?"

"Thank you, but I have another client coming here tomorrow and the road from Fuchū has left me tired."

Lord Abe cleared his throat.

"You'll stay in the castle of course, Kumada."

Sadahiko bowed.

"Ah!" said the warden. "Of couse, I can't compete with Lord Abe's hospitality, but you're welcome to stay the night here."

Sadahiko had no desire to tarry with this young buffoon, but a thought occurred to him that perhaps there would be more executions in the morning. He might convince the warden to allow him to stand in as decapitator as a further demonstration of his prowess. The thought of sating his obsession stayed his initial instinct.

"It *would* be more convenient . . ."

"By all means, Kumada," Lord Abe said, perhaps too quickly. "Stay and rest up."

For his part, Lord Abe had no great wish to have this corpse cutter staying in his castle. He had saved the young warden's face, true, but the warden had done him a service unwittingly. Kumada

Sadahiko made him uneasy, with his pale complexion and unblinking eyes. They only lived when they cut into dead flesh.

Let him stay at the prison tonight, in smelling distance of the killing ground. He would be more at home than in the castle.

Red Dog knelt before the warden's office, covered by three *doshin* guards and bound with chord. The cold numbed his bruised and trembling knees through his pale prison clothes. Blood stiffened invisible in his reddish hair.

The warden blew in his hands and rapped his gavel on the wood plank to the right of his *tatami* mat. He was a soft faced man, young, and new to the post. Dog had never seen him before.

"Prisoner," he said. "You have violated the rules of this institution and murdered the latrine boss of your jail room." He paused, then, and Dog glanced up from his mandatory obeisance (the snow was cold on the bridge of his nose) to regard the official.

*Get it over with, already!* he thought.

"I am curious, prisoner. You are a known bandit, but you have never killed anyone as far as the law is concerned. Yet scant hours after your arrest you strangle a fellow inmate to death. I would like to know your reason before I pronounce sentence."

Dog stared at the younger man dully.

*As far as the law was concerned he had never killed anyone*? Well, that was because he had never been caught. It was a harsh world, and there were men in it who did not balk except to be killed. Dog had met a few men that way. He was one himself. He had necessarily spilled blood before, but no, not *as far as the law was concerned*. He had never killed anyone important.

How to explain his actions to this privileged youth? Had he any inkling of the goings on at his prison or in the world around his estate for that matter? After Dog was caught robbing a ferry at knifepoint on the shore of the Seto Sea (by old Jinza, the captain of the prison guard, of all people) he had undergone the usual treatment. First a sound drubbing around his middle in the drilling room with the arresting officer's iron *jitte*, then a humiliatingly thorough strip search, a round of *muchiuchi* whipping that left his back singing, followed by the *ishidaki* torture when he'd refused to give any name other than Red Dog to the prison interrogator.

The torture had nearly done him in. He had knelt lashed to a stake all morning with six slabs of heavy stone on his lap while the interrogator demanded again and again to know his family name and han of origin. The sharp, dancing needles in his knees had melted into rivulets of liquid fire that coursed up and down his thighs, but he had borne it until the exasperated torturer gave in at last and grudgingly marked him down as 'Bingo Inu' in the ledger. 'Bingo' from the name of the neighboring province, and 'Inu'—Dog. Funny how Jinza hadn't recognized him . . . but he'd been little more than a boy the last time he was inside Fukuyama prison.

He had considered giving a false name to ease his suffering, but the pain of the pressing slabs had driven all creativity from his mind. He had nearly blurted out Kawaramono as a surname, but that would've cost him his head then and there. Kawaramono—'dry riverbed people'—was the name they gave to the unclean ones who lived along the River Ashida. *His* people. The leatherworkers and the butchers and the corpse handlers whose undesirable professions spiritually defiled them, made them 'eta'—the lowest of the low, not even allowed by law to cultivate rice in the fertile black riverbed dirt. Immediate decapitation was the only justice the untouchable son of an *eta* could expect.

So he'd held out.

But then, had it ended? No. Once put stumbling on dead feet among his fellow prisoners in the crowded lesser jail he'd found more of the same goddamned system. The prisoners themselves, led by the fat bastard of a *dairyo* and his eleven trustee officers had laid into him as soon as he arrived, shaking him down for money. They'd stretched him out and beat his ass black and blue with a hard plank bearing the prison rules when they'd found not so much as a brass *mon* tucked into his jaw or clenched between his buttocks.

He'd crawled off to one of the corners, every part of him tenderized by the rough morning's treatment. All he'd wanted to do was curl up on the hard floor and sleep. He didn't even care about finding himself a goddamned *tatami* mat.

Then, as shadows inched further along the floor, he'd begun to drift off, and he heard the latrine boss whisper to his assistant to ladle some piss into his *miso* and be sure the *honyaku* served it to him later on. He'd pretended not to hear, but he turned on his side and watched the man through slitted eyelids from then on.

Koda Moan, his name was, a lanky, wiry haired pickpocket with a foolish overbite, a brushy beard, and a sagging bag of a belly. He whispered too loud and laughed too long, and the droopy, fleshy wattle under his chin danced when he did either.

After hours of listening to the man's grating laugh, Dog just hadn't been able to stand it anymore. He'd surreptitiously unfastened his loincloth, limped up, and whipped it fast around Moan's chicken neck from behind. He'd brought him face down onto the floor and driven both his shaky knees into the man's back. Before anybody could raise the alarm or beat him away, he'd jerked Moan's head back with a harsh crackle.

The other prisoners might've killed him if the *doshin* hadn't heard the commotion, rushed in and pulled him out. Maybe it would've been better if they had.

Dog shrugged in answer to the young warden's question. He breathed through his mouth. The fog of heat rose in the chilly air, backlit like a lightning cloud against the deepening shadows by the lantern light on the warden's porch.

*Just get it over with.*

The warden frowned and sighed as though he had tried to help, as though any answer Dog might've given him would've made the slightest difference in his living or dying.

"Very well. Then you are sentenced to *shizai*. In the morning you will be beheaded, and your body will be used for *o-tameshi*." Then, to the *doshin* guards, he said offhandedly, "Take him away."

The policeman to Dog's left cleared his throat.

"Pardon me, sir. Shall we place him in the death row cell, then?"

The warden looked aghast at being questioned.

"Of course! Where else?"

"Well sir, it's just that . . . Minoru's in there still, and he's made a mess of the place."

The warden seemed to recall something that vexed him.

"That damned monk . . . ! Well, we can't put him back in the lesser jail with the other prisoners. They'd tear him to pieces. He's only going to be there one night."

The policeman bowed.

"Yes sir."

Dog was hoisted to his feet as the warden rose, groaning and remarking about the cold, and retired to his warm office.

They led him shuffling across the twilight yard. He could hear someone chanting a *Nembutsu* over Moan's body. Apparently he'd been popular with the other inmates, though Dog couldn't see why. It sounded like it was coming from the lesser jail itself. The *eta* burial detail had probably left for the night.

*Pray all you want over that scrawny son of a bitch,* thought Dog. He knew how the *eta* disposed of prisoner corpses. Tossed them in the river, or by the side of the road as soon as they were out of sight of the prison. Let Great King Enma look for him in the muck. Dog's only regret was that he hadn't stuffed the fool headfirst down the latrine.

"Who is Minoru?" said one of Dog's guards, when they were well on their way.

"That's right, Gorobei's been sick," said another. "You'd better tell him, Kinpachi."

"Jinza brought him in," said Kinpachi. "He's a *kumoso* monk. The *eta* villagers down on the river complained that their brats were disappearing. Three of 'em in all. Well, they started going missing around the same time Minoru started staying in a hut out in the woods. Turns out he'd been luring 'em in with his flute playing and snatching 'em."

"What for?" said Gorobei.

"He was eating them."

"What!" exclaimed Gorobei.

"Yeah. He's completely crazy. He says he was a samurai but he died and came back as a *jikininki* and now he has to eat people."

"Then why does he eat *eta*?" quipped one of the other guards.

They all thought this was worth a laugh.

The guard holding Dog's rope gave his bonds a tug.

"That's some cellmate you've got, Red Dog. Ready to meet him?"

"That's not the worst of it," said Kinpachi. "I kinda feel sorry for this one. That Minoru's really made a mess of the cell."

"How?" said Gorobei.

"He sits there all day playing his flute and sculpting little *Jizō* figures out of his own shit."

Gorobei made a disgusted sound.

"Why the hell is he still here?"

"The warden doesn't know what to do with him. He's a monk, so he can't be condemned to *shizai*, and his victims are all *eta*, so they might have to ship him off to Danzaemon for judgment. He's waiting for word back from the *bakufu* in Edo."

As they walked, they began to take note of the low, trilling sound of a flute.

"What in hell's that?"

"That's him! Minoru, playing his *shakuhachi*."

"He's allowed to keep it?"

"Take it from him if you want, Gorobei. It's as filthy as he is."

They turned a bend and came to the eastern corner of the compound, looking out on the white sand execution grounds and the low mound that had been used in the day's *o-tameshi* demonstration. The ground seemed to glow eerily in the fading light, as though it had soaked up the blood of ghosts.

They drew up before the dark cell adjoining the grounds, and the flute cut off in the midst of its playing. The effect was like the cessation of a chorus of crickets in a foreboding wood.

Gorobei's breath hissed.

"Creepy bastard," he muttered.

As Gorobei stepped forward to let Dog in, the *doshin's* face grimaced. Dog could smell it too. Rank and overpowering as an open trench, the heavy smell of excrement emanated from within.

As Gorobei swung the door open, a dark, hunched shadow shuffled and stirred inside.

"Look!" said Kinpachi, giggling and reaching up toward the lamp to shine it inside.

"No, no," Gorobei insisted, but too late, his grinning partner cast a spot of light into the cell, briefly illuminating a yellow skinned, bug-eyed figure with a bald pate and dark, shabby robes. The monk held up one thin arm against the sudden intrusion of light. That hand and arm were splotched with dried, muddy stains that matched the finger marks smeared on the walls in the corner in which the monk sat. Dark little figurines, half a dozen in all, were neatly ordered against one wall.

Gorobei pushed aside Kinpachi's lantern and the scene was doused again in shadow.

"Gah!" exclaimed Gorobei, retching. "I feel for the poor *eta* that has to scrub that out."

The others laughed at Gorobei's reaction. Kinpachi roughly undid Dog's ropes and shoved him inside.

"Enjoy your last night on earth, Red Dog!" he offered.

Gorobei slammed the cell door with a clatter, and the *doshin* shambled off across the yard, talking of *sake* and women as their voices faded away.

Dog limped to the far side of the cell and put his back in the opposite corner, pulling his sleeve across his face to hamper the stench.

The only sound for some time was the unhurried breathing of the two men. The cell would have been black but for the white ground visible through the crossed cell bars and a single shaft of moonlight that slid through the tiny window high up on the back wall and pooled on the floor between the two men. As it was, Dog could just make out the thin form seated in the filthy corner, pop eyes shining like the unblinking gaze of an old *koi* fish. Each man's breath hung like fog and intermingled high in the moonlit space between them.

He did not know how long they sat in silence before the monk produced his *shakuhachi* and began to play again, a meandering tune that seemed to wend in and out between the wood bars of their cell.

Abruptly as it had begun, it stopped.

"The world is ending tonight," said Minoru in a plaintive voice, deep and gravelly, halfway between a moan and a growl.

Dog said nothing.

"They say," Minoru went on, "no masters of the arts will appear when the world is coming to its end. So tell me, have you seen any great works of art lately? Even the flowers are gone in this season of death. Some would say there is art before our eyes, out there on the killing sand. But those so-called artists . . . *feh!* They do not call the *eta* butchers artists. If there is no art in butchering an animal, tell me then. What art in butchering men? No. The world is at its end."

Dog only stared at the floor and rubbed life into his deadened feet, thankful for the abundance of space. He could stretch out for his last night of sleep if nothing else.

"Everything in the world is but a sham, and death is the only certainty," said Minoru.

Dog paused, considering. The danger of lunatics was that they sometimes made sense.

"Would you like to know about my *Jizō*?" said Minoru, gesturing in the dark to the little excrement sculptures flanking him.

Dog shut his eyes and lay his head back. Maybe there would be no sleep on his last night after all.

"No," he said. "Shut up."

Dog could tell by Minoru's voice that a grin had split his ghostly face.

"Ah! I thought maybe you were deaf and dumb. The *doshin* told you what I am, didn't they?"

Dog shifted on his side, resting his ear on his palm.

"Yeah," said Dog. "They told me."

"As a *jikininki*, I am cursed to go digging for corpses in graveyards at night and to eat the dead. I eat every part. Their tongues, noses, their genitals . . . I eat their assholes. In life I was a samurai, proud and vain. These *Jizō*," he said, as he again gestured to the invisible figurines. "They are both my curse and my salvation."

"I don't want to hear this," said Dog. "Shut up."

But Minoru went on as if he were deaf himself.

"You know how children who die before their parents are doomed to pile stones at the banks of the River Sanzu because they have not lived long enough to purify themselves with good karma? It came to me, while I was chewing on the leg of a nun I had dug up near Hiroshima that although the blessed divinity Ojizō-sama hides these children from demons beneath his robes when they are prayed for, there were still some children who might never make it across due to the unfortunate circumstances of their birth. I mean *eta* children. Who is more defiled spiritually from the womb to the grave than these poor, filthy creatures? *Eta* are a living blight, surely, but their little children . . . who prays for them, that blessed Ojizō-sama would deign to hear?"

Dog stared across the cell now, his blood beginning to simmer.

"And so I thought, what better savior for these muddy little souls, than a poor, damned *jikininki*? You see, I serve these unfortunates in two ways. Firstly, in cutting their lives short, I spare them a pitiful existence of uncleanness and spiritual debasement. Secondly, when I consume them, my body transmutes them, breaks down their impurities, and what I at last eliminate is their refined selves. I fashion these into little *Jizō*, to honor Ojizō-sama, so he may then take these neglected souls at last across the River Sanzu. Do you see how fine and loving a *jikininki* I am? In all of human history there has never been a *jikininki* like me. I am a savior to the *eta*. At night I hear their little voices calling to me from the banks of the River Sanzu, calling my name and thanking me. Thank you, Uncle Minoru! (they say) Bless you, *jikininki*! Bless you!"

Dog watched him splutter and shout in his excitement, watched the tears spill from his fish eyes. In the end, the monk was so overcome that he sobbed into his filthy sleeve.

Dog wanted to tell the fool he was *eta*. But why die at the disgusting hands of this monster, or dirty himself killing him? He was going to die anyway. Why not die as no *eta* ever had? By the *shizai,* like a legitimate person. Let him take that joke with him to the next world.

Minoru returned to his flute, and played haltingly for some time.

After a while, snow began to fall, and Dog heard a pair of wooden *geta* crunching across the grounds. In a few moments a samurai in dark clothes flaked with white came to stand before the cell. He was very pale, and meticulously groomed, obviously a person of worth and not any prison official he'd seen about. Surely he was no *doshin*.

Minoru continued to play, and the stranger listened. Then he moved and lit the lamp outside, shining light into the cell and becoming a featureless shadow.

Minoru lowered his stained flute and bowed respectfully to the stranger.

"'Evening, samurai," he said, smiling a gap-toothed grin.

Dog could barely stand to look at him.

"You are the monk, Minoru," said the stranger, in a cultured tone.

"I am he."

"That *honkyoku* you're playing . . . I've heard it before."

"It's called *Shika No Tone,*" said Minoru, and he smiled. "Do you remember it from your youth, young master Kamada?"

Dog looked sharply at the monk. What was he playing at?

Sadahiko stiffened at the sound of his own name. But this man had been here earlier today. He had probably watched the *o-tameshi* demonstration from his cell. He might have heard Lord Abe speak his name. Still, the monk's familiarity was off-putting. He knew the heinous crimes this man had committed. The warden had told him all about them over tea before he'd excused himself to walk the grounds and take in the cool air.

But, he did remember having heard the tune as a boy. It was strange to be called 'young master' again, after so many years. He peered through the bars at the older man. He was skeletal and filthy, like the hungry graveyard ghost he claimed to be, and his stench was extremely offensive.

"It was in Edo during the Kanda festival that you first heard it,"

Minoru said, "in the spring of your eighth or ninth year. You heard a *komuso* monk playing, and you wandered from your mother's side to listen."

Sadahiko cocked his head at the strange man. He did remember going to Edo to the Kanda festival with his mother and father. He remembered the bright little shrines bouncing on the shoulders of the boisterous Edokkos as they paraded through the streets singing and dancing. And he remembered the tune, and the strange, basket headed monk solemnly breathing in and out of his flute in a quiet alley away from the tumult. It was the same tune.

"Yes!" said Sadahiko, taking an inquisitive step toward the cell, in spite of his disgust. "But how could you know this? Were you the monk I saw?"

"No, young master," said Minoru patiently, as if he were correcting a guessing child. "In life, I was a retainer to the Kumada family. I saw my young master wander off, and I followed him to the alley where he heard the monk playing *Shika No Tone*. I told him what the tune meant."

"Two deer," said Sadahiko, amazed. "Ready to mate, calling to each other in the forest."

Minoru smiled, almost pleasantly, and nodded.

"You remember."

Red Dog leaned back against the wall and blew through his lips loudly.

Sadahiko turned to the scruffy, unshaven man in the other corner. He had asked the warden about him too, and after *sake*, the warden had agreed to let him conduct the man's execution on the morrow.

"What is the meaning of that?" Sadahiko demanded.

Dog looked at the samurai and shrugged.

"Forgive me, samurai. My feelings about this touching reunion between a child eater and his old employer's son moved my lips of their own accord. It's a small world, isn't it?"

He didn't know why he said it. It was worth a beheading on the spot. But he was tired of this mean world and wished it would end like the mad monk said.

Sadahiko turned from the old man. In truth, he had only a vague recollection of this onetime retainer. It was known that not all of his father's samurai had followed his suicide in the obligatory *tsuifuku* ritual. Some had become masterless *ronin,* and it was said that many wandering *komuso* monks were onetime samurai. It would have to wait.

"You're the bandit, Red Dog," Sadahiko said.

Dog nodded.

"I was. Tomorrow . . ."

"Tomorrow, I will take your head."

Dog stared at the samurai, looked into his eyes. There was a perverse fire there. He had said that with lust in his voice, as if he had made an intimate promise to a lover.

Dog could not resist.

"Are you willing to stain the execution sand with an *eta*'s blood, samurai?"

"What!" said Minoru, stiffening in his corner and putting his back to the wall.

Sadahiko recoiled from the man as he had not from the filthy monk. His first instinct was to throw open the cell and cut the bandit down then and there. But he stayed himself. What if a swift death was all he wanted? This was a bold man indeed, to make such a claim. But no, it was no claim, for who would pretend to that?

"A filthy *eta*!" Minoru hissed, his face coiling into an ugly mask.

Dog jumped to his feet.

"That's right, you bastard! Why don't you come and purify me?"

The monk made a disgusted face.

"*You?* Full grown as you are you would turn this *jikininki's* stomach!" he clenched his belly as if it were a precious treasure. "You would expel my poor children from me. *Kill* him, young master!"

Sadahiko curled his lip at the monk, whose madness had begun to show. He looked again at the Dog.

"Why tell me this? I can kill you right now."

Dog shook his head. He walked toward the bars.

"So I choose between a death in this shitty cell or on that pretty sand in the morning in front of all those soft-skinned hypocrites? I don't care which I get. My father was an executioner at this very prison. He performed the *haritsuke*. You ever watch a crucifixion, samurai? I never knew what my father did for our living. Just thought he swept up around the prison. Then one day he brought me here when I was eleven years old. I guess he meant to make me his apprentice. My father . . . we'd fished together, and I'd watched him bounce my little sister around on his shoulders. Then I watched him string a crying, pissing burglar up on a wood frame, and stab him twenty times in the side with a spear, till the blood and the rice, and his stinking guts spilled out of his wounds . . . like wet meal from a ragged sack. The smell . . . it's even worse than his smell," he said, nodding to Minoru and wrinkling his nose with the memory of it.

"After he stripped the body, I realized all those years, the new clothes he'd brought home for us, the dresses for my sister . . . taken from the dead. The corpse handler's bounty. I didn't want any part of it, so I fled. Never saw my family again. I tried to live on my own. I stole. I was caught. They brought me back here and sentenced me to *irezumi*." He held his hair away from his forehead, displaying the flat, ugly scar there. "My father's best friend, a man I had called 'uncle' when I was a little boy, branded me with 'dog.' When I got out, I held a hot trowel in a fire and burned it off my flesh. Still there was no one who would hire me on as anything. I had to travel far. I went across the sea. Tell me, samurai. Do men smell an *eta*? I never killed a man till I was thirteen. I never butchered an animal, I never worked in a tannery. But it was as if they smelled it on me. I didn't believe I was different. I tried to find a place. But all the places were taken. So I became Red Dog. It was all I could do. I made sure never to kill above my station."

He laughed, and gripped the bars, peering out at the pale man. "But what the law didn't know was, everybody was above my station. The lowdown beggars and pickpockets and thieves, the gamblers and the pimps I had to kill over the years, even this filthy, crazy bastard who plays with his own shit. Somehow, you're all above me . . . so I don't care anymore samurai." He pressed himself against the bars, and pulled open his shirt, baring his chest.

"Go ahead."

But what Sadahiko would have done next neither of them would ever know, for at that moment a shrill, strangled scream pierced the stillness and men began to shout, prisoners and *doshin* alike. The lamps were lit, and feet pounded the boards and broke the snow.

Sadahiko backed away from the strange pair of men in the death cell and hurried after the commotion.

Dog watched him go and sighed, closing his jacket and returning to his wall.

Minoru huddled, watching him.

After a minute, he began to chuckle.

"Foolish *eta*," he murmured. "None of it matters. The world is ending tonight."

Sadahiko rushed across the compound and arrived at the site of the disturbance before the warden. Two *doshin* guards were standing at the door of the lesser jail, T-shaped *tsukubō* polearms brandished at the mass of wide-eyed prisoners huddled against the bars and yelling all at once.

The *doshin* rapped the groping hands, and these recoiled only to be replaced by others. Desperate faces framed in the jail bars. Eyes bugged and lips spluttered.

Sadahiko stood back for a moment and tried to understand what was going on, but the prisoners, nearly half the jail room's compliment with more pushing behind them, were all shouting over each other at the guards. He could discern a few calling for the door to be opened.

"What is it?" the warden demanded, stumbling over and fastening his coat. "Is it a riot? Kinpachi! Gorobei! Report!"

The guards looked over their shoulders, as panicked as the prisoners.

"I don't know, sir!" said Kinpachi. "Somebody started screaming, then they were all yelling and rushing the door!"

"Get us out of here! Get us out! A monster!" shouted one of the prisoners over all the others. He was a thin man, and he was pressed against the door.

The warden stalked forward and pointed the man out.

"What's that you said?"

The other prisoners heaved at the door and the thin man grimaced as he was forced against the bars. There were shrill screams coming from the back of the mob.

A dozen more guards came rushing over, bearing a variety of arresting polearms from the guardhouse. They took up a defensive formation in front of the jail. The guard captain, Murasame Jinza, was in the lead.

"Where is Kikuchi?" the warden called to the prisoners. "Where is your *dairyo*?"

"Dead! He's dead!" several of them yelled. "Open the door!"

The thin man in front gave a shrill, dwindling scream and fell slack, lips dribbling blood.

Sadahiko watched in fascination as the prisoner slumped and was dragged down by the men behind him.

"They're killing each other! *Jinza!*"

The warden turned, and the captain stepped to meet him.

"Fetch some muskets, and call out the entire guard!"

Jinza nodded and selected a four man detail to do so. These four broke off and headed for the armory at a run. A bell rang wildly in the night.

"Stand down!" the warden shouted at the prisoners, marching up and down behind his guards. "Stand down or I will shoot every man in front!"

They were heedless, and shoved at the door, some of them climbing the grate like monkeys to avoid the crushing fate of the thin man.

"What is going on?" the warden demanded again, when the guards returned, the fuses of their arquebuses trailing smoke.

The four musketmen knelt in a line before the guards.

The sight of the primed and ready muskets calmed the men in the front somewhat, but the prisoners in the rear continued to howl and press the others forward, until several were screaming as the thin man had.

The warden cursed as there was a groan and the cell door began to buckle in its housings.

He lifted his hand to Jinza, shaking his head in disgust and turning away as he did so.

"Ready!" Jinza bellowed.

The musketmen raised their weapons to their cheeks.

Now the men who were not being crushed against the door scrambled for the rear, while the men in the back pushed, unaware of the guns.

"Fire!" yelled the captain.

Sadahiko watched the red flashes of fire alight from the barrels of the long guns, and the bright explosions of blood and smoke that rose from the twisting mass of prisoners. Chips of wood splintered and flew as the lead balls glanced off the grating.

Three men went down dead and a fourth slapped his hands to his face and wailed. He was quickly dragged down with the others.

Then Sadahiko saw something that made him grip the handle of his sword.

One of the men on the floor reached a trembling hand up and

grabbed a hold of the naked leg of one of the men standing on him. Craning his neck, he sunk his teeth into the fat part of the offender's calf.

The standing man screamed shrilly and the men around him looked down. They began to scream too.

A semicircle cleared around the bitten man and the man on the floor.

"Look! Look!" someone gibbered.

It was the thin man who had been crushed.

The crushed man pulled away from the prisoner's leg, taking a hunk of bright, stringy flesh in his teeth.

"Help me!" the bitten man cried as he fell to one knee.

The crushed man grabbed a hold of the wounded man's kimono and pulled him down as if to kiss him with his bloody mouth, but instead clamped his mouth on the soft part of his throat and tore it open in a gush.

The warden, the guards, even Jinza and Sadahiko were speechless at the grisly sight.

The prisoners scrambled to get away, but men in the back were still pushing forward, and some stumbled and fell. Then, the men who had been shot began to move. They held the fallen down, and these began to scream and fight furiously, but there was no room in the tangle of flailing limbs and stomping feet to escape. Teeth tore through skin and blood spurted. Sadahiko saw a belly rent and quivering intestines pulled out by manic, clawed fingers, strewn like parade ribbons across the shoulders of the confused prisoners. He could smell the hot blood.

"Sir?" Jinza called, unable to keep his voice steady.

The warden shook his head.

"Shoot them again!" he mumbled.

"No!" Sadahiko heard himself yell. "Can't you see? Open the door! Let them out! Shoot the ones on the floor!"

The warden looked at Sadahiko and slowly nodded.

"Yes! Yes! Gorobei, let them out! Polearms!"

The *doshin* formed a semicircle as Gorobei gingerly stepped toward the cell door with the key and looked over his shoulder to see that all was ready.

In that instant an arm shot through the bars and grabbed his face, fingers hooking into his mouth and jerking him toward the door by his cheek.

Gorobei screamed as he was held there. He yanked his policeman's *jitte* from his belt and beat at the fingers holding him until they let go. He stumbled back and fell on his knees in the snow, blood flowing from the empty place his ear had been.

Sadahiko jumped forward, taking the keys from the snow and drawing *Tasogare* as he went.

With one hand he jabbed the point between the bars again and again, not caring who he stabbed so long as they kept away. He jammed the key in the lock and turned it, then retreated as it swung open.

Men tumbled out like bales of hay. Some of them were biting furiously. Those bitten screamed in agony and thrust out elbows, even kicking to get away. They scrambled through the snow, trailing blood. The guards parted for these, and thrust their blunt-headed *tsukubō* and their spiked *sodegarami* sleeve-catchers and their sharp, U-pronged *sasumatas* at the biting prisoners, entrapping them on the ground like wild dogs so the others could escape.

There were some forty prisoners lodged in the lesser jail, and they streamed out in a rush, inadvertently bowling over some of the guards, freeing the crazed, biting men to snap at their ankles and trip them up as they rushed by, pulling them down.

Sadahiko found himself in danger of being overrun himself, but he planted his feet and swept back and forth at the mob of men, describing a deadly arc of silver with *Tasogare*. The skin on the back of his neck rose with secret glee as *Tasogare's* edge tore through four living men, spilling their guts and blood in a shower of scarlet. They tumbled to the ground, one of them nearly cut in half, forming a natural barrier that the men behind pitched clumsily over and the rest avoided, parting around him like a rushing river around a jutting stone.

He looked on the four dead men with satisfaction, thinking how only a few hours ago he had remarked how difficult it was to cut a man in two at the waist.

Then the bisected man began to twitch.

At first he thought it was the natural muscular reflexes of the dead. Sometimes the bodies of men he beheaded continued to shake and jump. It was why women tied their legs together before committing *jigai*—so the throes of death would not shame them.

But the upper half of the dead man did not simply tremble. It lifted itself on two hands and began to drag itself towards him. Its eyes were wide open and regarded him, though they were clouded over with strange, blue gray cataracts. Its nose twitched like a hunting animal's, and its teeth gnashed and snapped.

He took a step back and regained himself, then struck off its head. It slumped, lifeless once more.

In a moment, the other three men he had cut began to stir.

He did the same for these, decapitating each in turn. But he did it with a dread deep in his chest that harrowed him to the core. *What madness was this? What monstrosity?*

He fell back toward the line of guards. Something gripped his pant leg. He glanced down and saw one of the *doshin* on the ground, bleeding from a bite wound in his neck. That same cloudy glaze was in his feral eyes.

Sadahiko split the guard's head down to his teeth.

Hands gripped his elbow and Sadahiko nearly cut the young warden down.

"What are you doing?" the warden stammered.

Sadahiko shrugged him off and leapt over the four bodies into the oncoming rush. He dodged through the prisoners until he reached the cell door. Jamming *Tasogare* into the ground, he flung his shoulder against the door and slammed it shut, knocking back a half dozen men still trying to funnel out the exit.

He turned the key in the lock and pulled his sword from the ground.

He backed away quickly as outthrust hands clawed at his clothes.

The warden had followed him.

"What are you doing?"

Sadahiko grabbed him by the throat.

"Listen to me! No more can come out, and all that will die must be killed!"

He dragged the warden over to the men he had twice killed and, gripping him by the nape like a wayward pet, forced him to look.

"Look! I cut these men down and they rose again. The men you shot attacked the others."

The warden tried to shake his head, but Sadahiko would not let him.

"The *doshin* I killed. Go and look at his body. He was bitten in the throat. He was dead *before* I split his skull." Sadahiko released the man. "Go! Look!"

The warden backed away from Sadahiko.

All around them, the sudden fight had subsided.

The prisoners who had escaped the jail room were huddled in a corner near the prison wall, penned in by guards. Across the yard, curious faces pressed sleepily against the bars of the greater jailhouse.

A few of the biting prisoners were writhing and snarling like animals on the ground, pinned by the *doshins'* poles.

Some of the men, prisoners and guards alike, sat or lay in the disturbed snow, hands clasped to bleeding wounds. None of these looked too serious.

The men still locked in the lesser jail begged to be let out. There were groans from the darkness behind them.

The warden went to stand over the *doshin* he had seen Sadahiko kill.

"I tell you, he was dead. These others were dead. But they *moved*." Sadahiko turned to regard the four men being restrained by the *doshin*. "Look at their eyes. Look at their wounds. There! From the muskets! You saw them fall!"

"Listen to him!" shouted one of the prisoners huddled against the wall.

The warden marched over to where the prisoners were being guarded, and the pleading of the men still locked in the jail became shrill.

"What are you talking about?"

A spindly man with wiry hair spoke above the others until they quieted down;

"When the new man killed the latrine boss, Koda Moan, we laid his body out on his *tatami* in a corner and old Denzo said prayers over him," the man related breathlessly. "When we all lay down to sleep and the lights were put out, we heard Denzo scream. Some of us went over there and found him wrestling with someone in the dark. A couple of us, Ichige and Entaro, they tried to pull them apart. Ichige, he got bit bad in the arm. We dragged the biter close to the bars to see who he was by the moonlight. It was Koda Moan."

The warden bunched up his lips, disbelieving.

"He kept fighting, snapping at us. Then old Denzo crept up on somebody and started gumming them. We thought he'd gone crazy.

Then Ichige bit Entaro . . ."

"What is this madness?" the warden chuckled, waving the prisoner away and stalking back to the jail room. "I'll see for myself."

But as he came to the door of the jail, he stopped. The dozen who had been standing there begging to be let out had fled back into the dark and were apparently hiding. Three men stood at the door of the lesser jail, moaning and reaching out beseechingly. Their eyes were all a milky gray and they bore the marks of terrible wounds. One of them was trailing his own coiling intestines. Another's forearm hung twisting from the elbow by a ragged thread of bloody flesh, and a third had a gaping, blackened bullet wound in the middle of his chest.

The warden took a hesitant step backward.

There were exclamations from the guards, and one of them nearly let go of their charge, a pale eyed prisoner covered in blood lying on his back in the snow, pinioned by two *tsukubō*. It—for by its behavior Sadahiko could not consider it a man—gave an obscene spasm of effort, spitting and growling and snapping its jaws. The noise seemed contagious, for the other three trapped creatures did the same before they all succumbed once again and lay still, groaning, gathering their strength.

A blubbering noise erupted from the dark jail room and was quickly silenced.

The four horrors at the cell door turned in unison and walked slowly back to hunt for the others who were hiding. The disemboweled creature stumbled on its own entrails heedlessly. They were the last thing to recede into the shadows, sliding across the floor like eels, leaving a trail of blood.

Sadahiko stepped up to one of the trapped prisoners and thrust the point of his sword a few times into its torso. It howled and struggled, but not from pain. Blood welled up from the wounds and spilled onto the snow, and as it writhed, flecked the terrified guards who held it in check.

The warden made a move as if to stop him, but waited.

Sadahiko watched it for a moment. They all did. It continued to snap and struggle, never diminishing in strength. Then he swung his sword and struck its head from its neck. Instantly it lay still, though its dead eyes were unchanged. It simply ceased to move.

"Murderer!" the warden whispered.

"*Jikininki*," said Gorobei, the *doshin* whose ear had been bitten off. His eyes were red rimmed, his lips trembling.

The others looked at him.

Gorobei spluttered as he spoke, the red stained cloth clamped over the side of his head making him look all the more unhinged. "We are cursed . . . by that old monk. He really is some kind of master *jikininki*. He's cursed us!"

"Shut up!" the warden spat. "Nonsense! All nonsense!"

Sadahiko regarded him quietly.

"The same must be done for these others. And the ones in the lesser jail."

A scream came from the lesser jail, and wet, terrible sounds, as of bones breaking and skin tearing, of stomachs emptying onto the wood floor.

"Jinza!" the warden growled. "Transfer the lesser jail prisoners into the greater jailhouse. Take the wounded men to the infirmary and see they're tended to."

"The surgeon won't be in until the morning," Jinza reminded him.

"Yes I know," the warden said. "Do the best you can."

"If their wounds are fatal, they'll have to be beheaded," Sadahiko said plainly.

Jinza looked from the warden to Sadahiko. The warden looked at the ground.

"I know what I saw," Sadahiko said.

"I'll take some men in there after those four madmen myself. There are still prisoners in there that need help."

"Sir!" said Gorobei, who had been listening. "Please, don't make me go in there!"

"Gorobei!" Jinza barked, disgusted at the guard's nervous tone.

"You're hurt, Gorobei," the warden intervened. "Go to the infirmary with the other prisoners."

Gorobei flushed and bowed deeply.

"No matter. The ones still inside are dead anyway," Sadahiko said.

The warden looked at Sadahiko, hissing.

"Please, stop this. You're inciting panic."

"I would burn the lesser jail down if I were you."

"Captain," the warden said to Jinza. "Before you carry out your orders, please escort Kumada-*sama* to my residence and see him to bed."

"Bed?" Sadahiko said, disbelieving.

"Your services won't be needed tonight," said the warden. "Please feel free to retire. My men and I will handle this crisis. Don't trouble yourself." He gave a short bow.

"You think you can put me under house arrest?" Sadahiko challenged.

"I didn't say that. You must have misunderstood . . ."

"You little cur!" Sadahiko snapped, touching the hilt of *Tasogare*.

Instantly three *sasumata* were leveled at him, and Jinza brandished his *jitte* baton, ready and able to trap and break his sword.

"The law requires that you be detained until the matter of officer Samidare Kinpachi's death can be investigated," the warden told him coldly.

"Who?"

"The *doshin* I saw you kill," the warden said, glaring.

"Please feel free to resist, samurai-*sama*," said Jinza, unsmiling.

Sadahiko looked from Jinza, to the warden, to the three *doshin* covering him. He let his hand drop from the handle of his sword.

He knew what he had seen. Dead men had moved. They had attacked the living. This pup of a warden thought this was some kind of sickness, or hysteria. Sadahiko did not believe in *jikininki* or curses, but he had lived with death long enough to know it when he saw it. He was familiar enough with its finality to know its nature had somehow been suspended. Altered. Something unnatural was going on at the prison, and he was afraid, but not for his sanity. He did not doubt what he had seen.

"Very well," he said. "But you will pardon me if I do not relinquish my sword."

Jinza looked to the warden uncertainly.

"Let him keep it," the warden sighed. "Just see he stays put."

It was half past midnight when it stopped snowing. The screams and the musket fire grew sporadic.

Dog had lain awake listening to them.

Minoru too remained wakeful, playing his flute. He paused once to squat in the corner and sculpt a new *Jizō* for the wall. The crazy bastard knelt there saying sutras over it, clasping his filthy hands together and rocking where he sat, touching his head to the grimy floor like a supplicant, heedless of whatever was going on outside.

After the first volley, Dog stood at the grate and peered out through the bars, though he could see nothing. The trouble was far across the compound. What in hell was going on? He heard orders barked, and the alarm tolled. No one came to their part of the prison. They had no news other than what could be gleaned from what they heard.

After the alarm, things were quiet for an hour, the strange, tense silence broken only by the occasional shout from the direction of the lesser jail. Then there came another loud commotion, followed by a second volley of rifle fire, and a tremendous crash as of a wall collapsing somewhere. The alarm sounded again, and there was a lot of yelling back and forth amongst the *doshin*. Orders and counterorders, nothing much discernible beyond the calling out of various areas of the prison. The lesser jail, the upper rooms, the infirmary, now the greater jail and the armory. Dog thought maybe a fire had broken out and was spreading across the compound. *Good. Let the whole damned place burn around them.*

But they saw no lights, smelled no smoke. The intermittent cries and screams continued off and on for hours. Soon he heard women too. Whatever it was, it had engulfed the entire western quarter of the prison.

Dog went from pacing the cell to sitting against the back wall and staring out into the night. It was nerve wracking to hear the screams of men and women. The air was heavy with a dread more terrible than if it had been thick with wood smoke and fire. Minoru's crazy words about the world ending poisoned his thoughts.

Minoru finished his prayers and returned to his flute, wordlessly, as if he knew exactly what was going on outside and it didn't concern him.

That was when the shambling figure came to stand before their cell.

They heard it first, the shuffling steps across the snowy ground. It was like the step of a tired man, without cadence or rhythm, more a stagger than a stride.

The thin, shadowed form crossed in front of them. Dog saw unkempt hair and long, ropy arms. But the most standout thing about the stranger was the angle of his head. It was bent sharply to the right, so that the right ear seemed to touch the right shoulder. Yet the man's posture was not hunched. There was a snuffling sound, and the man emitted a low, almost plaintive moan and shuffled closer to the bars.

He stepped into the beam of moonlight.

That was when Dog saw the face of Koda Moan, the latrine boss. His neck was broken still, by all appearances, and yet he lived. His eyes were glazed with a white film, and the jaw hung loose. His mouth was splashed with black, like the ink on a woman's teeth.

He was expressionless, and as Dog flattened himself against the wall, Koda Moan pawed at the grate as though he were unfamiliar with the concept of a door. His thin arms snaked in between the bars and his long fingered hands reached imploringly out to him. His head lolled about his shoulders, flopping between his chest and back without reason.

Minoru stopped playing his flute and stared silently. He slowly got to his feet.

"It's Koda Moan!" Dog exclaimed.

"Oh. He's *your* visitor, then," Minoru said, sitting back down and picking up his flute. "I thought he had come to see me."

"He's dead!" Dog stammered. "I killed him!"

"Well," said Minoru, "maybe you should appeal to the warden and see if he will agree to hear your case again in light of this new development."

Koda Moan rattled the wooden grate and groaned again.

"He's certainly anxious to see you," Minoru went on. "Go and get the keys, if you want in," he called to Moan.

Moan answered with an animal snarl and a disconcerting wobble of his broken neck.

Minoru cocked his head, and stood up again.

Dog trembled all over, his hairs straight on end. He hugged himself for fear that he might shake the soul loose from his body. He had killed this man with his hands. Heard his neck break, heard his last breath rattle out of him. He had heard prayers being said over his corpse. Hadn't he?

Minoru approached Moan, stopping inches from his grasping hands. He watched his fingers clench and unclench, peering through the dimness at his face.

Dog forced himself to stand also, and stared over Minoru's reeking shoulder.

Minoru's hand snaked out suddenly and touched Moan's face,

eliciting an outburst of violent growling.

Minoru held his hand up to his own face and licked his palm.

Dog winced, imagining the flavor.

Minoru held out his hand to Dog. It glistened with the black substance all over Moan's face.

"Blood," said Minoru. "And he's cold to the touch. I'm afraid there'll be no appeal for you." He chuckled.

"Blood! Is it his?"

"No no," said Minoru, licking his hand again. "This is fresh. And look, there's no mark about his face. Well, besides what you put there. No open wounds. He's been drinking it. I think he wants more."

Dog reeled and had to steady himself with one hand against the wall.

Moan snarled.

Minoru turned to him and spoke in mock sympathy, as if to a puppy or a child.

"Yes, yes, I know," he cooed. "But we don't have the key, my friend. I'll play you a tune. You'll feel better about it."

He went to his corner and picked up his stained flute again.

Dog's eyes bulged and he gripped his own arms till his knuckles were white. The *shakuhachi* played *Shika No Tone* again. He wished this was a nightmare. He wished that he would awake and find Minoru chewing on his ankle. Anything would be better than what stood before him. He never prayed, but he prayed now to awaken.

In almost immediate answer, Koda Moan suddenly straightened and pressed his narrow face against the grate, as if he were trying to force his head and somehow the rest of his body through one of the squares. There was a sickening crunch, and his body fell entirely away, while his head remained in the air, jaws working, milky eyes rolling.

Dog gasped aloud and bit his hand to stifle a shriek. As a boy in his village he had heard tales about *nukekubi*, monsters whose heads could float away from their bodies and hurtle through the air screaming, to suck the life from the living. The tale had terrified him as a child and now the old chest squeezing fear came back to him in a flood.

But then the head too fell to the ground, and there stood the samurai sword tester, Kumada Sadahiko, withdrawing a policeman's U-bladed *sasumata* polearm. He had neatly separated Moan's head from his body with one thrust.

Sadahiko came to the bars. His eyes were wild and his hair disheveled. He was not the collected gentleman who had come earlier to assure Dog of his own death.

"Are you both alive in there?"

"No," said Minoru.

"Yes," said Dog at the same time.

"We're both alive," Dog said, when Sadahiko hesitated.

"Ah! Young master Kumada!" exclaimed Minoru, sounding genuinely pleased.

"Yes." He looked around fervently, then laid the bloody *sasumata* aside and drew out his sword. "Do you know this sword, monk?"

Minoru answered immediately.

"It's called *Tasogare*. Muramasa Murashige made it. You had the signature altered to avoid the shogun's ban on Muramasa swords. It was the sword you cut off your father's head with."

"Then you are who you say you are," said Sadahiko.

Minoru smiled faintly and nodded, closing his pop eyes.

"Yes."

"I know why you became a *kumoso*. When my father was ordered to commit *seppuku*, you were one of the ones who left us instead of following him in death as a loyal retainer."

"When I was alive, I thought that to cut open my own belly for the petty crimes of a greedy accountant was absurd. And I thought I was more of a samurai than the young master."

Sadahiko curled his lip at that.

"That is the sin of pride which I died with," Minoru continued. "Now I am a *jikininki*," said the monk, bowing low. Then he stared up at Sadahiko from beneath his downturned brow. "And I know something else too, young master Kumada. I know that at night that sword, *Tasogare,* calls out to you for blood, and nags like a dissatisfied woman when you put it away clean. Tonight it will get its fill."

"What do you know about tonight?" Sadahiko said sharply.

"I know the world is ending, as it does each day and night for some man somewhere, as it did for the dying star I saw streak across the sky last night."

"What *is* happening?" Dog broke in impatiently.

Sadahiko looked to the bandit.

"I will show you."

Sadahiko unlocked their cell and they stepped over the corpse of

Koda Moan. Dog paused to toe the face skyward, still not wanting to believe. He glimpsed the bloodstained overbite on the dead, brushy face and looked away, pushing aside panic.

The snow in the yard was ankle deep. They navigated the dark avenues of the prison, clinging to the wall shadows like creeping rats. Dog was last in line, Minoru's stink heavy in his nose.

Each section of the compound was divided into courtyards by high walls capped with rows of discouraging iron spikes about two *shaku* long. The prison was surrounded by a wide moat only passable by the main gate drawbridge, lending it an isolated, labyrinthine feel, particularly if one did not know one's way around.

Dog had practically grown up here, fetching his father home to the *eta* village every afternoon. He'd had relatively free reign about the compound, and had explored it thoroughly as a boy. He had seen the crucified men outside the main gate almost everyday, marking when the corpses changed, but giving them little thought until the day he'd watched his father perform his duties. They'd been in the midst of removing the stiff, gray bodies from the crosses when Jinza brought him in this morning, the frozen blood shimmering like candy on the wood poles.

He shook these memories away. They left the gate that led to the execution grounds (which was ajar and unguarded—an unpardonable dereliction of duty) in the northeast corner and moved stealthily along the first wall towards the neighboring upper chamber jail, where the infrequent high ranking prisoners were incarcerated.

The shouts continued to come from the west, and glancing to the south as they neared the upper jailhouse, Dog could see the guard-house adjoining the armory and interrogation chambers and the southeast gate leading to the warden's office and residence. The door was broken in, the snow around it marred with scattered footprints. A barricade composed of an overturned cart and some firewood had been smashed to pieces.

They came to the upper jailhouse. Sadahiko produced his ring of keys (*whose* ring of keys? Not even the *doshin* guards were given *all* the keys to the prison . . . only the captain and the warden carried master sets) and tried them until he unlocked the door. They slipped inside. Dog noted that Sadahiko locked the door behind them.

The upper jailhouse was smaller than either the greater or the lesser jails, where the majority of prisoners were kept. Wishful thinking on the part of the architects, that the higher classes did not often wind up in jail, but true to some extent, for they often had the resources to hide their crimes. The upper jailhouse was unoccupied tonight, and the halls were dark, only the silver, broken moonlight filtering through the barred windows showed the way.

Sadahiko did not reach for one of the oil lamps. Dog didn't ask why. Light could attract trouble.

They climbed the stair. This was the only two story building in the compound. They opened the empty jail room and Sadahiko held them back. He held the *sasumata* before him and called out;

"Jinza!"

"Here," came a weak voice from the corner, near the western window, which looked out over the spiked walls and building rooftops.

The man who had arrested and beaten Dog that morning sat in the corner, his leg bleeding through a tightly bound linen bandage. He looked pale.

Sadahiko propped the *sasumata* against the wall and knelt beside Jinza.

Dog stood over him. The red tasseled iron *jitte* the man had laid up against his head and shoulders was stuffed in his belt. So this was where the keys had come from.

"Jinza came to get me from the warden's residence," said Sadahiko. "Tell them what you told me, Captain. So they believe."

Jinza gathered himself up and nodded.

"The warden led a couple of *doshin* into the lesser jail to fetch the four mad prisoners and the dozen who were hiding in there. The rest of the prisoners were separated. I took the wounded ones to the infirmary. We put the others in the greater jail with the rest of the population. I'd just finished sorting them out and was seeing to their wounds when we heard the warden scream. I took some guards and went into the lesser jail after him." Jinza paused, shaking his head. His face was beaded with sweat. "We found more than a dozen of them in the back of the jailhouse. They had . . . they were *eating* them."

Dog looked at Minoru. Minoru nodded and smiled.

"They'd made a circle on the floor and they were . . . tearing them to pieces. The warden and the four *doshin*. Just like ravenous dogs."

Jinza coughed, and seemed to enter a paroxysm of some sort. Sadahiko steadied him, but when it had passed, he stood up, wary.

The captain went on;

"The gunners I had left to guard the greater jail started firing, so we left two men outside the lesser jail and went back. We must have missed a wounded man or two . . . put them in with the other prisoners. They . . . the creatures were inside, and the prisoners were screaming. And the infirmary . . . some of the wounded had succumbed while we were gone . . . and they . . . they rose up again. Gorobei told me one of the men they'd thought was sleeping just rolled over and bit into another man lying beside him . . ."

"What are you saying?" Dog snapped, pacing in front of Jinza. "That the dead are eating the living?"

Jinza nodded coldly.

Dog laughed out loud, but he cut himself off, thinking of Koda Moan. He went to the window and looked out. The yard beyond the western gate was still lit up, and Dog could see crowds of figures milling about in the lantern light. The doors to the infirmary were open, and the snow covered roof of the greater jailhouse was sagging; one wall had fallen, the source of the crash Dog had heard earlier.

"Was there a riot?" Dog wondered aloud.

"There's something else," Jinza mumbled, ignoring him. "Something I didn't tell you, Kumada-*sama*."

Sadahiko took a step back.

"I told you I hurt my leg when they pushed the jailhouse wall down," he said. He shook his head.

"Gorobei . . . Gorobei bit me. He only lost an ear," Jinza muttered. "I didn't think . . ."

Sadahiko drew his sword without a word and passed his blade through Jinza's neck. The old captain's head rolled across the room and bounced into one of the dark corners. The blood that erupted out of the stump left a red flare on the wall like a stylized candle flame.

Dog stared. Though the man had been friendly to him as a boy, he felt nothing at his death. Still, he had to admit the action had been swift and cold.

Sadahiko turned to them.

"Do you understand now?"

"Yes. The world is ending for everyone tonight," said Minoru.

"You have to destroy or sever the head to stop them," Sadahiko said. "Nothing else will stop them. I saw them crawl without any legs. They feel no pain. Their bite is a swift poison. Anyone who dies for any reason comes back as one of them."

Dog looked out over the slow moving mob to the west. No time for disbelief, no time for reasoning. To think about such things would only cause hesitancy, and Dog had learned as a bandit that to hesitate was to die.

"The only way out is the main gate drawbridge," Dog said quietly.

"They're all locked in the west half of the compound," said Sadahiko, picking up the *sasumata*. "We can go out without seeing any of them."

"On the way in here I saw the guardhouse door broken in. A few must've gotten out. Maybe some of the *doshin* let them out, trying to get to the armory."

"We can deal with a few," Sadahiko said.

"There's something else, samurai," Dog said, turning to look at him. "They lock the drawbridge mechanism during a riot."

Sadahiko shrugged and held up the ring of Jinza's keys.

"The captain of the *doshin* always gives his main gate key to the warden."

"I've never heard of this."

Dog scratched his chin.

"Jinza was here back when my father was an executioner. He instituted the policy so if he was taken hostage the prisoners couldn't escape."

*The warden!* Sadahiko leaned tiredly on the *sasumata*.

"The warden was killed in the lesser jail," Sadahiko muttered.

Minoru looked out the window and smiled, laughing a hissing laugh between his ugly teeth.

They locked the upper jailhouse behind them and followed the western wall, happening upon a discarded polearm, a *tsukubō* that one of the *doshin* had dropped after impaling himself on the wall spikes trying to climb over. His body was transfixed in two places and he was bootlessly moving his limbs and moaning, trying to free himself. Whether the *doshin* was alive or one of the *jikininki* (for what else could they call them, even if they weren't exactly *jikininki*?) they didn't know.

Sadahiko took the T-headed *tsukubō* and passed it to Minoru, giving the crescent bladed sasumata to Dog and drawing his own sword. They were all armed now.

They came within sight of the western gate. It was ajar. A few of the *jikininki* were hunched over, wetly savaging the open trunk of a dead *doshin*.

They heard another musket shot from the west followed by a high pitched scream that was swiftly cut short.

"Only three," said Sadahiko, moving forward. "We can kill them easily."

Dog grabbed his sleeve.

"There are too many on the other side of that gate. We should try to find another way in. We might be able to get into the lesser jail by the roof. There's a fire bell tower in the corner of the east wall."

Sadahiko shrugged him off impatiently. He *wanted* to kill these three *jikininki*. He had gone twenty nine years without killing to survive, and this night had gotten his stagnant blood going.

"How do we get over the spikes?"

"It can be done, if we don't hurry," said Dog. "We could grab a couple of the *tatami* from the upper prison and lay them across. I used to climb over these walls that way when I was a boy. 'Course, I was smaller then."

"Climbing like a monkey, little *eta*," muttered Minoru. He was smiling and leaning on his *tsukubō* like a hermit's staff.

"We should have left him in the cell," said Dog.

"Oh but I'm useful," Minoru assured him. "I have this."

He took out his flute from where he'd tucked it in his robe.

"What'll you do with that?" Dog said warily.

"I'll play a tune to my *jikininki* brothers," he said.

"Like hell you will," said Dog, shifting the blade of the *sasumata* in his direction.

"Where?" said Sadahiko.

Minoru pointed to the fire bell tower, a swept gabled silhouette peering over the wall where Dog had said it would be.

"That will be my stage. I'll play a tune they'll all come to hear."

"We can slip by them while they're distracted," Sadahiko said to Dog.

"If they like his music," Dog scoffed. "Personally, I'd go the other way."

"If it works, they'll swarm you. I don't know if they can climb or not," said Sadahiko.

"They won't hurt me, young master Kumada," Minoru grinned. "No animal attacks itself."

Sadahiko stared at the madman. He didn't know what had driven him to this state. Was it shame at his dereliction of the responsibility of *oibara*, or just common dementia? Was he, in his strange way, trying to make amends for his long ago disloyalty? It was an odd twist of fate that had led to their reunion.

"Alright," he said.

After retrieving a pair of the sleeping mats from the upper jail, they moved to the quiet corner of the wall nearest the bell platform. Minoru planted his *tsukubō* butt first in the snow. They boosted him up to the lip of the wall.

"Watch the spikes," said Dog, not knowing what else to say. He had heard of samurai self sacrifice, but he'd never seen any example of it personally. Most samurai he'd known were selfish bastards. Even this one, for all his good intentions, was a lowlife child killer. Yet if this worked, and he died as their decoy . . . well, he couldn't say he would miss the old man. It was just *gou* working itself out.

Minoru was nimble as a spider. He hung by his fingers, bracing his feet against the wall, and was able with one hand to lay the sleeping mats they passed up to him over the spikes. He straddled the wall and motioned for his *tsukubō*. When he had it, he slipped out of sight.

Dog and Sadahiko headed back to the west gate, moving between the buildings and the wall. Rounding a corner they came face to face with one of the *doshin* who had led Dog to the killing grounds earlier. His eyes were white and his clothes were splashed with blood. He lunged silently at them. Dog dropped to one knee and thrust the crescent blade of the *sasumata* under the *doshin's* chin and sent his head end over end into the air. The body took a step and fell silently into the snow.

Sadahiko had been startled by the *jikininki's* appearance, but even more so by the swiftness of the bandit's reaction. Met with sudden danger, he had counterattacked without hesitation. He was a killer, this one, no matter what the warden had thought.

They paused at the corner and looked out at the gate. The few they had seen feeding earlier had gone, leaving an unrecognizable mass of splintered bones sucked dry of marrow and strewn with partially chewed viscera.

Keeping to the wall, they moved to stand behind the open gate and waited.

Now their clouds of hot breath were a reassurance. Dog had

noticed that the *jikininki* didn't seem to breathe. Minoru had said Koda Moan was cold, too. They truly were dead. He closed his eyes, fighting down hysteria again, swallowing it in a lump and shoving it deep into the pit of his stomach.

Sadahiko almost wished the things would charge out of the gate in a mob. He remembered how he had cut the four men outside the lesser jail down with as many swings. How he looked forward to more of that sort of action!

Minoru's flute began to play, echoing hauntingly across the entire prison. Sadahiko didn't know the tune.

The music had the effect of a tidal wave. They heard the groaning begin near the bell tower, and then resound across the courtyard beyond the gate as the *jikininki* became aware of him.

They waited in silence, hearing the tramping of many feet pass by.

Then, directly in front of them, seven *jikininki* suddenly appeared, walking slowly through the snow. The two parties perceived each other at the same time, and the *jikininki* let out a terrible gnashing sound and doubled their speed.

Dog didn't know why they moved so slowly. Maybe their blood wasn't flowing, or the cold had some effect on them. Either way, he and Sadahiko charged at them side by side. They knew they didn't have long before Minoru was overrun or forced to retreat.

Plunging into the midst of the trudging creatures, Sadahiko struck with furious glee, chopping them down at the neck one after another like bamboo stalks, his sword whistling, cutting first air and then bone. Dog actually saw him smile. As for himself, he accounted for two, tripping them up with the butt end of the *sasumata* and then slicing their heads off as they struggled to rise.

Sadahiko turned wildly, and for a second Dog lifted his *sasumata* defensively, thinking he would feel that sharp sword next.

"Let's go!" Sadahiko hissed.

He ran back to the west gate, and Dog struggled to keep up.

They passed through the gate into the large western courtyard. Directly before them, the infirmary was a shambles, as was the adjoining greater jail. How many prisoners had that jail housed? Seventy? Ninety? Dog didn't like to think about it.

To their right they saw the backs of the hundred or more infected prisoners waddling toward the bell tower in the far eastern corner, behind the lesser jail (which still appeared to be locked and intact).

Dog could see the scaffold of the tower, and make out the dark iron bell on the flat platform. He supposed any one of them could have simply gone up there and rang the bell, but hell, he wouldn't have been crazy enough to do it. Then he saw Minoru. The man was marching solemnly around the bell, the flute to his lips. As he watched, a few of the *jikininki* crowding the base of the tower began to tentatively scale it. They wobbled and fell back into the crowd, but always two or three rose to replace them. He wouldn't last long up there.

Then they heard a sound that made their skin rise. They had not stopped running toward the lesser jail, but they did look over their shoulders to see the source of the strange, high wail that rose above the noise of the *jikininki*. What they saw nearly caused them to pitch face first into the snow.

It was the women.

Last to be infected, last to leave their sequestered jailhouse nestled in the southwest corner of the prison, they were coming steadily across the snow—all of them. At least thirty, Dog thought. In their pale prison garb and with their deathly skin and chalk eyes, they melted into the winter white but for their streaming black hair and splotches of bright red blood. Truly, they were like a retinue of *Yuki-onna* spirits storming across the snow, ephemeral and beauteous, yet terrifying for all their anachronistically savage expressions. The queer, high-pitched sound that burst from their slender throats was mangled as it passed through their gnashing teeth. The sight of Dog and Sadahiko enraged them, and it chilled Dog's soul.

Sadahiko felt it too, and he hissed;

"Don't look at them! Run!"

They ran, but it was hard going through the snow. They reached the lesser jail door well before the women, but when Dog leaned against the bars panting, Sadahiko jerked him back. Five pairs of arms thrust through and grabbed the space he had narrowly vacated.

Dog landed on his ass in the wet snow and nearly lost his *sasumata*. He fished for it frantically. When his fingers closed around it, he was already standing.

The women were coming up on them, stumbling over each other in their haste.

Sadahiko hacked at the groping arms, lopping away hands and fingers like candle wax. The things did not recoil but prodded him with bleeding stumps protruding shorn bone.

He stood back and tore the keys from his clothing.

"Hold them back!" he shouted.

Dog glanced back and saw the ones behind the door, but he was unsure if Sadahiko meant them or the approaching women. Keeping the blade of the polearm angled toward the onrushing mob, he shoved the butt-end through the gaps in the bars hard, knocking a few of the *jikininki* inside flat on their backs.

It was enough. Sadahiko thrust the key into the lock and turned, then swung the door open.

He stepped across the threshold and gaped.

A dozen or more *jikininki* were staggering out of the dark room.

Dog looked over his shoulder and saw the trouble. They were trapped. His eyes fell . . . and there, struggling to get up, face half torn away and one eye plucked out, was the warden himself.

"Look there! On the floor!" he shouted, and turned back to the women just as the first of them charged him with open arms and mouth roaring.

Dog shoved the crescent blade into her open mouth and with the help of her own momentum, sheared off the upper half of her face, sidestepping the flailing, spurting body in time to meet two others whom he battered down with the haft.

Sadahiko saw. He jumped into the room and swung down at the disfigured warden as he sat up. *Tasogare* parted the warden's head and wedged halfway down his chest in his breastbone. It was the most magnificent cut he'd ever made.

As the body sank back, the upper head and neck peeling into two bleeding halves, one whole the other a nightmare of exposed tissue and bone, he pulled the sword free and chopped the *jikininki* on his left down at the knees. He pushed the other back with his foot and thrust his hand frantically into the warden's robes as the dozen advancing on him howled and stretched their arms towards him.

Dog swept the *sasumata* back and forth. He had fought off a gang once the very same way with a whip-like bamboo fishing pole, but in that instance, fear of pain had driven the superior number back. These women stepped heedlessly into his arc and fell, some only to rise once more, not even stunned by the force of his blows or the horror of their wounds. He whimpered. This was hellish work, cutting into a crowd of women.

He was nearly overcome when he recognized one of the women

as Oyuki, the old white haired crone who had worked as the prison *asaji*, attending to the female prisoners and washing the heads of the executed. Auntie Oyuki, he had always called her. She had washed his feet with cool water from the courtyard well on hot, dusty days. He split the side of her old head open above the ear and sent her down hard. Doing it nearly made him vomit.

But it wasn't Old Oyuki and they weren't women, he told himself. Not anymore.

Then he thought, what if his father still worked here at the prison? He had no idea if he was even alive. But no, the *eta* corpse handlers had gone home, hadn't they? Yes, otherwise Koda Moan's body wouldn't have stayed in the lesser jail overnight.

If his father still lived, he was sleeping down by the river in the *eta* village in the old hut. And his mother? His sister? If he lived through this nightmare . . . no.

He wouldn't think about that.

Sadahiko ducked out, curling fingers tearing his sleeves. He slammed the cell shut and broke off the key, then turned in time to cut a woman from her shoulder to her armpit.

"I've got them!" Sadahiko shouted, feeling the cold iron ring against his belly.

Dog shoved two of the women back. He couldn't cut them anymore. Though they were swiftly trapping them in a semicircle in front of the lesser jail, he just couldn't.

"The flute!" Sadahiko exclaimed.

*What flute?* Dog thought, and then realized what he was getting at. The absence of it was deafening.

Then they heard a roaring noise from behind the lesser jail. They both knew what it meant. Minoru was dead. The mass of *jikininki* would return, attracted by the sounds of the women.

Sadahiko lashed out, cutting the women to pieces like dolls. Delicate, porcelain heads spun through the air, long black hair whipping about.

Dog was using the back end of his *sasumata*, shoving them away like unruly livestock.

"What are you doing?" Sadahiko screamed. "Cut them down!"

Dog shook his head, tears in his eyes. It was too horrible. They were so beautiful, even in this horrendous state. He had no right.

Then the crowd of *jikininki* came surging around the corners of the jailhouse, relentless, infinite. They pressed through the trilling women, bloody and terrible. Dog turned his blade on them, unable to discern anymore. He and Sadahiko were two threshers in a field, two trees groaning before a broken levee.

Then, from the sky, a T-shaped *tsukubō* descended between them. Sadahiko glanced up.

Minoru was braced on the lip of the jailhouse roof, holding the *tsukubō* down to them by the butt.

"Grab on, young master!" he called.

While not bladed, the 'T' on the *tsukubō* was studded with small barbs up to about a *shaku* down the length of the haft, so that a criminal couldn't grab it and force it away without tearing up his hands. Minoru had wrapped the T end in cloth torn from the hem of his prison robe.

Sadahiko whipped the blood off his sword and took the blade in his teeth. He grabbed the *tsukubō* with both hands, leaping up as Minoru swung. He left the ground and reached out, hands clamping on the edge of the roof. He drew his feet up.

Minoru swung the *tsukubō* back down to Dog.

Dog thrust his own weapon lengthwise at the front row of the *jikininki*, forcing them back, then turned and grabbed the proffered lifeline. He fumbled, almost fell, but Sadahiko, who had pulled himself up in the interim, grabbed his arm and held him.

One of the things reached up and hugged his ankle, teeth seeking his flesh.

He screamed and kicked out, pulping its nose, but it would not let go.

Sadahiko lay on his belly on the roof and pushed the point of his sword into its eye. When the blade finally broke through the back of its skull, it released Dog and dropped into the crowd below.

Sadahiko pushed Jinza's keys into Minoru's hands.

"Lock them in! We'll head for the main gate."

Minoru nodded and smiled in his way, clutching the key ring like a treasure.

They ran across the roof of the jailhouse, slipping on the snow, the *jikininki* following their progress on the ground, stumbling to keep up.

They dropped down on the south edge, collapsing in the snow and pulling themselves up as the army of *jikininki* came lumbering like a single, massive creature across the courtyard.

Rushing through, Sadahiko and Minoru turned and pushed the ponderous gate closed as Dog picked up the *tsukubō* and kept watch.

The gate slammed shut and Minoru fitted the key in as it began to thud from the impact of the bodies colliding on the other side.

"Go, young master!" Minoru shouted. "My *jikininki* won't wait long."

Dog and Sadahiko ran, turning south, slipping and crashing in the powder in their haste.

Dog marveled that the old man had survived. What this crazed killer had done to deserve the protection of karma he didn't know.

Sadahiko's eyes swept the courtyard lanes and the dark doorway of the guardhouse almost hopefully. His heart was racing. He could almost feel every drop of blood that coursed through his limbs. The air in his stinging lungs was pure as a wind from heaven. He was more alive than he'd ever been. Tonight he was not the dispassionate slaughterer his father had called him in his final hours. Tried in glorious battle, he had cut down scores of men like a storied warrior.

Dog was the first to reach the gate. He could see the sky paling over the treetops through the arrow slits.

He turned, and watched Sadahiko looking all around as he approached.

Dog was alive, and more, there was life ahead of him. His family's village lay no more than a few minutes further down the road. And past that? Across the sea? No. Across the ocean, maybe. Somehow. To Chūgoku, Kankoku, anywhere. He was going to get the hell out of Japan. He didn't understand what was happening in this prison. Maybe somehow the gods existed, and all the tainted blood of his *eta* ancestors, of all the people who had bowed down to this government of slaughter and death had sown the ground with some evil and the *jikininki* were the shoots breaking the killing grounds to tear down the shogun and the *bakufu* and the weakling emperor, the unavoidable fist of *gou*. Maybe this world was ending as Minoru said and the start of it all had been born here tonight, bloody and screaming and white eyed.

Whatever.

He didn't want to be Red Dog anymore. He didn't want to live in madness and death. He swore if he could find a way, he would leave this land behind him forever. There had to be a place where no one had ever heard of *eta*.

Sadahiko handed him the keys.

With supreme satisfaction, he unlocked the gate crank housing and put his all into lowering the drawbridge.

Sadahiko paced back and forth before the gate, staring up the way they'd come. Surely this wasn't the end. Surely there was more death to be dealt, more cutting to be done. But the night was ending. Even now the east gleamed brightly as the wavy *hamon* on the face of Japanese steel.

"Where is that old man?" he said aloud, giving voice to his annoyance.

"I don't care," said Dog, panting at the wheel, yet blessing the fire in his arms and the wonderful clanking of the drawbridge lowering. "I'm done. Finished. I'm getting the hell out of here."

Sadahiko breathed in the cool morning air.

The drawbridge thundered onto the far bank of the moat beyond the heavy gate doors. Dog locked it into place, feeling its final settling reverberate through his bones, through his heart.

He ran to throw up the heavy bar.

As he stopped to raise it, they both heard the unearthly flute.

It was so still. As still as it had been at twilight, when the newly fallen snow had muffled the earth. Even the riotous sounds of the *jikininki* were suspiciously absent. Maybe the light of dawn had put an end to them. Maybe such things could not thrive beneath the sun.

Then they saw Minoru walking across the courtyard toward them, playing his flute.

Behind him, the entirety of the cannibal dead marched, as if in a Shinto procession.

Sadahiko's lips parted, but he said nothing. Did Minoru truly hold some sway over these creatures?

When the creatures saw Sadahiko and Dog at the far end of the compound, they began to howl and groan as they had before.

Minoru kept up his pace and his playing, even as the things all around him limped past hurriedly.

Dog heaved the bar off the gate and let it crash to the ground. He pushed with all his strength, swinging the heavy doors wide and rushing out onto the drawbridge.

Halfway across he stopped.

Against the sky he saw the dark silhouettes of the crucified dead, still lashed to their execution frames, flanking the path, the *bakufu's* visual deterrent to the would-be criminals and upstarts who might dare to oppose the shogun's edicts.

They were twitching and rocking on their crosses.

They began to moan.

He stared, horrified. Then he saw the others.

There was a mass of dark figures moving slowly beneath the trees on the far bank of the moat, lining the road that led to the river.

Dog dropped to one knee and sat down heavily.

Behind him, Sadahiko backed onto the drawbridge, staring.

"Minoru!" he screamed. "What's happening?"

Minoru stopped playing his flute. He was weeping. He raised his arms, the sleeves falling back to his shoulders.

His spindly, shit-mottled arms were red, perforated over every inch with bite marks and coursing blood, the white bones exposed in some places where the fatty flesh had been eaten away.

"You're welcome, my children!" he called in a breaking voice. "You're welcome! I love you!"

His voice dwindled as the mindless creatures passed him by. Sadahiko could almost imagine he saw Minoru's bulbous eyes clouding white.

Sadahiko stood over Dog's shoulder, gripping his sword with both hands, ready to die fighting.

"*Eta* or no," he said to Dog. "We will die together as warriors. As samurai."

"What?" said Dog distractedly, watching the dark figures approaching from the far bank. He turned away and looked up at Sadahiko. He didn't want to see their faces.

"Tonight, you and I fought with distinction. Those we slew will attest to that in the next life."

Dog chuckled.

"The *next* life? You damned samurai, always looking for honor in slaughter," Dog smirked. "We may as well have been mowing grass. They didn't fight us, we fought *them*. *Feh!* It doesn't matter."

He shook his head and put his hands over his ears and closed his eyes, tired.

"You're an idiot, corpse cutter," he muttered.

The drawbridge underneath them shook with the march of the *jikininki*.

# ZOMBIE SAFARI
## by Ben Cheetham

Ben Cheetham's short fiction has won awards and been published in numerous magazines and anthologies in the UK, US and Australia. Most recently *Voice From the Planet* (published by Harvard Square Editions) and *Fast Forward: The Mix Tape, A Collection of Flash Fiction*. He's a 2010 Pushcart Prize nominee. He's recently completed his first novel—a dark psychological tale touching on themes such as the corrupting power of money, grief, love, infidelity, schizophrenia, murder and end-of-the-world paranoia—for which he's currently seeking representation. Sometimes he thinks a zombie apocalypse would change his life for the better.

## Day One.

We got up at six a.m. and packed our gear into the boat. I took my APR Single Shot hunting handgun and my Safari 850 rifle. The APR has proven itself over many years as the handgun of choice for serious hunters—shot by seven of the top ten competitors at the International PZH (Pro Zombie Hunter) Championships last year. It's the only gun in its class to have twice broken the world record for one shot knockdowns at 550 metres. Last year, on a trip to the South Western Reserve, I made a 450 metre shot. Luckily Tommy was with me otherwise no one would've believed it.

I firmly believe there's no finer hunting handgun on the planet than the APR Single Shot. Of course, Bob reckons that's a load of crap. He maintains that the F-33 Contender is the superior pistol. Now don't get me wrong, in terms of versatility and user friendliness in the field the F-33 is unmatched by any other handgun. If it's accuracy and proven long range performance you're looking for, though, the APR comes out on top every time.

When it comes to rifles, Bob and me are in complete agreement. For anyone who prides themselves on using only the best then the Safari 850 must be the rifle of choice. Power, reliability, beauty—the Safari 850 truly has it all. The only reason Bob doesn't own one is because he can't afford to. Mine belonged to my dad. I inherited it when he went missing in the Southern Reserve last July. He didn't have his Safari 850 with him because it was in the workshop for repairs to its walnut stock.

By 9 a.m. the sun was already hot and we were well on our way to

Robertson Island. Tommy and Jim were waiting for us on a shingle beach on the south side of the island. Both looked tired. Tommy especially seemed strung-out. He complained that they were being worked too hard.

Robertson Island was uninhabited until last February and its new residents are still struggling to assert their dominance over nature. Flash-flooding and infestations of caterpillars have decimated their crops. Their fresh-water well has been contaminated by saltwater. And a bush-fire burnt their biodiesel processor to the ground. Worst of all, though, a flesh-eater somehow managed to find its way onto the island and the first anyone knew about it was when it took a bite out of a kid walking his dog.

Jim is Tommy's cousin and only living relative. Most people mistake them for brothers because they look so alike, but any similarities begin and end there. You see what a man's really about when you're in a tight spot with him, and you can take it from me that Tommy's a crack-shot, but liable to panic if it comes to a fight at close-quarters. Jim, on the other hand, can't shoot for shit, but doesn't mind getting his hands dirty. In fact, I'm beginning to think he enjoys it a bit too much, if you know what I mean.

Personally, I get twitchy if there's much less than half a mile between me and a flesh-eater. I've seen close up what one of those things can do if it gets its teeth into you. It can get real messy. If you've ever seen video footage of a lion chowing-down on a zebra, you'll know what I'm talking about.

That's why I always hunt with Bob, because he never rattles no matter how up close and personal things get. If I had to describe him in a word I'd say consistent. Bob would be the first to admit that I'm capable of making an occasional shot he couldn't make in his dreams, but he'd also point out that if it came down to say five rounds of ten shots at under 300 metres he'd come out on top nine times out of ten. That's partly because, as my dad always used to tell me, I've got the attention span of a flea and partly because in some ways I'm more like Tommy than I'd care to admit.

As the boat motored across the bay towards the mainland, I turned to Tommy. "What did you go for?" I asked, glancing enquiringly at his holstered rifle.

"The 550 Custom Deluxe."

"Can I?"

"Go ahead."

I took the rifle out and ran my finger down the cold hammer-forged barrel to the bolt. "Jesus, that's nice."

"The bolt's machined from a single forging, there are no weldings."

I examined the rifle's handcrafted rosewood stock. "Beautiful."

Tommy grinned, pleased by my approval. "I can knock a fly off a wall at a hundred paces with it."

Jim scoffed. "We aren't gonna be shooting any flies. Take a look at this." He unzipped his kit-bag and took out an SMG (Sub Machine Gun) that looked very similar to an Uzi.

"What's its rpm?" I asked.

"640 at full tilt. This little beauty'll cut one of those fuckers in two."

"Tell him what else you've got," said Tommy.

Jim grinned. "Only the best automatic rifle in existence."

"M-16," I said.

"Did you hear that?" laughed Jim. "Mikey thinks the M-16 is better than the AK-47."

"You've got a Kalashnikov," I said, impressed.

Jim's grin reached from ear to ear as he took out the weapon. "Say hola to the AK-47 Kalashnikov Assault Rifle," he announced as proudly as if he was showing off his firstborn. "First developed in World War Two for the Soviet army, it subsequently became the most popular automatic weapon worldwide. Gas-operated, highly-reliable and—"

"It can't hit shit beyond three hundred metres," interrupted Tommy.

"Who cares? Where's the fun in using one of those?" Jim jerked his chin at Tommy's rifle. "I like to see the look in their eyes as the bullets go in."

"I can see Cutshaw," Bob called from the front of the boat. I eased up on the accelerator and guided us into the pier.

Bob threw out the mooring-rope and Cutshaw secured the boat while we gathered up our gear. Cutshaw nodded at me as I stepped onto the pier. We stood in silence as the others clambered out of the boat. I knew better than to try and get any conversation out of Cutshaw. Like anyone who spends a lot of time on the reserves, he's a silent, morose man. He's also the best guide in the business—cool, calm, and absolutely collected. I sometimes think if you sliced him open you'd find wires inside him. Dad introduced him to me on my first hunting trip with the words, "Be nice to this man, son. One day he might save your life."

I disliked Cutshaw straight away. I don't like him much better now, but I respect him. I haven't got a clue what he thinks about me or, for that matter, anybody else. I can't remember him ever expressing an opinion on anything other than hunting. And I've never known him to be wrong. I swear, if there was a single stone out of place on his patch he'd know about it.

We slung our packs into the back of the HMMWV (pronounced hum-vee). Cutshaw climbed the ladder beside the gate and scoped the landscape for flesh-eaters while we settled into our seats. His Labrador dog, Franz, jumped on me and licked my face. I ruffled his fur, laughing. They say dogs grow alike to their masters, but in Franz's case the opposite seems to be true. Every time we meet he seems more affectionate while Cutshaw seems more aloof.

Jim wrinkled his nose in disgust. "How can you let that thing lick your face like that? He was probably licking his balls before we got here."

"Franz is a good boy, aren't you," I said, scratching behind his ears.

"Aww man, he's getting a hardon."

"Mikey or the dog?" put in Bob.

"You're just jealous," I said, and I meant it. Franz was a relentless tracker and, if need be, a ferocious bodyguard. My dad once said, "I swear, that dog's nose has eyes." Whoever Franz favoured was likely to bag the best trophies of the trip.

We fell silent as the gate slid open. I knew there was no danger because the land had been cleared and flattened for half a mile, but even so my hand dropped to the grip of my Beretta 92FS. Bob fingered the hammer of his Magnum Revolver. We glanced at each other and a shudder of excitement passed between us. The mood heightened as Cutshaw got into the Humvee and drove through the gate. My mouth was dry, my stomach was fluttering and I felt light-headed. This may not sound like a particularly enjoyable mixture of sensations, but believe me you quickly grow to like, even crave it. Anyone who's hunted dangerous game knows what I'm talking about. The surge of adrenaline coupled with the sense of normal duty being suspended is a heady mixture.

Suddenly I couldn't help but grin. I knew without having to look at the others that all of them—except Cutshaw—were grinning like

Cheshire cats too. As the Humvee rumbled along, Franz settled down at my side with his head on my lap. I felt the tension drain out of my body, secure in the knowledge that for the next three weeks I'd be doing what I liked best in the world with the people I liked best.

"Has there been any action today?" asked Bob.

"No," replied Cutshaw, succinct as ever.

"I heard there was some trouble over in the Southern Reserve," said Tommy. When Cutshaw nodded, he continued, "It's true then, three hunters and their guide were eaten."

"Yes."

"Jesus."

"What happened?" I asked.

"They went after a thinker."

"Jesus," Tommy said again.

Now, as you know, most flesh-eaters are creatures of pure instinct, but a few of them, perhaps one in ten thousand, seem to possess a rudimentary intelligence of the sort that evolutionists are nowadays fond of comparing to tool-using chimps. The obvious absurdity of such comparisons notwithstanding, these 'thinkers' are an especially dangerous and highly prized quarry.

"Has anyone bagged it yet?" asked Jim. I guessed at once what he was thinking. So did Tommy.

"Forget it," he said. "We haven't got time to get down to the Southern Reserve."

"Yes we have, if we only spend a few days up here."

"But the hunting's better here."

"No it isn't."

"Is."

"Isn't."

"Give it a rest," I said. Franz barked as if in agreement and pressed his nose to the window, staring across a flat expanse of scrubland to the edge of a pine forest about 300 metres away. His ears were pricked and his fur stood on end, which could only mean one thing.

Cutshaw stopped the Humvee, slid back a reinforced-steel panel in the roof and stood through it.

"Do you see anything?" I asked as he scoped the densely-packed trees.

"No, but there's something in there."

Cutshaw has the eyes of a hawk. Often when we're out hunting he'll point to what appears to me as a smudge of colour and say, "Target." But even his eyes are no match for Franz's nose.

"Let's bag it," Jim said eagerly.

Cutshaw shook his head. "I'll radio it in. We don't start until tomorrow."

Jim didn't argue—no one ever argues with Cutshaw—but I could tell he was disappointed. We all were. None of us had shot anything but tin cans and crows since the previous autumn. It'd been a long hard winter and we were ready to let off some steam. In another way, though, I was relieved. I used to know a pro-footballer who never pulled on his shirt until he was running onto the pitch. I'm a bit like that with hunting. There are certain rituals I like to perform before I go out. For instance, I always bring a bottle of single-malt whiskey with me to share round the campfire on the first night. Dad got me started on that one. I also get everyone in the party to kiss my rifle, which they're usually happy to do because they've just drunk my whiskey.

"Possible activity nine miles out from Pier 12. No confirmed sighting," Cutshaw mumbled into his radio as we pulled away. Franz settled back down on my lap. Forehead puckered, I stared at the dark band of woodland blanketing the hills to the south.

I glanced at Bob as the Humvee passed a dirt-track that branched off the sealed-road, skirted the woods and ended at a derelict farmhouse. Behind the house a sandy trail was faintly visible rising into the forest. You have to be a brave man with a steady nerve to hunt there. Apart from flesh-eaters, hungry packs of wolves and bears roam in ever increasing numbers. Bob and me went up there once, against my dad's advice—he'd hunted there and knew how the wind moaning through the trees and bringing the shadows to life can play with your imagination. What he didn't tell us was how the mist can roll down off the hilltops so that before you know it you're groping along like a blind man.

I cringed inwardly at the memory of that day. From Bob's face it was plain he felt the same. Neither of us was yet ready to admit how close we'd come to losing it in those woods. It was only through dumb luck we got out of them alive.

"Hey didn't you guys hunt that trail a couple of seasons back?" said Tommy. A low grunt from Bob was the only response he received. "Man, you wouldn't get me up there for any money."

Sensing my unease, Franz lifted his head to look askance at me. I smiled at him, pushing my fingers through his fur.

It was late afternoon when we rolled into Camp 14. A gate made of platted iron slats slid back and a guard waved us through. We scanned the compound for a spot to pitch our tents. Luckily there were only a couple of other parties in.

As soon as the tents were pitched we got down to the serious business of sampling Bob's homebrew—an evil-smelling moonshine he called Skull Cracker. "What do you think?" he asked as I took a slug.

I nodded approval, trying not to choke. "It's smoother than the last batch."

"It's a new recipe."

I hadn't eaten since breakfast and the stuff made my head buzz like a swarm of bees. Jim tutted and chuckled. "I always suspected you were a lightweight, Mikey."

Bob nudged me, eyes wide with awe. "Over there," he said quietly as if he was in church.

A stone's throw to our left a skinny old guy with a straggly beard was crouched outside an old-fashioned Whelen lean-to tent struggling to open a tin of beans with a pocket-knife.

"Jesus," I murmured.

"Exactly."

"You think it's really him?"

"It's him alright."

"Do you reckon I should ask him if he wants to borrow our can-opener?"

Bob looked horrified at my suggestion. "That's Jesus Martinez. That guy's wasted more flesh-eaters than you've seen weekends."

Just in case you don't know, Jesus Martinez is only the greatest living hunter. A whole lifetime spent on the reserves (most people don't last more than a couple of years before their brain turns into jelly). More confirmed kills than every hunter I know put together. Always hunts alone. Just him and The Viola, his rifle—a weapon of near mythical status. A real living legend right there in front of us.

We reverently watched him labour at the tin. After a couple of minutes he threw it down. "Puta," he spat, glaring at the tin as if trying to bore a hole in it with his eyes.

I dug out the tin-opener and, despite Bob's protests, took it over to Jesus Martinez.

"Que chingados quieres?" muttered the old man without taking his eyes off the tin, which roughly translated means, *What the fuck do you want?* Whether this remark was aimed at the tin or me I wasn't sure, but I held out the tin-opener.

Jesus Martinez looked at me. I was struck by the blackness of his eyes. They were like a shark's eyes, absolutely unreadable. He accepted the tin-opener, levered the tin open and handed it back with a slight nod. I stood there awkwardly a moment, a starry-eyed idiot vainly trying to think of something to say, then turned and headed back across to the others.

"What did he say?" Bob asked eagerly.

"Nothing."

"Not even thanks?"

"He said thanks."

We sat down to a meal of bacon, eggs and beans, followed by tinned fruit in syrup—a real luxury in these times. Most of the talk concerned our plans for the following day. There was also much hushed speculation about what Jesus Martinez was doing here. As the sun went down, the midges started to bite and we retreated into our tents—Bob and me in one, Tommy and Jim in the other. Bob couldn't get over having seen Martinez in the flesh. He'd spent half his youth listening to tales of The Mexican's exploits. He said that for damn sure he was going to speak to him in the morning. He was as excited as a kid on Christmas Eve. I heard him tossing-and-turning in his bag for hours. My own sleep was fitful and disturbed by ugly dreams. I didn't mind, though. I knew that tomorrow night with the first kill of the season under my belt I'd sleep like a baby.

## Day Two.

Bob prodded me awake at first light. From the look of devastation on his face I knew Jesus Martinez was gone. "I can't believe I didn't speak to him," he said.

"Don't worry, you'll get another chance."

"No I won't." Bob got into his sleeping-bag and pulled it up over his head. After five minutes of silence I left the tent. I was surprised and a little concerned by Bob's reaction. He was usually so steady. I was supposed to be the emotional one.

It was a damp morning with a high, blue sky. I headed for the toilet-block. A guy about my age was stood outside it. "I see Martinez is gone," I said.

"Left an hour before daybreak."

"Do you know where he's headed?"

"South, I reckon."

"That figures."

After answering nature's call, I busied myself with making breakfast. Tommy poked his head out of the other tent, sniffing. He looked like he hadn't got much sleep either.

I handed him a mug of coffee. "Looks like it's gonna be a hot one."

"Hope so."

From inside the tent came a groan. Jim crawled into sight. He grunted at me before shuffling off to the toilet-block. I called to Bob that breakfast was ready and got no reply.

"What's up with him?" asked Tommy.

I shrugged. When Jim returned we ate a big breakfast. I didn't have much of an appetite—I never do on the first morning of a hunt—but I forced myself to eat until I was full. I knew from past experience that Cutshaw would push us hard to see what sort of shape we were in.

Cutshaw was leant against the Humvee smoking a cigarette. I approached him and asked, "Have the spotters seen any activity?"

"Some."

"Where?"

"Colt Creek."

"How many?"

"Two."

"What type?"

"Stage three."

This news got my adrenaline pumping. As you probably know, zombies go through five stages of decomposition characterised by progressive physical degeneration. A stage one zombie is at the height of its physical powers. By stage three, with the onset of black putrefaction, the zombie's bloated body begins to deflate like a punctured tyre, fluids ooze out of its mouth and nostrils and its flesh takes on a creamy consistency. Also, the bones fuse giving the zombie its familiar stiff-limbed walk. A word of warning, though, stage three zombies may be slower on their feet than an arthritic old man, but they're as powerful as a grizzly and can bite through bone like it was butter.

Jim rubbed his hands together excitedly when I gave him the news. Tommy looked apprehensive. I ducked into the tent. Bob was rummaging through his kitbag.

"Everything alright?" I asked.

He nodded. I told him about the sighting. "We're heading out in ten."

Ten minutes later we were in the Humvee rumbling along Route 56 towards Colt Creek. Already you could see the heat shimmering on the unsealed road and the brushy meadows to either side. Tommy giggled at Jim's terrible jokes. Bob was silent. I sipped constantly at my canteen to stop from feeling like my mouth was full of cotton-wool.

Cutshaw pulled-up north of Colt Creek where we were downwind of our quarry—a zombie can smell living human flesh from up to several miles away depending on the wind's strength and direction.

We checked our weapons and got out of the Humvee. Franz was instantly alert, prowling forward, stiff-tailed, nose pressed to the dirt. Cutshaw followed him, slightly hunched over. We fanned out to either side of them.

I glanced at Bob and was relieved to see that he was totally focused. The hunt was on, nothing else mattered.

All around wildflowers were coming into bloom. The landscape was awash with purple thistles and bright yellow sundrops, with scattered patches of Virginia bluebells, Rocky Mountain beard tongue and red-pink creeping phlox. You could get drunk on the smell of it. The air hummed with bees.

A ring-necked pheasant rocketed up out of the grass. Jim squeezed off a short burst from his AK-47 and it fell from the sky with a thud.

"Jesus, Jim," hissed Tommy.

Jim stuffed the fat bird into his rucksack. "At least we won't go hungry tonight."

I laughed. Cutshaw didn't look amused, but then he never does.

We started up a long slope. By the time we were halfway up it I was wheezing like an asthmatic buffalo. Bob was only doing a little better. I could tell from Cutshaw's frequent glances that he was irritated by the amount of noise we were making, but so long as we were going after nothing worse than a stage three it wouldn't make any difference if we belted out a couple of verses of Jake Leg Blues. All zombies go deaf shortly after turning.

At the top of the slope Franz stopped suddenly, fur bristling.

Cutshaw dropped onto his belly, motioning for us to do likewise. About 300 metres away was a steep-banked creek. Cutshaw scoped it, then handed me the binoculars, saying, "In the water, beneath the river birch."

The zombie was standing waist-high in the stream. It was a stage five in about as advanced a state of necrosis as any I'd seen, a real ugly mother. Only a few tatters of putrefied skin still clung to its skull, its eyes had rotted away, most of its teeth were missing and it'd lost an arm.

"Who wants it?" asked Cutshaw after we'd all taken a turn with the binoculars.

"I'll take it," said Tommy, unslinging his rifle. There were no complaints. A stage five kill might be something to brag about when you're a novice hunter, but not when you're a veteran of seven seasons. What's more, this one probably didn't have more than a couple of months to go before the billions of microbes, maggots, flies, beetles and moths feeding on its mouldering body killed it off.

"I almost feel sorry for it," said Jim as Tommy sighted the flesh-eater.

There was a sharp crack and the zombie dropped back into the water. I watched it go over through my scope and knew it wouldn't get back up. We congratulated Tommy. It was a pretty good shot considering it was his first kill of the season. We took turns drinking from Bob's canteen while Cutshaw got on the radio to see if any of the spotters knew where the stage three had got to.

"Any luck?" I asked.

"It was seen an hour ago four miles south of here," answered Cutshaw, starting towards the creek.

The zombie was bobbing about in the water face down, flies swarming over it. Cutshaw cut a branch off the birch, hooked it through the zombie's tattered clothing and pulled it into the bank. Tommy and me dragged it out of the water, struggling to get a firm grip as it was slimy as a rotten fish. The stink was hard to take. All zombies smell bad, but when they're that far gone they have a smell that's difficult to describe. It's like a cross between rank cheese and raw sewerage, only much worse.

"How far gone do you reckon?" asked Tommy.

"Christ knows," I said. "It's probably older than us."

We washed our hands in the creek while Cutshaw doused the

body in ethanol and set it alight. As smoke mushroomed into the sky, we made our way south. The sun felt hot enough to fry an egg.

We hiked alongside the creek for about two miles on an overgrown trail, then climbed a hill crowned by pine trees. We looked out over a broad, grassy country dotted with thickets of birch and ash. Cutshaw pointed at something I couldn't see. I squinted through my scope and spotted the stage three about three-quarters of a mile away, goose-stepping its way southward. I wanted it straight away. So did Bob.

"Flip you for it," he said.

"Tails."

He flipped a coin. Tails came up. The stage three was mine. I started down the hillside, blood pumping with the thrill of the chase. Franz was ahead of me, nose to the ground. At 350 metres I brought the zombie into sight, centring the crosshairs on the back of its skull. I took a couple of breaths, trying to relax, holding myself still, waiting for the right moment. My shot echoed around the valley, the zombie went down.

Jim whooped. "You got it."

"No he didn't," Cutshaw stated.

I said nothing. I knew he was right. I'd felt myself tense on the shot. The zombie was sitting up slowly, arms outstretched, black blood oozing out of its throat. It rose stiffly to its feet and resumed walking south.

"That's odd," said Jim, starting after it.

"Wait," said Cutshaw, his hawk-eyes slitting.

A shot rang out dropping the zombie again. Cutshaw nodded as if something he'd privately suspected had been confirmed.

"Where the hell did that come from?" wondered Jim.

I scoped the landscape and fixed on two figures emerging from a knot of pines to the south. "There," I said, pointing.

"It must have caught their scent."

We hurried across to the kill sight. One of the hunters was bent over the zombie. The other watched our approach. I recognised him as the man I'd spoken to outside the toilet-block. "Sorry about that," he said. "I had to take the shot, it was onto us."

"What the hell did you expect when you were upwind of it?" said Jim.

The man frowned. "Like I said, I'm sorry."

"Hey, Dean, you've bagged a beauty here," said his partner, a pale-faced kid. He pointed at a clean round entry wound big enough to put your index-finger in. "You got the bastard straight between the eyes."

"Nice shot," I said, trying not to sound as cheated as I felt.

"Thanks." Dean turned to his partner. "Let's get moving, Al."

"Where you headed?"

"Burke's Ridge."

"The old tin mine?" asked Tommy. Dean nodded and started walking.

"See you back at camp," I called after him. He raised a hand.

"They must be crazy going up there," said Tommy as we watched the men make their way eastward towards a craggy range of hills.

"They've got balls," said Jim in a tone of begrudging respect.

Bob snuffed down his nose. "No brains, more like. That boy can't be more than sixteen. No one's got any business taking someone as green as him up there."

Jim rolled the zombie over, exposing a large exit wound with the skull pushed outwards at its edge like the rim of a moon-crater. "We'd better burn it," said Tommy. Cutshaw was already unscrewing the ethanol canister's lid.

We climbed a bare hill to the west on top of which was a hut stocked with food, water and firewood where you could hole up for the night if you got in a fix. We ate our lunch in the hut. Jim and Tommy argued the whole time we were eating. Jim was on for following Dean and Al up to the tin mine. Tommy said he'd rather hike back to the Humvee alone than go up there. I was inclined to agree with him. Flesh-eaters just love to congregate in dark, dingy holes like those mines. Anyone who went up there without a small army at their back was liable to be biting off more than they could chew. Cutshaw put an end to the argument when he told us we were heading to a derelict farmhouse two miles to the southeast.

"What have the spotters seen?" asked Bob, but Cutshaw wouldn't say.

We hiked those two long miles through waist high grass and marshland swarming with biting midges. By the time we sighted the farmhouse all I wanted to do was lie down in a shady spot. We staked the tin shack out for an hour with no luck. Eventually Cutshaw and Jim went in the front-door and found nothing but dust and cobwebs. I felt like burning the place down. I half-suspected Cutshaw had deliberately led us on a wild-goose chase just to knock us into shape. A glance at Bob told me he thought the same.

The sun was setting by the time we got back to the Humvee. We were all dog-tired, except Cutshaw, the bastard. Every moment spent in his company made me like him less.

There was drama back at the camp. A large party had come up from the south full of crazy stories about a legion (their word not mine) of zombies that'd attacked several camps and which seemed to be driven by an intelligence that went far beyond simple remembered behaviours from their mortal existence.

We were full of scepticism. Bob wanted to know about Martinez. A wild-eyed kid strung out on hillbilly pop told us he'd seen The Mexican two days ago sat up a tree fifty miles to the south. He shook his head when we told him Martinez had been here the night before, saying, "No way, Martinez was headed south. Everybody's headed south. That's where it's all happening. We only came up here to meet with some friends then we're headed back south."

Jim's eyes shone with excitement. "Didn't I say that's where we ought to go. The country round here's all hunted out anyway."

The wild-eyed kid whose name was Hooch nodded feverishly. "You're welcome to come along with us. It's gonna be a blast."

The mood was contagious and after a couple of turns each at the homebrew Jim, Bob and me were ready to pack up and head south. Tommy couldn't stand it. He mooched off sullenly to his tent after Jim shouted at him, "What the hell did you come on this trip for anyway?"

A bonfire was lit. Hooch jumped whooping through the flames as gun muzzles flashed all around. The whole camp was drunk. A brawl erupted. The guards were afraid to get involved. Hooch was off his head on anything he could get his hands on. He wanted to go on a night-mission, but the guards refused to open the gate. He yelled at them that he had enough dynamite to blow the motherfucking gate down. When one of the guards made a grab for him, he broke away screaming that he'd kill anyone who touched him. Guns were drawn and someone would've got shot for sure, if Bob hadn't floored Hooch with a wicked right hook.

## Day Three.

It didn't occur to me until I crawled bleary-eyed out of the tent in the morning that something was seriously wrong. I went in search of a guard. "I didn't see Dean and Al come in last night."

The guard eyed me sourly. "Who?"

"The guy about my age with the kid in tow."

The guard frowned in realisation. We checked Dean and Al's tent. It was empty. The guard hurried off to find out when they'd last made contact. It turned out they'd radioed in a couple of hours after we'd seen them to say they were heading up Hungry Hill. My stomach clenched like a fist. "But they told us they were making for Burke's Ridge."

"Well they changed their minds."

I returned to the tent and gave Bob the news. He shook his head. "That's the last we'll see of them."

"They might've made it."

"You reckon? You know what it's like up there when that mist comes down."

"We made it."

"Only just and we were damn lucky."

News of Dean and Al's disappearance spread quickly through the camp. A search party was assembled. Hooch approached us, a pair of revolvers hanging off his hips, a sawn-off shotgun balanced on one shoulder. There was an ugly bruise on his chin.

"No hard feelings," said Bob.

"Forget it," grinned Hooch. "I know what an asshole I can be when I get like that. We're going after those missing dudes. You coming?"

I exchanged a glance with Bob, then nodded. The thought of going into those woods again made me feel sick to my stomach, but what choice did I have? Bob wordlessly started getting his gear together while I looked in on Jim and Tommy. Jim looked barely alive.

I told them what was happening. Jim tried to get up and almost passed out with the effort. He was distraught at having to miss out on a trip up Hungry Hill. "Goddamn, sonofabitch moonshine," he croaked.

"I'd better stay with him," Tommy said sheepishly.

I nodded. To be honest, I was relieved he wasn't coming with us. The shape he was in, if things went bad, he would've been more hindrance than help.

Two hummers rolled out of camp with twelve men armed to the teeth crammed into them. Franz lay across my lap, breathing his meaty breath in my face. More than once during that journey I thought

I was going to puke. Hooch hitched a ride with us. He talked non-stop. I switched off listening after a few minutes. Jim had insisted I take his AK-47 and I occupied my mind by admiring its genius simplicity. Forget Tolstoy and Lenin, as far as I'm concerned Mikhail Timofeevich Kalashnikov is the greatest Russian ever.

The sun was hot and high by the time we reached Hungry Hill. My mouth was sawdust dry as we started up the trail behind the farmhouse. Cutshaw and a Ranger named Nash led the way. A guttural moaning drifted out from under the trees. Nash raised a hand and we raised our guns.

The zombie, when it appeared, was almost comical, a real pathetic specimen. Some half-starved wild animal must have had a go at it because both its arms were missing and its guts trailed over the ground like a string of sausages. Cutshaw dropped it with a single shot. The corpse was quickly doused and set alight.

"Keep close together," said Nash as we started moving again.

It was gloomy and silent as a tomb beneath the dense forest canopy. Every sound we made felt like a violation of a sacred silence. I concentrated on taking controlled breaths, fighting a creeping sense of claustrophobia.

Franz barked suddenly, pressing his nose to the dirt and pulling tight on his lead.

"He's picked up their scent," whispered Bob.

We found the boy half a mile further on. His skull had been smashed open like a hard-boiled egg and the brains scooped out. The flesh had been stripped off his bones by teeth hungry for marrow. There was no chance of him turning, but we dismembered his remains just in case. It was grisly work.

Franz snuffled about until he picked up the scent again off to the left of the trail. A compass reading was taken and we headed deeper into the woods.

We hadn't gone much further when we found the dead zombie. Half its head had been blown away. A trail of dried blood led away from it. Franz growled, back roached, fur bristling.

"What is it, boy?" said Nash.

"Look," hissed Hooch, pointing. I glimpsed a flash of grey fur moving through the gloom thirty or so metres to the west.

"Wolves," said Cutshaw.

Hooch cupped a hand to his mouth and gave out a high-pitched howl, which was greeted by a chorus of plaintive howls and yips.

"They're all around us," said a man with popping blue eyes who'd travelled up from the south with Hooch.

"That ain't nothing to worry about, Lyle," said Hooch. "They ain't hunting us."

"They're hunting something," Bob said.

We followed the blood-trail, moving with even more urgency than before. Every so often Cutshaw bent to examine a spatter. After about three-quarters of a mile, he said, "It's wet." The words were barely out of his mouth when a shot rang out nearby. The woods suddenly came alive with howls that were reflected and scattered by the tree trunks until they seemed to be coming from everywhere at once.

Franz dragged at his lead. We hurried after him. Shadowy forms moved with incredible swiftness through the closely packed trees on either side of us.

"Hold your fire," shouted Nash when Lyle squeezed off a couple of shots at them.

Cutshaw signalled for us to halt. He advanced a couple of steps into a sunny clearing with a white pine at its centre. Dean was slumped against the base of the tree. About five metres away from him was the corpse of a huge wolf.

"Stay back," Dean called out.

"Are you infected?" asked Cutshaw.

Dean levelled his rifle at him. "I said stay back."

"What happened?"

"It wasn't my fault. The sonofabitch came out of nowhere."

"Where did it get you?"

After a pause, taking a shuddering breath, Dean said, "My leg."

Nash immediately started circling around to the right of the clearing. I turned my back, knowing what had to happen. Everyone else stood grimly fixated. Hooch licked his lips as if he was hungry. An echoing shot rang out. I looked over my shoulder and saw that Dean was fallen to one side.

As we retraced our steps, the mist rolled down behind us. The mere sight of it made my hair stick lankly to my forehead. Luckily, we reached the edge of the woods before it overtook us. We walked in file, like a funeral procession, each man making sure he didn't lose sight of the man in front of him. The going was deadly slow. After what felt like a long time, the dark shape of the farmhouse loomed through the mist. We piled into the Humvees, breathing sighs of relief. Everyone was silent during the journey back to camp.

Jim and Tommy were full of questions. Bob answered most of them. I couldn't bring myself to say much. "Jesus," murmured Tommy when he heard about Dean. We all agreed that we'd move camp the following day. None of us felt like hanging around after what'd happened.

## Day Four.

At sunup we rolled out of camp waved off by Hooch. He threw his head back, howled and danced a crazy little jig that cracked Jim up. Bob and me exchanged an uneasy glance. "That kid'll be lucky if he survives the season," said Bob.

We were heading for Camp 24, fifty miles to the south. It would take most of the day to get there. Jim was itching for some action. I was glad of the chance to rest-up after the exertions of the previous two days.

At noon we pulled over to eat. Jim got out of the Humvee. He could barely keep his finger off the trigger of his Kalashnikov. After a couple of minutes we heard him shouting.

We ran over to where he was stood at the edge of a field of scrubby grass. "Over there," he said, gesturing at a weed-choked drainage ditch about 250 metres away.

I put the glasses on it and my heart missed a beat when I saw how fast the flesh-eater was moving. It'd caught our scent and its face was horribly contorted by its lust for living flesh.

"It's a stage one," said Jim.

"Stage two, just," corrected Cutshaw.

"Better take it down," Tommy said nervously.

Jim took careful aim and squeezed off a volley that punched the zombie into the air as if it'd been hit by a charging rhino. He lowered his gun, grinning.

"It's not dead," said Bob.

"What are you talking about?" retorted Jim. "Its head came apart like a rotten melon."

"Look."

Jim's jaw dropped as the zombie struggled to its feet and started towards us again. Two thirds of its head must have been missing.

He shouldered his gun and fired a whole clip into the creature. This time it stayed down for a full minute before rising up and staggering forwards. Its face had been obliterated. We looked at each other in silent astonishment. Of course, the only way to make absolutely certain a flesh-eater stays down for good is to incinerate it, but to encounter one that can survive such a massive loss of brain tissue is almost unheard of.

The creature was less than 200 metres away now. "Get back into the Humvee," said Cutshaw. We obeyed unhesitatingly.

Cutshaw took an RPG-7 out of a steel box and loaded it with a HE (High Explosive) round. He checked the back-blast area, sighted the flesh-eater, calmly waited until it was within optimum range and fired. The warhead detonated and when the smoke cleared the zombie was gone.

"Have you ever seen anything like that before?" I asked Cutshaw as he got into the Humvee.

"No."

It gave me a bad feeling when he said that. I thought about Dean and Al and about all the improbable tales Hooch had told us and for a second I was tempted to suggest we call the whole trip off. I couldn't bring myself to do it, though. I'd worked my balls off all winter for this chance. Besides, I'd never be able to look anyone in the eye again if I arrived home without a single kill under my belt. I glanced at the others, wondering what they were thinking. Jim looked dazed. He kept shaking his head and murmuring, "How?"

Bob seemed unperturbed. "I reckon it was a one-off," he said, "nothing more."

Tommy nodded. "Yeah, a one-off that's what it was."

I could see he desperately wanted to believe Bob was right, but there was little conviction in his voice. He looked to me for it.

"What do you reckon, Mikey?"

"I reckon Bob must be right," I said, more because I didn't want Tommy freaking out on us than because I believed it.

"I don't know about that," said Jim, "but I'm gonna get one of them RPGs and next time one of the bastards refuses to stay down," he made as if taking aim, "ka-fucking-boom!"

There was little talk during the remainder of the journey. We stared at the changing landscape, lost in our own worlds. The pine-clad hills were gradually petering out into dusty plains and in the west there were mountains with patches of snow on their peaks. A vast turquoise lake fed by glacial melt-water lapped against their feet.

Camp 24 had its back to this lake. There were lots of serious looking characters in camp, men whose faces told dark stories. They gave us sly, appraising looks and quickly decided there was nothing we could tell them that they wanted to hear. It started to rain as we pitched our tents. We ate a miserable cold meal and hunkered down for the night.

## Day Five.

After breakfast we hired a boat with an outboard motor and took it across the water. Conditions were perfect. Not a breath of wind disturbed the lake's surface which reflected a cloudless sky. All of us were in good spirits, even Tommy. It may sound like a cliché, but the rain seemed to have washed away our fear and uncertainty.

We moored at a jetty in the shadow of an imposing buttress of black rock and hiked along an unsealed road that led to an opencast mine on a high plateau. To one side of the road was a rusted railway track that'd once been used to transport millions of tons of coal a year to the coast where it was shipped to steel-mills in Japan, China, South Africa and Brazil. All around were signs of recent rock-fall.

About two miles along the road there was a stone-built bunkhouse. We let Franz sniff the place out before taking a look ourselves. The walls inside were scratched all over with names and dates, some going back more than a hundred years. Coats and hardhats still hung on pegs with steel-toed boots neatly arranged beneath them. I pictured miners fleeing barefooted as the Apocalypse came down.

"It's like they were here just a minute ago," Tommy said in a hushed voice.

Not far from the bunkhouse was a rusty old pickup truck with a flesh-eater sat behind its steering-wheel. Bob shot it through the glass. There was a moment of tension as we waited to see if one shot would be enough. When it became apparent that the creature was dead, Bob gave me a look as if to say, I told you so.

We shot three more on the way up to the mine. They lined up on a hump in the road like tin cans on a wall. Tommy took the first one, a grossly fat woman who toppled off the side of the road and bounced away down a thousand foot scree-slope. Me and Jim took the other two. I dropped mine cleanly. Jim chopped his into meat with the AK-47 going full tilt. We threw them both down the scree slope just for the hell of it.

Further on was a rail terminal to which coal was once carried by an aerial ropeway that ran for several miles down vertiginous slopes. We ate lunch in the terminal, which had been fortified for use by hunting parties.

Two hours of hard slog took us from the terminal to the mine. We looked out over the vast workings marvelling at what our ancestors had been capable of. The sheer scale of it was difficult to comprehend.

Cutshaw pointed to a bunch of shadowy forms emerging from a cave 100 metres to our right and almost 400 metres below us. There were four of them. Their mournful groans reached us faintly. We picked them off at leisure, making amazing shots. Jim smashed his PB by 55 metres. We finished the last one off by rolling a huge boulder into the hole, cheering when it scored a direct hit.

The walk down felt easy. We motored across the bay, taking turns at the wheel. Back at camp, as the evening breeze soothed our sunburnt faces, we cracked open bottles of beer and congratulated each other on the shots we'd made. We all agreed it'd been the best day's hunting we'd ever had.

## Day Six.

At daybreak pretty much the entire camp was on the move. A line of hummers kicked up dust on the road south like a wagon-train out of an old cowboy movie. Jim was keen to follow them. Tommy wanted to stay put. We put it to a vote and Jim came out on top, so we hit the road. Mountains reared up on every side as we crossed an immense dustbowl. The wind whipped in from the east, stirring up clouds of reddish-brown dirt that shrouded the sun.

After we'd been going about six hours, Cutshaw slammed his foot on the brake. "There's something in the road up ahead."

I squinted through the glass, but it was impossible to see more than twenty paces. "Stay here," said Cutshaw when I picked up my rifle. He unfolded the stock on his Micro-UZI and got out of the Humvee followed by Franz. We fingered our weapons as the dust cloud swallowed them.

After a couple of minutes he reappeared, grim-faced, and hauled an ethanol canister out of the boot. We all knew what this meant. "One of you come with me," he said.

I was first out of the Humvee. I hurried after Cutshaw, shielding my eyes from the dust-laden wind. After thirty metres I saw a dim form that gradually revealed itself as a Humvee with its front end smashed in. A scene of carnage unfolded. All around the Humvee lay dead flesh-eaters, their oily blood pooling on the hard-packed dirt. A couple of them looked like stage ones. Grave-wax had only just begun to form on their cheeks (for those of you that don't know, grave-wax is a crumbly, white substance that starts to form on those parts of the zombie's body that contain fat within a month of turning). Inside the vehicle were three corpses in hunting gear. All of them had been decapitated.

"I knew these men," said Cutshaw. "They were in Camp 27 last night."

"Where are their heads?" I asked, unable to keep a tremor out of my voice.

Cutshaw knelt at the front of the Humvee, studying the road's surface and the crumpled bull-bars.

"Perhaps they hit another hummer," I suggested.

"No they didn't."

"What did they hit then?" I asked, but Cutshaw made no reply.

We dragged the bodies out of the Humvee and piled them up at the roadside along with seven dead flesh-eaters, working safe in the knowledge that Franz would warn us if we were in any danger. I stood well back as Cutshaw set fire to the heap. Franz barked as we pushed the damaged Humvee off the road. Cutshaw peered into the dust-cloud, Micro-UZI at the ready. After a moment, he signalled to me and we hurried back to our Humvee.

"Jesus Christ. What happened there?" asked Jim as we accelerated past the funeral pyre.

I told what I knew, half-listening to Cutshaw trying to contact the nearest camp on the radio.

"But what the hell did they hit?" wondered Bob. "There's nothing out here."

"This is bad," said Tommy.

"This is way beyond bad," I said.

"What do you think?" Bob asked Cutshaw, who'd given up on the radio.

"I don't know," he said matter-of-factly.

There was a long moment of silence. For a second time in the space of three days Cutshaw didn't have an answer. Once was bad enough. But twice! In my experience, such a thing just didn't happen. I don't mind admitting that I was shaken to my core. It was like the ground had shifted beneath my feet. I suddenly knew with absolute certainty that I'd been wrong not to follow my instinct and abandon the trip. Determined not to repeat my mistake, I opened my mouth to speak, but Bob beat me to it.

"How far are we from Camp 33?" he asked. I could tell from his voice that he was thinking the same as me.

Cutshaw knew what he was thinking, too. "We haven't got time to make it back to Camp 27 before nightfall," he said.

"Hang on, are you suggesting we give up and head home?" said Jim, frowning.

"That's exactly what I'm suggesting," said Bob.

"But why?"

"Because there's something happening down here that I don't want any part of."

"It was an accident, that's all."

"I don't think so."

Jim snorted. "Well, Bob, I never thought you were the type to buy into the kind of nonsense that whacko kid was spouting." He turned to Cutshaw. "Go on, tell him how wrong he's got it." When no reply was forthcoming, his forehead wrinkled with uncertainty.

All this talk was too much for Tommy. "Oh man," he groaned, covering his eyes with his hands. "This is great, just fucking great."

"Take it easy," I said. "Tomorrow we're heading back north."

"You too, eh, Mikey." Jim shook his head at me in a self-righteous, pitying sort of way as if I'd admitted to something shameful.

I stared hard at him. "You just don't get it do you, Jim?"

"The only thing I get is that I'm riding with a bunch of gutless wonders."

Jim had no right to say such a thing, and he knew it. I bit my tongue to stifle an angry response, realising it wouldn't do anyone any good if we had a big falling out. A year ago I'd have given him the hairdryer treatment, but since dad's disappearance I've thought a lot more carefully about what I say to people in the heat of the moment. Besides, I could tell from Jim's face that he was already regretting what he'd said.

"Sorry, Mikey," he mumbled after a few minutes of uncomfortable silence.

"Forget it."

"It's just that we've all worked so hard for this, I can't believe we're going to give it up. We might not get out here again until next year."

"At least this way there'll be a next year."

"I suppose," Jim said grudgingly.

"There's no suppose about it," said Bob.

Jim flashed him an irritated look, then settled to staring out the window. I didn't blame him for being so sore. I knew he needed this trip more than any of us after the year he'd had on Robertson Island.

A voice crackled over the radio. "Car 316, this is car 211, are you receiving us? Over."

As Cutshaw reached for the handset, the Humvee emerged from the dust-storm into an eye of calm. A couple of hundred metres away a black SUV was parked at the roadside facing us. Cutshaw pulled up alongside it, winding his window down. "You're looking for car 316," he said.

The driver of the SUV nodded. "We got a call off them an hour ago to say they'd hit a tree that was blocking the road." Rolling his eyes at the treeless plain, he continued, "I know it sounds crazy, but that's what they said. We thought maybe they were having us on."

"They weren't having you on," said Cutshaw, and he told the driver about our grisly discovery.

"Jesus," murmured the man. "Where you headed?"

"Camp 33."

"We've just come from there. I'll follow you back in."

Everybody who was anybody in the hunting world was in Camp 33. The place was as cramped as a battery hen's cage. There was a tacit hierarchy as to who camped where, with grizzled veterans towards the centre of the site and ambitious young guns at its outer edge. We pitched our tents in the shadow of the perimeter-fence. As news of car 316's fate spread, we found ourselves at the centre of attention. All those flint-faced men who hadn't wanted to know us the night before last sidled over to hear the tale. By dusk I must've told it thirty times. There was a general consensus that it was the work of a thinker whose intelligence far exceeded anything previously encountered. As one wiry old dude put it, "We're talking about the goddamn Einstein of zombies here."

Hooch was there, too, whacked out of his skull on Christ knows what. As soon as I saw him I knew there was going to be trouble. He staggered over to us waving the biggest revolver I've ever seen and yelling, "Where's that bastard who broke my jaw?"

"I think you mean me," said Bob, cool as ever.

Hooch glared at him. "I've been looking everywhere for you."

Here we go again, I thought, dropping my hand to the grip of my Beretta, but suddenly Hooch was grinning from ear to ear and embracing Bob like a long lost brother. "Man, it's good to see you guys," he said. "I was starting to think you'd pussied out." He turned to me, wild-eyed. "Look at this place. Just look at it! Damn, this is gonna be good."

"We're heading back north tomorrow," said Jim.

Hooch eyed him disbelievingly. "You gotta be shitting me."

"Afraid not."

Hooch scrunched his face up and scratched his head, then his grin returned. "That's a good one," he laughed, wagging his gun at Jim. He tottered off, shouting over his shoulder, "I'll see you guys later."

Pulling faces like a child that's been told it has to leave a party early, Jim ducked into his tent and yanked the zipper down.

We sat silent beside our campfire. There was a buzz about the campground that was impossible to ignore, a feeling that something momentous was about to happen. Just being around it was enough to make your hair stand on end. I resisted it for as long as I could, but it was no good.

"Maybe we were a bit hasty back there," I said.

"Maybe," said Bob.

"Shall we make some dum-dums?"

"If you want."

And just like that it was agreed. Both of us understood that we wouldn't be heading north in the morning. We carefully began pulling handgun bullets out of their cartridges with pliers. I hammered the end of each bullet flat, before Bob carved a cross into the even surface with a hacksaw. This causes the bullet to split open on impact, blowing a hole about ten inches in diameter through your target. Very nasty and totally lethal. The only problem is the bullet's effective accuracy is reduced to around ten metres—a hell of a lot closer than I've ever been to a live flesh-eater. Nevertheless, we always went through this ritual before a really dangerous hunt. I guess it's kind of a psychological prop.

Tommy and Jim stuck their heads out of their tent at the sound of my hammering. Tommy went pale when he saw what was going on.

A wolfish grin split Jim's face. "I knew you boys wouldn't let me down." He grabbed Tommy in a headlock and knuckled the crown of his head.

"Get off." Tommy jerked free, jumped up and stomped away.

"Tommy," I called after him.

"Go fuck yourself," he retorted.

"Leave him," said Jim. "He'll get over it."

As the light dropped, a swirling wind got up. Before getting into my sleeping-bag, I hammered extra pegs into the guide-ropes. The wind built until the tent quivered like a hovercraft about to lift-off.

"Do you hear that?" Bob said suddenly.

I listened hard, but heard nothing.

"There it is again," said Bob.

This time I heard a faint, guttural moaning that gradually increased in volume until it formed an unbroken wall of sound—a sound more heart-rending and terrifying than anything I'd ever heard before. I fought an urge to pull my sleeping bag up over my head and plug my fingers into my ears. A scream sliced through the unholy dirge.

I lurched out of the tent and tripped over Tommy, who was curled into a ball on the ground, hands clamped over his ears, crying repeatedly, "I can't stand it."

Jim was knelt at his side, saying, "Calm down."

The camp was a hive of activity. Everywhere figures were emerging from their tents, rifles gripped in their hands.

"They're attacking the fence," somebody shouted.

Figures wearing night-vision goggles streamed up ladders to lookout platforms. Within moments blue flashes were going off everywhere, the heavy boom of high-calibre rifles competing against the deafening rattle of automatic weapons.

I frantically rummaged through my kitbag for my Raptor S-63 night-scope. Bob was already busy attaching his night-scope to his rifle.

"Stay with Tommy," I shouted to Jim.

"You stay with him," he yelled back, snatching up his AK-47 and sprinting for the nearest ladder.

I slung my rifle over my shoulder and hurried after him. Four figures were already knelt on the platform, squeezing off volley after volley. The noise was enough to knock the wind out of you.

"Mother of God," I breathed, squinting into my scope, "there must be a thousand of them."

The flesh-eaters were about 450 metres from the fence, advancing in a thronging mass. Fear gripped me—the same kind of primordial fear the Romans must have felt when they looked out of their encampment at the Barbarian Horde. Suddenly, I understood what the great hunters like Jesus Martinez must have known all their lives: this wasn't a game, it was war. Out there in the darkness was the enemy.

I shouldered my rifle, centred the cross-hairs and, tensing slightly in anticipation of the recoil, squeezed the trigger. A zombie went down. I pulled the bolt back and fired again, shooting with mechanical efficiency, relaxing a little more with every bullet that slammed home.

Jim was in his element. Every so often, as he slapped another clip into his AK-47, I heard him laughing crazily.

Zombies were hewn down like corn beneath a pelting hail-storm. But still they came on, slowly, irresistibly. It was like we were trying to hold back a river with our hands. A hundred metres, fifty, ten. Then they were right beneath us, converging on the gate. The stink of decomposing flesh was overwhelming. I bent double, retching.

"Keep shooting you sonofabitch," screamed the man next to me.

As I swung my gun up, a series of explosions momentarily blinded me. Handfuls of grenades were being tossed into the seething mass below. Blood dampened our faces like spray from breaking waves.

Bob grabbed my arm. "Look what they're doing," he gasped.

My jaw went slack and, for a second, my brain refused to accept what I was seeing, but there was no denying it. The zombies were gathering their dead and stacking them against the gate to form a kind of crude siege-platform. They had no shortage of building material, either. The irony being that the faster we blew them back to hell, the faster the heap grew. In no time at all it was almost as tall as the gate.

The situation was getting desperate. Dozens of zombies, driven into a howling frenzy by the scent of our flesh, were clawing their way to the heap's summit. We concentrated our fire on them, but for every one we picked off there were five more waiting to take its place.

It was only a matter of time before they broke through.

Jim wasn't laughing anymore.

A jet of flame streamed down, engulfing the mound of necrotic flesh. Several years ago dad managed to get his hands on an M-9A1 flamethrower that'd seen use by US troops during The Vietnam War. The first sentence of the training manual stated that: 'Flame has a powerful psychological effect in that humans instinctively withdraw from it, even when their morale is good.' Well flesh-eaters are no different in this respect and they retreated from the gate with howls of pain and fear. The plain was soon lit up like, well, like the biggest goddamn bonfire you could ever imagine, as those zombies that'd been doused with the lethally combustible mixture of gasoline and diesel staggered about setting alight anything they touched. It was a scene worse than any nightmare you ever dreamed.

We continued firing until the horde was out of range, although the accuracy of our shooting was reduced by a thick pall of smoke. Jim punched his AK-47 into the air, whooping. I was too exhausted to do anything besides crouch down, wiping sweat out of my eyes. I gratefully accepted a canteen off the man at my side and took a swallow of water.

"I ain't never seen nothing like that before," said the man—a craggy-faced old hand of about fifty, not exactly the type to get easily excited.

"If I hadn't seen it with my own eyes I wouldn't believe it," I said.

"We owe Hooch an apology," said Bob.

"Where are you going?" I asked as Jim started down the ladder.

"To check on Tommy."

A shout went up on the far side of the campground. "Here they come again."

You didn't need night-vision goggles anymore to see the amorphous mass of zombies shuffling towards us, the blaze at the gate illuminating their flesh-hungry faces.

"What the hell," exclaimed Jim, returning to the platform. "There's twice as many of them as before."

"At least," said Bob.

"Where in Christ's name have they all come from?"

This question had already occurred to me. Zombies, as you know, are slow moving creatures. Even a stage one can't travel more than twenty miles in a twenty-four hour period. For the zombies to have reached the campground so soon after sundown, they must've been gathering somewhere within roughly a five mile radius of it. In which case, why hadn't they been detected by the spotters?

My train of thought was broken by a deafening barrage of gunfire. I joined in, concentrating every fibre of my being on the task at hand. Thousands of rounds a minute were being spent, the plain was as bloody as a butcher's slab, but it wasn't enough to stop the zombies. The first to reach the fence threw themselves on the ground, allowing others to clamber onto their backs. This process was repeated all along the fence. Spouts of flame swept over them. Fuel drums with grenades taped to them were flung onto their heads. The heat was so intense that even zombies that hadn't been sprayed with burning fuel started spontaneously combusting. The smoke made it impossible to pick out individual targets. We fired blindly, not knowing what else to do. It was getting difficult to breath. The man at my side suddenly dropped to his knees, clutching his chest and gasping.

"What's wrong, Harry?" asked one of his companions, flinging out an arm to stop him from keeling off the platform. "I think he's got a heart-attack," he said to me as Harry's face turned purple.

"There's someone coming up the ladder," said Bob.

We trained our guns on the ladder, waiting to see what would appear out of the smoke. A face so grimy with soot and sweat it took me a moment to recognise it emerged into view. "It's Cutshaw," I said. I swear I've never been gladder to see him than I was at that moment.

"What's happening?" asked Bob.

"There are zombies in the compound," said Cutshaw, po-faced as ever.

"Have you seen Tommy?" Jim asked.

Cutshaw shook his head. Jim started towards the ladder. I grabbed his arm. "Don't be a fool."

He tried to shake me off. "I can't leave him down there."

"He might have made it to another platform or even the bunker," said Bob (at the centre of every camp is a concrete bunker stocked with enough food and water to last fifty men a month).

"No way. You saw what sort of condition he was in."

"Whatever the case, there's nothing you can do for him," I said, one eye on Cutshaw who was drawing the ladder up onto the platform.

Jim glared at me. "Let go."

"No. You'll get yourself killed."

"I'm warning you—" Jim broke off mid-sentence as I released him. Seeing what Cutshaw had done, he yelled, "Put that fucking ladder back!"

Cutshaw faced him silently, immovable as a wall. Short of putting a bullet in the inscrutable bastard there was no way Jim was going to get his hands on the ladder. Jim's gaze swept resentfully over me and Bob as he turned and stalked to the opposite side of the platform. He emptied a full clip into the smoke, shooting from the hip, then yanked out the clip and hurled it away.

"I'm out of ammo," he said.

"Take Harry's rifle," said Harry's companion. "He won't be needing it anymore."

We all turned to look at Harry's contorted, dead face. He was about the same age dad had been at the time of his disappearance. Tears welled into my eyes. I lowered my head to hide them.

"We've got to deal with him," Cutshaw said.

"I'll do it," said Harry's companion whose name I later found out was Joe. He unholstered his pistol.

"Save your ammo." Cutshaw drew his hunting-knife and proffered it to Joe. I could've swung for the heartless swine.

Joe took the knife and held it against one of his friend's eyeballs. "Sorry Harry," he murmured as he pushed the blade in. Then he used the knife's serrated edge to saw through the spinal-column at the base of the neck. As a final indignity, Cutshaw stripped off Harry's shirt. After tossing the decapitated corpse into the inferno, we cut the shirt into strips and tied them bandit-style around our faces to keep from breathing too much smoke.

Visibility was down to almost zero. "Don't shoot unless you're sure of your shot," said Cutshaw as we took up our firing positions again. He settled down by the ladder, rifle balanced across his lap.

Sporadic crackles of gunfire continued for a while, before a spooky calm settled over the camp. Once or twice I glimpsed shadowy forms at the base of the platform, but it was impossible to tell whether they were friends or foes.

"If it comes to it, you'd do the same for me, wouldn't you?" said Bob. "I don't want to end up like one of those things down there."

"You don't have to worry about that," I replied. "But it's not going to come to that."

"Yes it will, one day."

I glanced uneasily at Bob. What he'd said was obviously true, but it's a truth you learn not to think about too deeply. After all, what good can come from dwelling on something you've no control over? It's like that crazy king in that old English play said, 'That way lies madness.'

## Day Seven.

Sunrise revealed a scene of devastation. It looked like a twister had ripped through the camp. Tents had been shredded, their contents strewn over the ground. Vehicles lay overturned. The gate had buckled from the heat and the sheer weight of bodies pressing against it. Flies swarmed around the corpses that littered the plain. There were no live flesh-eaters to be seen.

Cutshaw radioed for news of Tommy. Jim's head dropped when the last platform reported back that Tommy wasn't there. We lowered the ladder. Jim scuttled down it and rushed off in search of Tommy. We followed cautiously, handguns at the ready as we picked our way through the carnage.

"Over here," shouted Jim. He was squatted by the tattered remains of our tents. He held up a bloody rag. "It's Tommy's shirt," he said, voice choked. He looked at us pleadingly. "We've got to go after him."

Considering everything that'd happened, it was madness to even suggest such a thing. I was about to point this out, when Bob said, "Don't worry, Jim, we'll find him."

I looked at him in astonishment. "You can't be serious. It'd be suicide to go after Tommy."

"Have you forgotten what you said last night?"

"No, but this is different."

"How is it different?"

I spread my hands to indicate the encircling destruction.

"You do as you want, Mikey, but I'm going after Tommy." Bob held my gaze a moment, letting me know with his eyes that there was no point trying to change his mind.

"And just how the hell are you gonna find him in all this mess?"

As if in answer to my question, Franz ran up to us wagging his tail. His fur was slightly singed, but otherwise he was fine. "This is crazy," I muttered as Jim held the bloody rag under Franz's nose. I turned to Cutshaw. "Tell them it's crazy."

"We'll need a serviceable hummer," he said, scanning the campsite. He approached a Humvee that lay on its side like a beached whale, followed by Bob and Jim.

"Has everyone but me lost their mind?" I said as I watched them struggling to tip the Humvee onto its wheels. Franz whined at me. "What do you reckon?" I asked him. He barked and ran towards the Humvee. With a resigned shake of my head, I followed him.

I braced myself against the bonnet. "Heave," I shouted, pushing with all my strength.

The Humvee's axles groaned as it tilted over. For an instant it tried to rock back onto us, but a figure charged into the gap between me and Bob and it dropped onto its wheels. Hooch grinned at me. "You looked like you needed some help. I heard about Tommy. I'm coming with you."

"Trust me, you should give this one a miss."

"You gotta be kidding, I wouldn't miss this for the world." Hooch sprinted off to salvage extra ammo from the wreckage of his tent.

There wasn't much visible damage to the Humvee. Cutshaw tried the ignition. The engine fired up first go. We piled in, drove over to the gate and contemplated the jumble of twisted metal and blackened corpses that blocked our path.

"That's gonna take hours to shift," Jim groaned.

"Not if we use this." Hooch took out a stick of dynamite.

"How old's that stuff?" I asked, eyeing it dubiously. Fresh dynamite's pretty insensitive to impact, friction and shock, but over time the nitro-glycerine can sweat out of it, forming into pure drops on the surface of the stick. When this happens even a small physical shock such as being dropped can cause it to explode.

"I only bought it last month."

We each took a bundle of sticks and blasting caps and a length of time (safety fuse). We weren't worried about doing further damage to the gate. The camp would have to be abandoned anyway until a team of engineers could be brought in to repair the fence.

I could feel the heat through the thick rubber soles of my hiking-boots as I clambered up the heap of corpses. I buried my bundle of dynamite near the top of the pile and threaded a long length of time into the bitter end of the blasting cap. I looked at the others and when each of them had given me the nod I lit the fuse. "Fire in the hole!" I shouted, hoping the heat wouldn't cause the cap to detonate before

I'd retreated to a safe distance.

We ducked behind the Humvee, hands over our ears, mouths hanging open. An explosion rocked the Humvee. Body parts rained down around us. A severed head landed near my feet. By some incredible, awful coincidence it belonged to Harry. Its tongue protruded out of its mouth as if blowing a raspberry at me. I kicked the thing away.

Hooch whooped when he saw that a broad channel had been blasted down the middle of the mound. Only a few more bodies needed to be shifted to allow the Humvee to get through. The bodies were so badly burnt that their flesh crumbled like ancient parchment as we heaved them out of the way.

Cutshaw walked out of camp holding Franz on a lead. The rest of us followed in the Humvee. It didn't take Franz long to pick up Tommy's scent. We tracked it for a couple of miles over the plain to the south of camp before Franz lost the scent in a muddy creek. Jim's face twitched impatiently as Franz snuffled about. Franz rediscovered the scent on the far side of the creek a hundred or so metres to the north. Bob ploughed the Humvee through the mud.

"A large pack of zombies passed this way a couple of hours ago," said Cutshaw.

"Was Tommy with them?" Jim asked.

"Yes. Most of the tracks lead south, but a small number, Tommy's included, lead northwest."

"What does that mean?" I asked.

"It may just mean the pack broke up." Cutshaw's voice was uncharacteristically hesitant. He stared at the tracks as if he was trying to solve a riddle.

"What is it?"

"There's something not . . ." Cutshaw frowned. I swear, the inscrutable sonofabitch actually frowned.

"We're wasting time," said Jim.

Cutshaw allowed Franz to lead him on. The sun broke through and heat gathered in shimmering pools on the plain. It was as hot as an oven inside the Humvee. The terrain grew steadily rougher. Around noon, we were forced to abandon the Humvee at the edge of an immense boulder-field on a high plateau.

"Nine hours till sundown," said Cutshaw.

"Where's the nearest hut?" asked Bob.

Cutshaw spread a map over the bonnet. "Six miles north of here."

"We need to be back here by seven at the latest then," I said.

"That gives us seven hours," said Bob.

"Hurry it up, will you," said Jim, his face haggard with anxiety.

Cutshaw folded the map away and we started hiking through a broken country of snaky ravines and flat-topped sandstone hills with dark, crusty caps. The sky darkened as it receded into the north.

There was little talk, even from Hooch. The memory of the previous night's horrors was still fresh in our minds. We were ready for anything. If a horde of flesh-eaters had risen out of the gravel plain I don't think any of us would've been surprised.

We'd been walking for roughly an hour when we reached the gorge. Tiers of crumbling sandstone cliffs, dotted with caves, ledges and overhangs, fell away from our feet. There was nothing left of the river that must have once rushed in a frothing torrent through the belly of the gorge.

We descended a steep, loose slope, arms spread like surfers trying not to wipeout. After twenty minutes of scrambling, palms bloodied, trousers torn, I slithered to the base of the slope.

"They can't have got much further," panted Bob, uncorking his canteen.

"They shouldn't have got this far," said Cutshaw.

"Must all be stage ones," said Hooch.

A few hundred metres further on we found the dead zombie. It was lying spread-eagled on a boulder at the base of a cliff. Fragments of its skull were spread over a radius of several feet. It was a stage one. Its body appeared relatively fresh on the outside, but its face was swollen by fluids and gases building-up under its skin.

Bob glanced up at the cliff. "It must have fallen."

Cutshaw studied the blood congealing over its shattered skull. "This happened less than an hour ago."

Franz lifted his head, sniffing. His gums drew back, his fur bristled. Jim, who'd continued ahead to a bend in the dry riverbed, gave out a sudden shout. He dropped to one knee, shouldered the rifle he'd inherited from Harry and squeezed off a shot. Then he jumped up and sprinted forwards.

"Wait," I yelled, chasing after him.

I reached the corner in time to see Jim disappearing around another bend. Cutshaw whistled and pointed and Franz raced ahead of us.

A second shot echoed around the gorge as we reached the bend. Jim was stood on a flat boulder about thirty metres away. "Come on," he called, flashing us a wild-eyed look. "I've seen Tommy." He jumped off the boulder.

"Watch out," I cried as a flesh-eater lurched out of the boulder's shadow. The zombie was fast, but Franz was faster. He sprang at the creature, knocking it off balance.

"Get down," Bob and Hooch shouted in chorus. Jim flung himself to the ground and before the flesh-eater could regain its balance a torrent of bullets blew its head apart.

Bob puffed his cheeks. "Damn, that was close."

"How many did you see?" Cutshaw asked Jim.

"Six or seven." He got to his feet. "Tommy was with them, I'm sure of it."

"Why haven't they attacked us?" I said. "They must have caught our scent by now."

Jim pointed at the dead zombie. "What do you call that?"

"Yeah, but what about the rest of them?"

"Who gives a shit? Come on." Jim charged onwards.

As the riverbed tumbled down in a series of steps, the gorge narrowed until only a ribbon of sky was visible. Stunted screwbean mesquites with spiny, twisted branches dotted the parched channel, indicating that there was moisture not far below the soil's surface.

We caught up with the zombies as they were about to enter a cave. A distinctive mop of curly ginger hair at the pack's centre told us Tommy was with them. Jim swung his rifle into position for a shot. Cutshaw knocked down its barrel so that the bullet kicked up a puff of dust.

"What the hell did you do that for?" snarled Jim.

"He's still alive."

"That's impossible," I said.

"Alive," murmured Jim. "How?"

No doubt, this question occupied all our minds as we charged towards the cave. None of us had considered it even a remote possibility that Tommy was still alive. Out of all the unlikely occurrences of the past few days this was by far the unlikeliest. A zombie's primary instinct is to feed on living flesh and brains. In this respect, there's no more single-minded creature on Earth than a zombie. The idea that these zombies were able to resist taking a bite out of Tommy with the smell of his flesh in their supersensitive nostrils was utterly incredible.

Before entering the cave, Cutshaw and Hooch pulled on night-vision goggles. The rest of us checked our infra-red scopes. The flaring entrance soon narrowed into a tunnel wide enough for two men to walk abreast. Jim and Cutshaw took the lead, followed by Hooch and Bob, then me. The cave was cool and dank. From somewhere far beneath our feet came the muted sound of running water.

Suddenly, a voice shrill with fear cried out, "Help me."

Jim surged forwards. "Hold on, Tommy, we're coming."

"Wait, we've got to stick—" I started to say, but was silenced by the ear-splitting boom of Cutshaw's rifle. He drew back the bolt for another shot, dropping onto one knee so we could shoot over his head. Squinting through my scope, I saw that the tunnel ahead of us was clogged with zombies falling over each other in their eagerness to get at us.

A vice-like grip closed around my arm. The noxious stink of dead flesh hit me full in the face as I jerked my chin around. I mouthed a silent scream, knowing I was on impossible terrain. In full daylight a zombie is a dangerous opponent, but in darkness and at close-quarters it's absolutely deadly. I dropped my rifle and fumbled at the grip of my Beretta, tensing in anticipation of feeling the zombie's teeth sink into my flesh. Franz's fur brushed against my face. I pitched myself backwards, tucking my head down so my shoulders would take the brunt of any impact. My breath whistled through my teeth as I hit the ground. Then I was sliding on my back headfirst down a rock-chute. I groped at the smooth rock, desperately trying to check my pace.

The chute spat me into thin air. I tumbled head-over-heels into a channel of swift-flowing, icy water. I kicked hard for the surface, water rushing up my nostrils. There was a small gap between the channel's surface and the roof of the cave. I pushed my hands against the rock to keep from having my head split open. In places the channel grew so narrow I became stuck until the pressure of water building behind me propelled me onwards like a torpedo. At other times the roof came down so low I was forced underwater until my lungs came close to collapsing. After what felt like hours, but was probably only minutes, a violent eddy buffeted me into the rock and I was knocked unconscious.

When I came to, I was lying on a muddy beach beside a river.

I struggled upright, feeling like I'd been worked over with an iron bar, but elated that I'd somehow managed to come through without serious damage. I scanned my surrounds. The river, which poured from a cave near the base of a sandstone cliff, was bordered by a narrow alluvial plain dotted with thickets of mesquite. Mesas, their slopes blanketed by clumps of sagebrush that perfumed the air with a pungent, turpentine aroma, formed an impenetrable barrier to the east and west.

My elation faded as it dawned on me just how tenuous my situation was. I was lost in a hostile environment with no radio or food and half a canteen of water. I faced a stark choice: remain where I was and hope the others managed to find a way through the cave-system or hike south and try to find a route out of the river-valley before nightfall. As I weighed up the pros and cons of either option, a low moan caused me to snatch out my Beretta.

The zombie lay on its back on the river-bank, hidden from view by a hump of mud. Its left leg looked as though it'd been put through a mangle and there were teeth-marks on its face. It stared at me, licking its lips as I took aim. The soft-nosed bullet did its job, fragmenting on impact and destroying two-thirds of the creature's skull.

As the echo of my shot died away, an agonised scream issued from a nearby mesquite thicket. I sprinted towards the thicket. A hot desert wind blew in my face, so I knew there was a good chance any flesh-eaters lurking in there hadn't caught my scent. My progress was slowed by a dense growth of crucifixion thorn that encircled the mesquites like a barbed-wire fence. The scream came again as I picked my way through the spiny tangle.

"Hang on, Tommy, I'm coming," I shouted, crashing though the remaining few feet of thorns, not caring that the spines lacerated my clothes and skin.

I halted in the shadow of a mesquite from which dangled fistfuls of screw-like, dull-green pods. I don't mind admitting that I was scared almost to the point of paralysis. I took several deep breaths and forced my legs to move step by trembling step.

Nothing, not even the events of the last twenty-four hours, could've prepared me for the sight that greeted my eyes as I entered the small clearing at the centre of the thicket.

Tommy was lying on his back. Most of his face was missing. His skull had been smashed open and a zombie was feeding frenziedly on his brain. Two more zombies stood at the back of the clearing. The feeding zombie was a late stage three. Dry decay had stripped away much of its hair and flesh and it was almost toothless. The other zombies were unmistakably stage ones, their green-blue skin was only just beginning to exhibit significant signs of putrefaction.

In every zombie pack there's a ruthlessly simple pecking order. The strongest zombies feed on the most nourishing parts of their kill, i.e., the brains and bone marrow, while older, weaker pack members make do with whatever's leftover (usually assorted internal organs). Understandably, then, my thoughts were thrown into turmoil by the sight of the stage ones allowing a stage three to feast on Tommy's brain. Read any book on evolution and you'll find talk about how one of the standards by which humanity is judged is the way we provide care for old and sick members of our society. It's this behaviour that separates us from the beasts in the jungle. By that reckoning I was witnessing something that cast into doubt not only what it meant to be a zombie, but what it meant to be human.

You may dismiss such talk, as others have done, as the product of a mind unbalanced by what happened next. But I know what I saw. I only wish I understood what it meant.

I unloaded into the stage ones. The force of the dum-dum bullets hurled them into the air like rag dolls. As I reloaded, the feeding zombie jerked its head up. There was something about its eyes, some gleam of intelligence that was horrifyingly familiar. My mouth opened and shut soundlessly. I could feel my eyes bulging with the effort of trying to speak. The word finally came out in a dry croak, "Dad."

The zombie hissed, rising slowly to its feet. It shuffled towards me as if its ankles were shackled. I tried to pull the trigger, god help me I did, but I couldn't do it. My arms dropped limply to my sides. Tears ran down my face.

The zombie was less than a metre away when blood ballooned out of the back of its head. I heard the shot a fraction of a second later. It was the perfect shot, the bullet entering dead centre of the frontal bone and exiting through the parietal bone. I found out later that it'd been made from nearly a mile away without the aid of a telescopic sight.

I blinked, then glanced around as though emerging from a trance. Unsurprisingly, the shooter was nowhere to be seen. The zombie lay on its back, arms outstretched like someone about to enter an embrace. There was a gold ring on one of its fingers. I worked it over the knuckle and put it in my pocket. Then I bowed my head.

I was still sat like that when a heavily accented voice said, "Everything ok, cabrito?"

Jesus Martinez entered the clearing. He prodded the zombie's carcass with his foot as if to make sure it was truly dead. "I've tracked this one many months. I never encountered its like before." He bent to peer at its face as if studying a specimen through a microscope. After a full minute, shrugging to himself, he turned to leave. "Come, I will take you to your friends." When I didn't move, he said, "Que pasa?"

"I need to bury him."

Martinez's eyebrows lifted. "There are many zombies nearby."

"Still, I need to bury him."

"How?" Martinez stamped his foot. "The earth here is like baked clay."

I took out my knife and began digging. Martinez watched me a moment. Then, with a sigh, he set his rifle down very carefully and joined me. The soil was looser under its crust. We buried the corpse just deep enough to keep the vultures off.

Beyond that there isn't much to tell. The thinker's death brought an end to the attacks on the camps. Poor old Tommy was taken back to Robertson Island for cremation. That was nearly a year ago. I haven't seen Jim since. I heard he got married and had a kid. Hooch is gone. The crazy sonofabitch's luck finally ran out on a night mission somewhere. Cutshaw is gone, too. He went missing on the Eastern Reserve last month. I hate to think what sort of zombie that bastard will make. I tried to find out what happened to Franz, but nobody seemed to know. Bob and me have got a hunting trip planned for spring. No prizes for guessing which reserve we're going to hunt.

www.ingramcontent.com/pod-product-compliance
Lightning Source LLC
Chambersburg PA
CBHW060435180626
46817CB00007B/2818